NEVADA

"Where you from?" Ben had asked. "Nevada" had been the reply. And that had been the only name by which Ben had ever known him.

Because he was a wanted man and he didn't like to see his friends involved in his troubles—troubles he won with the speed of his gun. But in the final showdown it was his skill with a pistol that won him his freedom and cut down the man who had forced him onto the outlaw trail.

Books by Zane Grey in the Ulverscroft Large Print Series:

THE DRIFT FENCE

LONE STAR RANGER

SUNSET PASS

THE HASH KNIFE OUTFIT

SHADOW ON THE TRAIL

SHEPHERD OF GUADELOUPE

ARIZONA AMES

THE BIG LAND

THE LOST WAGON TRAIN

RIDERS OF THE PURPLE SAGE

THE RAINBOW TRAIL

NEVADA

ZANE GREY

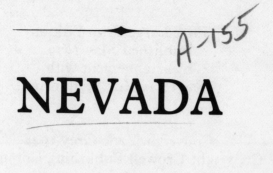

A-155

NEVADA

Complete and Unabridged

ULVERSCROFT
Leicester

First published in Great Britain in 1969
by Sphere Books Ltd
London

First Large Print Edition
published May 1979
by arrangement with
Zane Grey, Inc., California

British Library CIP Data

Grey, Zane
    Nevada.—Large print ed.
    (Ulverscroft large print series: western).
    I. Title
    823′.9′1F   PS3513.R6545N/

    ISBN 0-7089-0301-0

Published by
F. A. Thorpe (Publishing) Ltd.
Anstey, Leicestershire
Printed in England

CHAPTER 1

AS his goaded horse plunged into the road, Nevada looked back over his shoulder. The lane he had plowed through the crowd let him see back into the circle where the three men lay prostrate. The blue smoke from his gun was rising slowly. Ben Ide's face shone white in the sunlight.

'So long, Pard!' yelled Nevada, hoarsely, and stood in his stirrups to wave his sombrero high. That, he thought, was farewell forever to this friend who had saved and succored and uplifted him, whom he loved better than a brother.

Nevada faced the road down which his horse was racing, and the grim mood returned to smother the emotion which had momentarily broken it.

The last gate of the ranch was open, and Nevada flashed through it to turn off the road and go flying down the trail along the shore of the lake. There was no need now for this breakneck ride. The officers of the law would eventually get on his track, as they had been for years.

Five miles brought horse and rider far around to the other side of the lake. The trail wound down upon the soft sand, and along the edge of the lake, where the midday sun had thawed the ice. Nevada saw the long cuts and scars on the ice, where he and Ben and the freed outlaws had run that grand wild stallion, California Red, to his last fall. Nevada could not help but thrill, as he remembered the strange lucky catch of the wild horse Ben Ide loved so well. How mad Ben had been—to bargain with the rustlers they had captured—to trade their freedom for the aid they gave in running down the red stallion! Yet mad as that act had been, Nevada could only love Ben the more. Ben was the true wild-horse hunter.

Nevada reached the bluff where Forlorn River lost itself in the lake, and climbed the sloping trail to the cabin where he and Ben had lived in a lonely happiness. Ben, the outcast son of a rich rancher of Tule Lake—and he, the fugitive gunman, whom Ben had taken in with only one question.

'Where you from?' Ben had asked.

'Nevada,' had been the reply. And that had been the only name by which Ben had ever known him.

It was all over now. Nevada dismounted from his horse. 'Wal, Baldy,' he said, throwing the bridle, 'heah we are. Reckon the runnin's aboot over.' And he sank heavily upon the porch step. He gazed across the lake toward the dots that were the cabins of the Blaine ranch.

'Reckon I cain't set heah mopin' like an owl,' soliloquized Nevada, getting up. 'The thing's done. An' I wouldn't have it otherwise. . . . Dear old Ben! He was the only pard I ever had. Wal, Ben's name is cleared now. Old Amos Ide knows the truth now an' he'll have to beg forgiveness of Ben. Hart Blaine will know, too. They'll all have to crawl for callin' Ben a rustler. . . . Ben will marry Ina now—an' he'll be rich. He's got California Red, too, an' he'll be happy.'

From the lake Nevada gazed away across Forlorn River, over toward the wilderness whence he had come and to which he must return. To the hard life, the scant fare, the sordid intimacy of crooked men and women, to the border of Nevada, where he had a bad name, where he could never sleep in safety. But at that moment Nevada was exalted by the consciousness that he had saved Ben from prison, cleared his name, given him back to Ina Blaine, and killed his enemies. Whatever had been the evil of Nevada's life before he met Ben, it could not change the sweetness of the service he had rendered.

Nevada went into the cabin. It had been ransacked by violent hands. The pseudo-sheriffs, who had come at the beck of Less Setter to arrest Ben, had not hesitated to stoop to thievery. They had evidently searched the cabin for money, or anything of value.

Nevada gazed ponderingly around on this disorder.

'Wal,' he muttered, 'I reckon Less Setter won't be rammin' around heah any more—or any other place short of hell!'

With that remark Nevada strode out and down the path to the corrals. He caught a horse and securing packs, he returned to gather his belongings and food, blankets, ammunition. Then mounting his horse he drove the pack animal ahead of him, and rode down to the ford across Forlorn River.

From a ridge top a mile or more up the lonely river, Nevada gazed back at the cabin for the last time. Something told him that he would never see it again. The moment was poignant. It was not only good-by to it and to his friend, but to the most precious of all that had ever entered his life—Hettie Ide.

Nevada made that farewell, and then rode on, locked in thought. Sunset brought him to an awareness of the need of suitable camp for himself and his animals. While crossing the river he let the horses drink. He dismounted to fill his water-bag and canteen. Then he rode away in search of a secluded spot. He knew the country, and before long reached a valley up which he traveled some distance. There was no water and therefore an absence of trails, and he halted in a grassy dell to make his camp.

His well-trained horses would not stray beyond the grass plot, and there was little chance of the eyes of riders seeing his camp fire. The night was cold and still. A few lonesome insects hummed sadly. He heard the wail of coyotes. There were no other sounds.

Nevada sat cross-legged, like an Indian, before his camp fire. It was small, but warm. Nevada spread his palms to the heat, an old habit.

The moment came when Hettie's face appeared clearly in the embers, crowned by fair hair, with its gray eyes and firm sweet lips. It looked more mature than the face of a sixteen-year-old girl—brave and strong and enduring. Nevada had kissed those sweet lips and had been kissed by them! They would haunt him now, always, shining from every camp fire.

'Hettie,' he whispered, 'you're only a kid an' you'll forget. I'm glad Ben never knew aboot us. It'll all come out now after my gunplay of to-day. An' you an' Ben will know I am Jim Lacy! . . . If only I could have kept it secret, so you'd never have known I was bad! An', oh—there'll never be any one to tell you I cain't be bad no more!'

Beside that first camp fire Nevada's courage failed. He had never realized the significance of that moment when Hettie and he found themselves in each other's arms. What might have been! But that, too, had only been a dream. And some day he might have buried the past, even his name, and grasped the happiness Hettie's arms had promised. Ben would have joyfully accepted him as a brother. But in hiding his real name, in living this character Nevada, could he have been true to the soul Ben and Hettie had uplifted in him? Nevada realized that he could no longer have lived a lie. And though he would not have cared so much about Ben, he had not wanted Hettie to learn that he had been Jim Lacy, notorious from Lineville across the desert wastes of Nevada clear to Tombstone.

The loss of Hettie was insupportable. On the steps of friendship, love, and faith he had climbed out of hell. Never could he minimize the bloody act through which he had saved his friend from the treachery of a ruthless and evil man. That act as well, had saved the Blaines and the Ides from ruin, and no doubt Ina and Hettie from worse. For that crafty devil, Setter, had laid his plans well.

When he crawled into his blankets at

midnight the conflict within him had exhausted his strength. With the dawn his ordeal returned. The agony was that he could not be happy without Hettie's love. He wanted to seek some hidden covert, like a crippled animal, and die. He wanted to plunge into the old raw life of the border, dealing death and meeting death among those lawless men who had ruined him.

'Baldy, I've got a fight on my hands,' he said to his horse, as he threw on the saddle. 'We've got to find some place where it's safe to hide. Maybe, after a long while, we can cross over the desert to Arizona an' find honest work. But, if I have to hide all my life, an' be Jim Lacy to the end, I'll be true to the name Ben Ide gave me— Nevada—the name an' the man Hettie Ide believed in!'

Nevada traveled far that day. He began to get into high country, into the cedars and pinons. Above him the black timber belted the mountains, and above that gleamed the snow line. Dusk found him camped in a lonely gulch.

Camp was welcome. And once again a

sweet face gleamed in the heart of the camp fire.

The next day Nevada climbed the divide that separated the sage and forest country from the desert beyond. From a grassy saddle he gazed down to the canyoned strip of California, and on to the border of Nevada, bleak, wild, and magnificent. The desert stretched away illimitably, with vast expanse of hazy levels and endless barren ranges. Strange to tell, this wild Nevada called to something deep in him, something raw and deadly.

'Reckon I'll hide out awhile in some canyon,' he reflected.

Then he began the descent from the divide, and soon the great hollow and the upheaval of land beyond were lost to his sight. The trail zigzagged down and on down out of the heights.

Before Nevada reached the end of the slope he heard the hum of a stream, and turning off the trail he picked his way over the roughest of ground to the rim of a shallow canyon, whence had come the sound of falling water. He walked for a mile or more before he found a break in the canyon wall where he could get down.

Here was a lonely retreat. Grass and wood were abundant, and tracks of deer and other game assured him he could kill meat. A narrow sheltered reach of the canyon, where the cottonwood trees still were green and gold and the grass grew rich along the stream, appeared a good place to camp.

So he unpacked leisurely and ponderingly, and set about making a habitation in the wilds. From boyhood this kind of work had possessed infinite charm. No time in his life had he needed solitude as now.

Nevada did not count the days or nights. He roamed up and down the canyon with his rifle, though he used it only when he needed meat. He spent hours sitting in sunny spots. His horses grew fat and lazy. Days passed into weeks. The nights grew cold and the wind moaned in the trees.

The time came when Nevada knew that if he lingered there he would go mad. For there encroached upon his dream of Hettie and Ben, a dark mood in which the men he had killed came back to him. Nevada had experienced this before. The only cure was drink, work, action, a mingling with humankind, the sound of voices.

CHAPTER 2

IT was a bleak November day when Nevada rode into Lineville. Houses on one side of the road lay in California, and those on the other belonged to Nevada. Many a bullet had been fired from one state to kill a man in the other.

Lineville had been a mining town of some pretensions during the early days of the gold rush. High on the drab foothill stood the ruins of an ore mill. Gold was still to be mined in the rugged hills, though only in scant quantity. Prospectors arrived in Lineville, wandered around for a season, then left on their endless search, while other prospectors came. When Nevada had last been there it was possible to find a few honest men and women, but the percentage in the three hundred population was small.

Nevada halted before a gray cabin set well back in a large plot of ground just inside the limits of the town. The place had not changed. Corrals and sheds stood farther back at the foot of the rocky slope.

Nevada remembered the rudely painted sign that had been nailed slantwise on the gate-post. Lodgings.

Dismounting, Nevada left his horses and entered, to go round to the back of the cabin. Nevada hesitated a moment, then knocked. He heard a bustling inside, brisk footsteps, after which the door was opened by a buxom matron with ruddy face, big frank eyes, and hair beginning to turn gray.

The woman stared, then burst out: 'Well, for goodness' sake, if it ain't Jim Lacy!'

'I reckon. Are you goin' to ask me in? I'm aboot froze.'

'Jim, you know you never had to ask to come in my house,' she replied, and drew him into a cozy little kitchen where the pleasant odor of baking bread appealed powerfully to Nevada.

'Thanks. Shore seems like home to me. I've been layin' out in the cold an' starvin' for a long time.'

'Son, you look it,' she returned. 'Never saw you like this, Jim, you used to be a handsome lad. You're as bushy-haired as a miner. . . . What've you been up to?'

'Wal, Mrs. Wood,' he drawled, 'Shore you've heard aboot me lately?' And his gaze studied her face, but she gave no sign.

'Nary a word, Jim. Not since you left.'

'No? Wal, I am surprised, an' glad, too,' replied Nevada, smiling his relief. 'You couldn't give me a job? Helpin' around, like I used to, for my board.'

'Jim, I jest could, an' I will,' she declared. 'You won't have to sleep in the barn, either.'

'Now, I'm dog-gone lucky, Mrs. Wood,' replied Nevada.

'I don't know about that, Jim. Comin' back to Lineville can't be lucky. I'd hoped if you was alive you'd turned over a new leaf.'

'It was good of you to think of me kind like that,' he said. 'I'll go out an' look after my pack an' horses.'

Nevada went out thoughtfully, and slowly led his horses out to the barn. There, while he unpacked, his mind dwelt on the singular effect that Mrs. Wood's words had upon him. Perhaps speech from anyone in Lineville would have affected him similarly. Presently Mrs. Wood called him. Shouldering his bedroll and carrying a small pack, he returned to the kitchen. She had a hot meal prepared.

Nevada ate until he was ashamed of himself. 'I know what to call myself. But it tasted so good.'

'Ahuh. Well, Jim, you take some hot water an' shave your woolly face,' she returned. 'You can have the end room, right off the hall. There's a stove an' a box of wood.'

Nevada carried his pack into the room designated, then returned for the hot water, soap, and towel. When an hour later he strode into the kitchen to confront Mrs. Wood, she studied him with eyes as speculative as kind.

'Jim, I notice your gun has the same old swing, low down. Now that's queer, ain't it?' she said, ironically.

'Wal, it shore feels queer,' he responded. 'For, honest, Mrs. Wood, I haven't packed it at all for a long time.'

'An' you haven't been lookin' at red liquor, either?'

'Reckon not.'

'An' you haven't been lookin' at women, either?'

'Gosh, no,' he laughed. But he could not deceive her.

'Boy, somethin' has happened to you,' she declared, seriously. 'You're older. Your eyes aren't like daggers any more. They've got shadows. . . . Jim, I once saw Billy the Kid. You had the look of Billy, an' if you'd kept on you'd been another like him. But somethin' has happened to you. I ain't inquisitive, but have you lost your nerve? Gunmen do that sometimes, you know.'

'That's it. I've no more nerve than a chicken,' drawled Nevada.

'Shoo! An' I'll bet that's all you tell me about yourself,' she said. 'Jim Lacy, you left here a boy an' you've come back a man. Wonder what Lize Teller will think of you now. She was moony about you, the hussy!'

'Lize Teller. Is she heah?'

'She about bosses Lineville, Jim. She doesn't live with me any more, but hangs out at the Gold Mine.'

'Lize married yet?' began Nevada, casually.

'She never will be now,' replied Mrs. Wood, forcibly. 'She had her chance, a cattleman from Eureka. He knew he was buyin' stolen cattle. But for all that he was a mighty fine sort for Lineville. Much too good for that wench. She was taken with him, too. Her one chance to get away from Lineville! Then Cash Burridge rode in one day—after a long absence. 'Most as long as yours. He come back to lie low an' gamble. He had plenty of money, as usual. Lost it, as usual. Lize was clerk at the Gold Mine. She got thick with Cash. She went from bad to worse. You'll see.'

'Cash Burridge back,' rejoined Nevada. That name had power to make him want to hide the sudden fire in his eyes. 'Reckon I'd plumb forgot Cash.'

'Jim Lacy,' replied the woman, 'no one would ever forget Cash, much less you. I hope you don't meet again.'

'Wal, of course we'll meet,' said Nevada. 'I cain't hang round your kitchen all the while, much as I like it.'

'Jim, I didn't mean meet him on the street, or in the store, or anywhere. You know what I meant.'

'Don't worry, Mother Wood. Reckon Cash an' I won't clash. Because I'm not lookin' for trouble. Has Cash been up to his old tricks lately?'

'I haven't heard much, Jim,' she returned, thoughtfully.

Nevada knew it would do no good to press her further in this direction, which reticence was proof that Cash Burridge had been adding to his reputation one way or another. Nevada had a curious reaction—a scorn for his own eagerness to know. Old feelings were regurgitating in him. A slow heat ran along his veins.

'Lineville shore looks daid,' he said, tentatively.

'It *is* dead, Jim. But there's more travel along the road than ever before. Three stages a week now, an' lots of people stop here for a night. I've been busy all summer an' fall.'

'Wal, that's a new one for Lineville. Prospectors always came along. But travel. What you mean, Mother Wood?'

'Jim, where have you been for so long?' she asked, curiously. 'Sure you must have been buried somewhere. There's a new minin' town—Salisbar. An' travel from north has been comin' through here, in spite of the awful road. There's been only couple of hold-ups. None of this outfit, though. We hear the stage line will stop runnin' soon, till spring.'

'You mentioned aboot a cattleman buyin' heah since I've been away. Shore he's not the only one?'

'No. But cattle deals have been low this summer. Last bunch of cattle come over in June.'

'Wal, you don't say! Lineville is daid, shore enough.'

'Jim, that sort of thing has got to stop sometime, even if it is only a lot of two-bit rustlin'.'

'Two-bit? Ha! Ha!'

'Jim, I've seen thousands of longhorns rustled in my day.'

'Reckon you have,' responded Nevada, looking up at her. 'You never took me for a rustler, did you, Mother?'

'You was only a gun-packin' kid, run off the ranges. But, Jim, you'll fall into it some day, sure as shootin'. I want you to go so far away from Lineville that you can't never come back.'

'I'll go in the spring.'

'That's a promise I'll not let you forget.

Meanwhile you can be snug an' hide here till spring.'

'Mother Wood, when was Hall heah last?'

'In June. An', Jim, he's never been back.'

'Maybe he has shook the dusk of Lineville. He rode in heah sudden, so I was told. An' why not ride off that way? To new pastures, Mother Wood?'

'No reason a-tall,' she said, reflectively. 'Only I jest don't feel that way about Hall.'

'An' that high-flyin' Less Setter from the Snake River country. Did he ever come again?'

'No. That time you clashed with Setter was the only time he ever hit Lineville. I remember, Jim, how that night after the row you talked a lot. It was the drink. You'd had trouble with Setter before you come to these parts. I never told it, but I remember.'

'I came from the Snake River country, too,' replied Nevada.

'It was said here that Less Setter was too big a man to fiddle around Lineville,' returned the woman, passing by Nevada's cryptic remark, though it was not lost upon her. 'Hall said Setter had many irons in the fire. His game, though, was to wheedle rich cattlemen an' ranchers into speculations. He was a swindler, low-down enough for any deal. An' he had a weakness for women. He tried to take Lize Teller away with him.'

'Wal, you don't say!' ejaculated Nevada. That sickening something shuddered through his soul. Less Setter would never have a weakness for women again. He would never weave his evil machinations around Ben and Hettie Ide, for he and two of his arch conspirators had lain dead there in the courtyard before Hart Baine's cabins.

'Lineville has had its day,' the woman was saying, as if with satisfaction. 'Setter saw that, if he ever had any idea of operatin' here. Hall saw it, too, for he's never come back, Cash Burridge knows it. He has been away to the south—Arizona somewhere—lookin' up a place where outside travel hasn't struck. He'll leave when the snow melts next spring, an' he'll not go alone. Then decent people won't be afraid to walk down to the store.'

'Good luck for Lineville, but bad for

Arizona,' returned Nevada. 'I feel sorry for the ranchers over there.'

'I don't know. There are wilder outfits in Arizona than this country ever saw,' rejoined the woman, contemptuously. 'Take that Texas gang in Pleasant Valley, an' the Hash Knife outfit on the Tonto Rim. Cash Burridge isn't the caliber to last long in Arizona. Waters an' Blink Miller are tough nuts, I'll admit. I suppose Hardy Rue will trail after Burridge, an' of course that Link Cawthorne. But there's only one of the whole Lineville outfit that could ever last in Arizona. An' you know who he is, Jim Lacy.'

'Mother, I haven't the least idee,' drawled Nevada.

'Go 'long with you,' she replied, almost with affection. 'But, Jim, I'd rather think of you gettin' away from this life than lastin' out the whole crew. I've heard my husband say that gunmen get a mind disease. The gunman is obsessed to kill. An' if another great killer looms on the horizon the disease forces him to go out to meet this one. Jest to see if he can kill him! Isn't that terrible?'

'It shore is terrible,' responded Nevada,

gloomily. 'But killing for the sake of killin'! Reckon I don't know what to call that.'

Later when he went into his little room he performed an act he had repeated a thousand times in privacy, but not of late. The act of drawing his gun! Sight of it so gave Nevada a grim surprise. How thoughtlessly and naturally the fact had come to pass! Why had he done that? He sheathed the long blue gun.

'Reckon Mrs. Wood's talk about Cawthorne an' the rest of that oufit accounts for me throwin' my gun,' he muttered.

He had returned to an environment where proficiency with a gun was the law. Self-preservation was the only law among lawless men. He could not avoid them without incurring their hatred and distrust. He must mingle with them as in the past, though it seemed his whole nature had changed. Mingling with outlaws was never free from risk. The unexpected always happened. There were always newcomers, always some would-be killer like Cawthorne, who yearned for fame among his evil kind. There was always the possibility of meeting a gunman who would want to kill him solely because of his reputation.

'Reckon I'd better forget my dreamin' heah,' he soliloquized. 'An' when I'm out be like I used to be. Shore it goes against the grain. I'm two men in one—Nevada an' Jim Lacy. . . . Reckon Jim better take a hunch.'

The leather holster on his belt was hard and stiff. He oiled it and worked it soft with strong hands, until it began to grow dark.

It was still daylight, however, when Nevada went out to walk leisurely down the road into town. He came at length to the several stores and shops, a saloon, and a restaurant, that appeared precisely as they had always been. Then Nevada arrived at a corner store, where he entered.

The place had the smell of general merchandise, groceries, and tobacco combined. To Jones' credit, he had never sold liquor. There was a boy clerk waiting on a woman customer, and Jones, a long lanky Westerner, who had seen range days himself.

'Howdy, Mr. Jones!' said Nevada, stepping forward.

'Howdy yourself, stranger!' replied the storekeeper. 'You got the best of me.'

'Wal, it's a little dark in heah or your eyes are failin',' returned Nevada, with a grin.

The other bent over to peer into Nevada's face.

'Jim Lacy! Back in Lineville! I've seen fellers come back I liked less,' he declared.

He shook hands heartily with Nevada. 'Where you been, boy? You sure look well an' fine to me.'

'I've been knockin' aboot, lookin' for a job,' drawled Nevada.

'An' you come back to Lineville in winter, lookin' for a job?' laughed Jones.

'Shore,' drawled Nevada.

'Jim, I'll bet if I offered you work you'd shy like a colt. Fact is, though, I could do it. I'm not doin' so bad here. There's a lumber company cuttin' up in the foothills. Heard about Salisbar?'

'Yes. Reckon I'll have to take a look at it. How far away?'

'Eighty miles or so,' returned Jones.

'Some miners struck it right, an' that started Salisbar off as a minin' town. But it's growin' otherwise. Besides mineral, there are timber an' water, some good farm land, an' miles of grazin'. All this is wakin' Lineville up. There's business goin' on an' more comin'.'

'Shore I'm glad, Mr. Jones,' said Nevada. 'Lineville has some good people I'd like to see prosper.'

From the store Nevada went down to the Gold Mine. Dark had fallen and lamps were being lighted. The Gold Mine was a tavern for the outlaw elect, a gambling hell and a drinking dive not equaled short of the Mexican border.

Nevada turned into the long dingily-lighted barroom. A half-dozen men stood drinking and talking at the bar. They noted Nevada's entrance, but did not recognize him, nor did he them. The bartender, too, was strange to Nevada. A wide portal, with curtain of strong beads, opened into a larger room, which was almost sumptuously furnished for such a remote settlement as Lineville. Six men sat around one table; he recognized only one, that of a gambler called Ace Black.

His cold eyes glinted on Nevada, then returned to his game.

Nevada took the seat on the far side of the fire, where he could see both entrances to the large room. A rattling of the beaded-curtain door attracted his attention. A girl entered. She had a pale face, and very large black eyes that seemed to blaze at Nevada.

CHAPTER 3

SHE came slowly toward him, with the undulating movement that he remembered even better than her tragic face. Life had evidently been harsher than ever to Lize Teller.

'Jim Lacy!' she ejaculated, with stress of feeling that seemed neither regret nor gladness.

'Howdy, Lize!' drawled Nevada. 'Reckon you're sort of surprised to see me heah.'

'Surprised? Yes. I thought you had more sense.'

'Wal, now Lize, that's not kind of you,' he said.

'Sit down, Jim,' she rejoined, and as he complied she seated herself on the arm of his chair. 'I've been looking for you all afternoon. Lorenzo saw you stop at Mrs. Wood's.'

'Ahuh! Wal, no wonder you wasn't surprised.'

'But I am, Jim. Surprised at your nerve and more surprised at the look of you. You're improved so I don't know you.'

'Thanks, Lize. There was room for improvement. Nothin' much happened, except I've been workin' an' I quit the bottle.'

'That's a lot, Jim, and I'm downright glad. I'll fall in love with you all over again.'

'Please don't, Lize,' he laughed. 'I've quit throwin' guns, too. An' I reckon it'd be unhealthy for me, if you did.'

'Probably will be, boy. You sure have me guessing,' she replied, and she gazed at him with inquisitive eyes, 'But don't try to lie to me about your gun tricks, sonny. You forget I'm the only one around Lineville who had you figured.'

'Lize, I don't know as I remember that,' he said, dubiously.

'Jim, you forget easily,' she rejoined, a touch of bitterness. 'But God knows there was no reason for you to remember *me*. It was natural for me to miss you. For you were the only decent man I knew. But you treated me like you were a brother. And that made me hate you.'

'Lize, you didn't hate me,' he said.

'That was temper. Maybe you got a little miffed because you couldn't make a fool of me like you did the others.'

'Jim, you don't know women,' she replied, bitterly. 'I can do anything. Where'd you say you'd been—workin'— all this long while?'

'Wal, now Lize, I don't recollect sayin',' he drawled. 'Shore never liked to talk aboot myself. What have you been doin'?'

'Me! Can't you see? If I live another year I'll be in the street. I hate this damned life, Jim. But of course Mrs. Wood told you all about me.'

'Some,' replied Nevada. 'Wish I'd been heah when you made such a darn fool of yourself.'

'I wish to God you had,' she flashed, with terrible passion. 'You'd have shot Cash Burridge. He double-crossed me, Jim. Oh, I know I'm no good, but I'm honest. Cash actually made me believe *he* would marry me. I'm working here at the Gold Mine now—everything from book-keeper to bartender.'

'Lize, I heah you're thick with Link Cawthorne,'

'Bah! You can call it thick, if you like,'

she returned, scornfully. 'But I call it thin. I was half drunk, I guess, when I took up with him. And now he thinks he owns me.'

'Wal, Lize, wouldn't it be interestin' for me right now—if Link happened in?' drawled Nevada.

'Link could never be interesting to you. He's a bluff.'

'All the same, Lize, if you'll excuse me I'll let you have the chair,' Nevada rose.

'What the devil's come over you, Jim Lacy?' she demanded. 'Why, two years ago, if Link had come roaring in here with two guns you'd have laughed and turned your back.'

'Two years ago! Lize, I've learned a lot in that long time.' She queried, sharply, 'Jim, did you kill Less Setter?'

Nevada had braced himself for anything from this girl, so at the point-blank question he did not betray himself.

'Setter! . . . Is he daid?'

'Yes, he's daid,' she replied, mimicking his Southern accent. 'And a damn good thing. . . . Jim Lacy, I lay that to you.'

'Wal, Lize, I cain't stop the wanderin's of your mind, but you're shore takin' a lot upon yourself,' he returned, coldly.

She caught his hand.

'Jim, I didn't mean to offend,' she said hastily.

'Ahuh? Wal, there's no offense. Reckon I'm sort of hurt that you accuse me.'

'Jim, I notice you don't *deny* it,' she retorted, with her brilliant searching eyes on him. 'But listen. Only a few people in Lineville have heard Setter is dead. I heard it from a chance traveler who stayed here overnight. Setter had been shot by a wild-horse hunter over in California. That was all. That reminded me of something else. Last summer Steve Elkins saw you in a saloon in Hammel. So when I remembered that, I remembered you had a grudge on Setter, also that you loved wild-horse hunting, and I put two and two together and figured *you* had done for Setter. Cash Burridge was glad enough to hear the news, you can bet. He had been sent to Arizona by Setter on some deal only the two of them were in. Cash had a roll of money big enough to stop up a stovepipe. He went to Arizona. And he never saw Setter again. He didn't tell me how he'd benefited by Setter's death. I figured that, too.'

'Lize, shore I'd rather you didn't give me credit for removin' so many undesirable citizens from the world.'

'Have it your own way, Jim,' she returned. 'And now for what I was coming to. Did you ever hear of Hardy Rue?'

'Wal, yes. Never saw the man, though.'

'He wasn't here during your time. But he's here now, and he's the man for you to watch. I think he was Setter's right hand man and came to Lineville to check up on Cash Burridge. They don't get along. I'd say Rue is a dangerous man: seldom talks, never drinks, hates women, and has an eye like a hawk. He's . . . Hello! Somebody calling me. I forgot I have to work. I'll see you later.'

She ran from the room, leaving Nevada with plenty to think about. Yet he was considerably relieved that his name had not been openly used in connection with Setter's death. That would have made his position less secure in Lineville.

Gradually the gaming tables filled up. More than one keen-eyed player gave Nevada a curt nod of recognition. He was approached presently by two newcomers, one of whom he recognized as Blink Miller.

'Howdy, Blink!' he replied to the other's greeting.

'You're lookin' fust-rate, Lacy,' replied Miller. 'Shake hands with my friend, Hardy Rue.'

Nevada found himself under the surveillance of a quiet, penetrating gaze. He had a hard lined face, prominent chin and thin lips.

'Care to drink with me, Lacy?' he inquired.

'No, thanks,' replied Nevada. 'Reckon I'm not fixed to buy drinks, so I'm not acceptin' any.'

'Aint you grown awful particular since you've been away so long?' queried Miller, with a smile.

'Come to think aboot it, I have,' drawled Nevada. 'Particular aboot not owin' anybody favors an' particular aboot who I drink with.'

Nevada, could not help giving that tart answer.

Miller blinked. 'Reckon that's particular nice of you, Lacy. Nobody wants to buy drinks for a feller who's broke.'

Then Rue gave Nevada an inscrutable look.

'But you're not particular about throwin' a gun on—anybody?' he queried.

Nevada drawled: 'Not at all, Mr. Rue. Shore it's just a habit. I never mean anythin' uncivil.'

The two men passed on to a gaming table, where seats evidently awaited them. Nevada turned on his heel, muttering: 'Damn them anyhow. They just cain't let me alone.'

Among others who entered presently was Cash Burridge. He was a handsome, dissolute man, blond, with a curling mustache, almost gold, and light, gleaming, restless blue eyes.

Nevada knew that Burridge had seen him the instant of entrance, if not before. Burridge had been the ringleader in the stage hold-up to which Nevada had been a party. The one deed to which he owned with shame!

At length Burridge disengaged himself from his companions and walked around between the tables to get to Nevada.

'Jim, I'm dog-gone glad to see you!' he said.

'Howdy, Cash!' replied Nevada. 'Reckon I'm glad you're glad to see me.'

'It's good you blew in. I've often wondered what'd become of you, and I'm plumb interested in what you're goin' to do.'

'Why so?' asked Nevada, not without surprise.

'Are you goin' to hole up here this winter?'

'Reckon I am, as far as I know,' returned Nevada.

'Broke?' queried Burridge, with a knowing look. 'I'm not so well heeled myself, but I can stake you to a roll.'

'Thanks, Cash. But I cain't borrow. I don't like borrowin', an' maybe I never could pay back. I'll get a job for my keep heah. An' the cairds an' drinks won't bother me.'

'Jim, what'll you do after the snow flies?'

'I'll be hanged if I know,' replied Nevada.

'That's all I wanted to hear,' spoke up Burridge, with great satisfaction. 'I've got a deal on—the biggest I ever handled.'

'You're not goin' to ask me to rustle cattle with you?'

'No. I swear I'm not,' hastily returned Burridge, 'By Heaven! it's an honest deal, Jim.'

'Wal, I'm glad to heah you say that. An' I'll listen to you.'

'This ain't the place for us to talk. The deal is big; it's cattle, an' it's honest. I've got to have a hard-shootin' outfit, an' a leader with reputation like yours.'

'But, Cash, I heard you say this deal was honest.'

'If it ain't then I don't know what honesty is,' declared Burridge, forcibly. 'You wait till I tell you all about the deal.'

Burridge withdrew then, while Nevada returned to his chair by the fire. 'What the devil is Cash up to now?' pondered Nevada. 'Honest deal? Cattle? Hard-shootin' outfit . . .'

Nevada discovered that the word honest inhibited all his deductive powers in relation to what Cash Burridge might be engaged in. But he grasped at once the motive for Burridge's warm greeting. Where Burridge had any special interest he could be agreeable, and, if the case required, most persuasive and dominating. These traits, however, had never before been exercised upon Nevada.

A little later Lize Teller returned, and before he could get up to offer her the chair she had plumped herself over the arm.

'You sit still or I'll jump into your lap,' she threatened. She would have done it, too; therefore Nevada decided he had better be quiet.

'Lize, if you want to make a show of yourself, you don't need to pick on me,' mildly protested Nevada.

'Listen! If you want to make me your friend—I say *friend*—forever, just be lover-like for a few minutes, or make a bluff at it.'

Nevada laughed at her in spite of the annoyance he could scarcely conceal. 'What're you up to, Lize?'

'Link Cawthorne just came in,' she replied, tossing her black head defiantly. (She still had some of the charms of girlhood left.)

'So I reckoned,' replied he. 'Wal, Lize, it may be fun for you to use me in your little tricks, but it mightn't be funny for me. An' it might turn out bad for Link.'

'That's why. He makes me sick. I want him to come in and find me with you. He was up all last night, in a card game, and he doesn't know you're here.'

'Lize, it strikes me you don't want very much a-tall,' returned Nevada. 'I hate to be rude to a lady, but *I* want to get up.'

'All I want is for the conceited lout to *see* I can like some other man.'

'Lize, I reckon you must have given Link some reason for bein' so conceited. Now didn't you?'

'I suppose I did. I thought I was mad about him, but I guess I was only mad at Cash Burridge. . . . There he comes,' she whispered, in fiendish glee, and then leaned over Nevada, radiant with some feeling quite beyond his comprehension.

Nevada looked up, not without a stir in his veins. Link Cawthorne stood with the bead curtain parted.

Nevada doubted Lize's assertion that Link had been unaware of his return to Lineville. He certainly did not start, nor change his expression materially. But he looked steadily at Lize, while she babbled to Nevada, apparently oblivious to her lover's advent.

Nevada's feeling, in that moment, changed from a good-natured contempt for Link and a vexation at his own part in this little farce to something vastly different. It seemed to be premonition that amounted to shock. He saw something, as a dream might foreshadow a future event. The sensation was so sudden and dismaying that Nevada heard nothing of Lize's whispered pretenses. It took violent effort of will, which was effected with Cawthorne's stalking across the room, to return to his cool, keen self.

A year and more did not set lightly upon Link Cawthorne's features. Nevada judged all these men by the changes that had risen in himself. Cawthorne halted before Lize and Nevada. His right hand covered the butt of a gun belted high. Whatever he had intended to say or do manifestly yielded to the passion which arose at close range. Lize's glance traveled from Cawthorne's boots slowly upward, at last to meet his piercing gaze with surprise that seemed as genuine as insolent.

'Oh, you here?' she said. 'Link, have you ever met my old friend, Jim Lacy?'

'Cat!' he spat out, and his body jerked with the word.

'Howdy, Link!' interposed Nevada, thinking to pour oil on the trouble waters. 'Reckon Lize has forgotten you an' me was acquainted.'

'Forget—hell!' responded Cawthorne, in hard scorn. 'Never mind Lize. I'll settle with her. I'm addressin' you, Jim Lacy.'

Nevada seemed a long moment in replying, during which he looked steadily up at Cawthorne.

'Ahuh. Wal, strikes me you're not very civil aboot it.'

'Strikes me you're too familiar with Lize,' flashed Cawthorne, hotly.

'Familiar? Say, you're out of your haid. If it's any of your business, we're old acquaintances.'

'She was sittin' on your lap. An' that won't go with me.'

'Link, look for yourself,' returned Nevada, quietly. 'There's where she's been all the time. Shore that isn't anythin' to raise a row, even if you an' she are engaged.'

'Jim Lacy, you're a liar!' he burst out, stridently.

Nevada was gazing hard up at Cawthorne's face, which had suddenly turned white. In his ungovernable fury he had said what had not been calculated upon. A sudden cessation of all sound from the gamesters was proof that they had heard him denounce Nevada. Cawthorne stood as one transfixed with terror.

'Now, Link, I'm not a liar an' you know it,' replied Nevada, without evident stress. 'Reckon I can make allowance for your feelin's.'

The young outlaw's face lost its pallor and rigidity. It waved red, and all at once his hair appeared to bristle.

'I'll have no allowances from you,' he shouted. 'I'm invitin' you for a little walk outdoors.'

CHAPTER 4

NEVADA calmly rose to his feet and stepped aside from the chair. He did not believe that Cawthorne would attempt to draw on him, but as there was no certainty, he wanted to be on his feet.

Cawthorne shouted the louder: 'I'm invitin' you outdoors.'

'What for?' queried Nevada.

'You know what for.'

'I haven't an idee, Link,' went on Nevada. 'Shore I see you're riled. But I reckon there's no call for me to get riled, too, aboot your mistake. It's cold outdoors. An' I like this warm fire. If you've any more to say, why go ahaid.'

Cawthorne expanded under this wholly unprecedented experience. A few drinks had addled his brains and jealousy had set them on fire.

'Say?' he demanded with contempt. 'I've no more to say. I've called you, an' you're yellow. That's all.'

Whereupon he turned to the amazed

and discomfited Lize and, half leading, half dragging her, left the room. The business of the gamblers was resumed, with a loud laugh here and caustic remarks there. Nevada heard the content of some of them: 'What the hell's got into Lacy?' ... 'He always was a decent chap.' ... 'Reckon he couldn't kill thet durn fool right before the girl's eyes.' ... 'You're wrong, gentlemen,' said a cold-voiced gambler. 'That was a little by-play between a real gunman and a would-be. I've seen it often.'

For nearly a week Jim stayed away from the Gold Mine. Then one night at supper Mrs. Wood spoke up seriously:

'Link Cawthorne is braggin' you're afraid to come downtown.'

'Shore, I don't care what Link says.'

'Son, that's not the way of the West,' she went on, gravely. 'No man can afford to lose the respect of his associates, even if they are mostly a worthless outfit of gamblers, rustlers, an' sech. They can't understand it. Least of all Link Cawthorne can't. He's likely to shoot you from behind a corner an' swear he met you on an even break.'

'But, Mother Wood, what can I do?' queried Nevada.

'Well, as long as you're here in Lineville be Jim Lacy as *they* used to know him,' she declared, forcefully. 'If you let this towhead run amuck with his brag, pretty soon he'll get the nerve actually to draw on you. Now, Jim, you don't want to have to kill him. Lize was fond of him. An' if she's fond of anyone it keeps her straight. You go downtown an' slap Link's face. Take his gun away from him an' stick it down the back of his pants!'

'Wal, maybe you're right,' he said. 'By Gosh; I wish spring would come, so I could hit the trail.'

'Mark my words, son,' she replied, 'The best way for you to make sure of spring an' summer an' fall is to be yourself!'

Nevada went back to the Gold Mine, dubious that he could ever escape the consequences of his name.

Cash Burridge made at once for Nevada, with all show of friendliness.

'Where you been, Lacy?' he inquired, 'We've certainly looked for you here.'

'Aw, been workin' hard an' goin' to bed early,' replied Nevada. 'Then, Cash, I reckon I wanted to avoid meetin' Cawthorne.'

'Bah!' snorted Burridge. 'You'll have to shoot that damned brag, an' the sooner you do it the better we'll all be pleased.'

'Wal, we won't argue aboot it, Cash, but I'm not seein' it that way.'

'I'll bet you five to one Link will nag you to draw. I've seen a hundred four-flushers like him.'

'Wal, I cain't bet with you, that's shore,' returned Nevada.

'Let's go up to my room, where we can have a quiet talk,' said the other, and led the way through the hall and up-stairs.

'Shore, you're comfortable heah,' remarked Nevada.

'I like it nice when I'm not in the saddle,' returned Burridge. 'Take a seat, an' have a smoke. . . . One more word about this Link Cawthorne. He was harmless enough until Lize made him a snake in the grass. My advice is for you to beat the daylights out of Link or call his bluff an' kill him.'

'Reckon I'm some worried, Cash,' admitted Nevada.

'A man like you must always worry,' rejoined Burridge. 'It's bad enough to have sheriffs after you, an' natural enemies, but it must be hell to know there're men who want to kill you because of your reputation.'

'Wal, I hope I don't get sore an' go back to drinkin'.'

'Jim, I want to talk serious to you now,' went on Burridge.

'Wal! Fire away. You'll get my honest opinion, anyway.'

'Lineville is gettin' a little too much travel to suit me. In another year it won't be any place for me, let alone you. Now I want to tell you about my deal. I'll tell you straight. An' if you don't want to go in with me it'll be all right, only I want you to respect my confidence here in Lineville. Will you do it?'

'I reckon,' replied Nevada, soberly.

Burridge showed satisfaction at that assurance, but he plainly hesitated over the next disclosure.

'Jim, you knew Setter was shot over in California?' he queried, sharply.

'I heard it from Lize,' rejoined Nevada, matter-of-factly.

'I want to say that whoever killed Setter did me a good turn.'

'Me too. Setter did me dirt once, over on the Snake River.'

Burridge drew a long breath and laid aside his cigar.

'Listen,' he began, with tenseness. 'After he left here he sent for me to meet him at Klamath Falls. He had gotten in with big cattlemen an' had more money that he knew how to spend. He told me he wouldn't risk settlin' down in Oregon. He'd sell out there pretty soon, an' he wanted a new an' safe place. No more rustlin' or sharp speculation with other ranchers' money. He might marry. Anyway, he was goin' in for honest ranchin', an' wanted me as a partner. Well, the upshot was that he gave me a hundred thousand dollars to buy a well-stocked ranch in Arizona. I was to own half, an' to help him develop cattle an' horses on a big scale. He left the choice of place to me, makin' the provision that I find a wild an' unsettled range. Well, I went to Arizona an' bought out a rancher who owned a big ranch, had miles of grazin' range, an' ten thousand head of stock. I ain't tellin' you the location until you decide to accept my offer. I hustled back here an' sent word to Setter. No word came from him. I went back to Arizona—that was early last summer. Then I had my eyes opened. Our cattle were bein' rustled right an' left. I suspected the very cowmen I'd taken over with the property. There were many more ranchers an' cattle than I'd suspected. Some of these ranchers were rustlers, thick with the worst of the outfits. You've heard of the Hash Knife gang an' the Pine Tree outfit. But nobody seemed to know just *who* belonged to them an' *who* didn't. This country around Lineville even in gold-rush days couldn't hold a candle to that neck of the woods in Arizona. Now when I got back here a few weeks ago I sent word to Setter an' waited. No reply. Then we heard Setter was dead. Hardy Rue brought the news. I've a hunch he's got somethin' up his sleeve. That property in Arizona is mine. An' my job is to get back there to run it. Here's where you come in. Jim Lacy! That wouldn't sound so pleasant to those outfits. I'll make you foreman an' give you an interest. It'll take some fightin' to keep my cattle. I want a bunch of the hardest-ridin' an' hardest-shootin' boys that can be hired. An' you to lead them! An' now a last word, Jim. You know that many an honest an' prosperous rancher was once a rustler. What do you think an' what do you say?'

'Wal, Cash, reckon I'll think more'n I say,' returned Nevada, ponderingly. 'You shore talked straight. I savvy when a man's tellin' me the truth. It's a darn interestin' story. What the courts might say about it I cain't guess. But I reckon half that hundred thousand Setter gave you is honestly yours. Maybe the other half, too. Nobody could tell just how much money Setter earned an' what he got speculatin'. He was always careful to get the other fellow to take the risks. Yes, sir, I reckon the Arizona ranch is yours, all right.'

'Good. I'm glad you see the deal that way,' replied Burridge, rubbing his hands together. 'An' you'll accept my offer?'

'Cash, I cain't promise that yet,' responded Nevada slowly. 'Reckon to be honest, the day might come when I'd be glad to take you up. But now I want time to think aboot it.'

'Take all the time you want,' spoke up Burridge, heartily.

'Wal, I appreciate that, Cash, an' I'll think it over. What I hate aboot it is livin' up to my name.'

The short days passed, the snow fell, adding to Nevada's work. In the evenings he would drop in at the Gold Mine. Burridge had made another strong plea for Nevada to join him, and then had left for Arizona.

Lize Teller had passed from jest to earnest in her mood towards Nevada. She was vain, willful, and malignant when under the influence of drink. She broke her engagement with Cawthorne and took to wild flirtations and drinking bouts with the gamblers. She lost all restraint and began to fail in health.

When Nevada at length took her to task, he received an impression that gave him concern.

'No decent man wants me and I'm slated for Hell,' she told him, bitterly.

Nevada conceived the idea that somehow he had failed the girl. It could not have been otherwise, yet the fact hurt him. Another side of the situation was the peril she had incurred by jilting Cawthorne. There was, however, no use in talking to Lize about that. Whenever Cawthorne accosted her, she flouted him as she would have a repulsive dog.

One afternoon Nevada, actuated by an impulse, bent his steps towards the Gold Mine.

He entered the place by the side door, and paused in the hall before the entrance to the gambling room. The usual quiet of that den had been disrupted.

Nevada quickly opened the door. The room was full of men, all standing. Cards, coins, chips, glasses on the tables showed evidence of having been violently abandoned. The noise that had halted Nevada came from the saloon.

Nevada strode to the nearest group of men. Something terrible had happened.

'What's happened?' he queried.

'Jim, we was playin' our caird games, quiet as usual,' spoke up the gambler, Ace Black, 'when we heerd an awful row in the hall there. Then a woman's screams. An' after that a heavy fall. We all jumped up an' some one rushed out to see what it was. An' by Gawd—'

'Wal?' broke in Nevada, cool and grim, as Black choked.

'Lize Teller! She was layin' half naked, streamin' blood. Link Cawthorne had beat her over the head with his gun. She'll die! . . . An' listen to him!'

In three long bounds Nevada had reached and split the beaded door-curtain. His swift eye swept all.

'*Cawthorne!*' he yelled, in piercing voice that brought an instant breathless silence.

CHAPTER 5

IT was springtime in northern California.

Hettie Ide had awakened this morning twenty years old.

It wanted an hour yet before breakfast. As Hettie tripped down the stairs she heard Ina shrieking with laughter, no doubt at little Blaine's pranks. But Hettie had no envy in her heart this birthday morning. She was closer to Ben than ever, and she loved Ina and the child as if indeed they were her own flesh and blood.

Hettie found Ben sitting on top of the corral fence. California Red was inside, and indeed he did not like it. Hettie halted to peep through at him. She loved this wonderful horse, too, for his beauty, his spirit, and for another reason which only Ben would ever have suspected.

California Red had been in captivity four years. He had been broken, yet never had lost his spirit. He shone red, and his long mane was a flame. He was a big horse, yet perfectly proportioned. He looked indeed what he had been for years, the wild stallion king of the sage hills of northern California.

Hettie climbed to a seat beside her brother.

'Mawnin', pard,' she drawled, mimicking the Southern accent of one neither of them ever forgot.

'Wal, howdy there, old girl!' replied Ben.

'What're you doing, Ben?' she asked, brightly.

'I was just coaxing that red son-of-a-gun,' he replied.

'Red doesn't seem to obey you very well.'

'I'd have to rope him before he'd lay down those ears.'

'Ben, you mustn't expect him to grow tame.'

'Tame? No, I only want him to love me.'

'Perhaps love was left out of Red's makeup,' laughed Hettie. 'Or perhaps he can't forgive you for taking him from his hills.'

'It's four years now,' said Ben, thoughtfully. 'What a long time! I couldn't ask a finer, gamer horse. But I—I always seem to want something from Red—I never get.'

'Ben dear,' replied Hettie, pressing his hand, 'what you want is something—some one to tame Red.'

'I reckon. . . . The only man who ever could tame Red.'

'Your old pard, Nevada,' she whispered, leaning closer.

Not for a long time had Hettie dared to broach this subject and now that she had, she meant to follow it up in a way to help her, and perhaps Ben, too.

'Ben, this is my birthday,' she spoke up, softly.

'Well, so it is,' replied her brother, starting out of his reverie. 'Let's see, you must be eighteen—nineteen.'

'Twenty,' she added, gravely.

'How time flies! Why, you're a grown woman, and a darned fine handsome one, too.'

'Ben,' she spoke up, 'I don't want any present on my twentieth birthday. But I ask this. If I'm a woman now I'm old enough to be listened to. Let me talk to you as I want—as I need to.'

'Hettie, I'm sorry you had to ask me

that,' he returned, contritely. 'But you hurt so. . . . And I thought you just a—a sentimental girl—that you'd forget.'

'Forget *him*? Never,' she whispered. 'Have you forgotten?'

'If I ever do may God forgive me,' replied Ben, poignantly.

'Ben, I know your secret, and I think Ina knows, too,' went on Hettie, earnestly. 'We have talked often. You remember when Ina came home from college—when you were a poor wild-horse hunter of the hills and father almost hated you— remember how Ina and I plotted for you and Nevada. How we fought for you!'

'Ah, Hettie—I do remember,' said Ben, dreamily.

'Well, Ina and I know what ails you. It's loss of your pard, Nevada!'

'No, Hettie dear, *not* all loss of mine,' burst our Ben, passionately. 'I'm not so selfish as that. I could stand loss. But what has grieved and shamed me—and, well, broken my heart—is that Nevada saved me, made all my good fortune, my happiness, possible, by sacrificing himself. Father forgave me, took me back home to mother and you. Hart Blaine was proud to give me—*me*, the lonely wild-horse hunter—his talented and beautiful daughter, the richest girl in all this valley of rich ranchers. I had fame, family, home, love, happiness beyond belief. Then father died, leaving me rich. I should say leaving us rich, for half of all this wonderful ranch is yours, Hettie. Next little Blaine came to bless me—my boy! . . . And Nevada went back to where he came from. God only knows where that is. I've spent a lot of money searching the West for a lean-faced rider who drawled his Texas accent—and answered to the name of Nevada. And I can't find him.'

'Some day you will, Ben,' she whispered.

'I believed I would,' went on Ben. 'I lived on that hope. But it's four years now. Four years. And that Forlorn River Ranch of ours is now worth a fortune. Half of that is Nevada's. Half of the Mule Deer Flat Ranch is Nevada's. He's worth money. . . . Why didn't he come back? The whole country rose up to bless him for killing Less Setter and his two accomplices. Why didn't he ever write? Just a line—a word to let me know he was alive and hadn't forgotten.'

'Don't you understand that the reason he disappeared like that, and became as one dead to you, was not because he feared the law might hold him for killing those wicked men who had trapped you. No! But because he feared we would find out who he really was. Oh, I know, Ben. That was it. Nevada had been bad. How bad I dare not imagine. . . . Don't you remember that day when he rode so furiously into the crowd to face Setter? How the mere sight of him froze them with terror. . . . Oh, Ben, I fear Nevada had been some great and terrible gunman. . . . That gentle, soft-voiced boy who was afraid to touch me with his little finger!'

'Gunman?' queried Ben, almost harshly. 'He could be any desperado I ever heard the name of—and what would I care?'

'Ben, you quite overlooked something,' rejoined Hettie, bravely. 'Nevada loved not only you—but me too . . . and I—I loved him.'

'Well, now, Hettie,' replied Ben, strangely softened, 'I reckon that's no news, though you never declared it so openly. But even though that was true, why should it make such a difference?'

'The boy came of a good family,' replied Hettie. 'He had an instinct to disappear when there was danger of my learning who he really was. There can be no other reason. He had pride. And he loved me so well, he couldn't bear to shame me.'

'Hettie, did that son-of-a-gun make love to you?' queried Ben, struggling with his resentment and remorse.

'Did—he?' murmured she, with a little broken laugh. 'Ben, when he found out I cared—he—he made the most terrible love to me. . . . Oh, I can never forget—never get over it!'

'Well!' ejaculated her brother, amazed out of his own pain. 'How and when did he ever get the chance?'

'Wouldn't you like to know?' asked Hettie, archly.

'And you—my little sixteen-year-old sister! . . . Who can ever tell about a girl?'

'Ben, didn't Ina Blaine love *you* when she was five years old—and ten—and fourteen?' queried Hettie. 'And at eighteen after she'd been away from you four years?'

'Thank the Lord, she did. I've never begun to understand it. But it's beautiful, wonderful. . . . Did my pard, Nevada, ever know you, too, had that strange, glorious thing—woman's love—for him?'

'Yes, he knew,' replied Hettie. 'He knew he had my faith, too. . . . And, Ben, *that* is why I've never lost him. I know. Nevada is not dead. He is not false to me—to what I believed he had become. And somewhere, somehow, he will come back to me—to us.'

'My God! that's good to hear!' exclaimed Ben, with fervent emotion. 'You strike me right in the heart, Hettie.'

'I'm glad. I've wanted to speak for so long,' replied Hettie, simply. 'And there's another thing that touches us closely.'

'What's that?' he asked, anxiously.

'Mother is failing. Haven't you noticed it?'

Ben nodded, 'I reckon I try not to see, but I do.'

'She has brightened up since spring came,' went on Hettie. 'Mother loves the sun. She likes to be outdoors. But I believe this valley is bad for her. It's bad for me, too, in winter.'

'I've been afraid of that very thing,' declared her brother, thoughtfully. 'But there's a possibility of some organic disease.'

'Mother's not old,' said Hettie. 'She ought to live many years yet. But we must do something to help her. Ben, I suggest you take her to San Francisco. Get the opinion and advice of some up-to-date physician. Take Ina with you. Blaine will be safe with me. I'll run the ranch, never fear.'

'By George! it's a great idea,' declared Ben, 'Ina will be tickled.'

'Ben, I actually believe you've decided already,' replied Hettie, suddenly feeling radiant.

'Reckon I have, and I'll bet you Ina squeals with joy. Let's go tell her this minute.'

Ina was in the yard, gathering violets. Little Blaine babbled at sight of his father and ran as fast as his short fat legs could carry him.

'Well, good-mawnin', you-all!' said Ina, gayly. 'Say, you look excited.' . . . Then she kissed Hettie and continued, 'Many happy, happy returns of the day.'

Ben snatched the boy up and, holding him on his arm, he confronted Ina with a smile that held great portent.

'How soon can you get ready for a trip to San Francisco?' he asked, quite naturally.

'What! Oh, I knew something was up,' she cried. 'How soon? ... Fifteen minutes!'

'Ha! Ha! I though you'd hit the sadddle and ride that idea pronto,' said Ben. 'But you needn't be so swift as that.'

'Ben, are you really going to take me to Frisco?'

'Yes. It's all settled. But—'

'You darling,' she cried, kissing him. 'I wanted to go somewhere. The winter has been so long, so confining. Klamath Falls was my hope. But San Francisco! Oh!'

'Ina, I'm sorry I don't think of such things,' replied Ben, ruefully. 'I guess I'd fallen into a rut. You must thank Hettie.'

Whereupon Ina most heartily embraced Hettie, and then, coming down to earth, she said: 'Let's go in to breakfast. You can tell me there all about this grand idea.'

'We'll tell you now,' said Ben. 'The trip

to Frisco is on mother's account and we mustn't discuss it before her. The fact is, Ina, mother is failing. Something wrong with her. Hettie suggested we take her to San Francisco to see a competent physician. Blaine will be safe with Hettie and so will the ranch. What do you say, dearest?'

'I say it's a happy and wise suggestion,' returned Ina, with a nod of commendation toward Hettie. 'This damp cold Tule Lake does not agree with mother.'

CHAPTER 6

HETTIE'S folk did not return from San Francisco on the date they had specified, nor did she receive any letter from them. This, added to the increasing perplexity of the duties that had been left to her, wore her into such a nervous state that she failed to keep her boast about running the ranch.

One day several strangers from Klamath Falls called upon Hettie. They were business men, representing an Oregon syndicate, who were buying up land around Tule Lake Valley. The Ides had received offers before, but never anything like the one made by these men. Hettie was shrewd enough to grasp that some situation had arisen, such as the possibility of a railroad from Klamath Falls, to increase the value of the Ide property enormously. She neither refused nor accepted the offer, saying that control of the ranches was in her brother's hand. She scarcely ever thought of herself as sharing equally with Ben the fortune their father had left them.

Hettie happened to be out on the farm somewhere when her people returned: and upon coming back to the house, hot and dusty and weary, what was her surprise and joy to be waylaid in the hall by her mother and Ina. It took no second glance to see that the little trip had been happily beneficial, especially to her mother.

'Oh—Ben,' she cried. 'I—I fell down on running the ranch! . . . The silly fools nagged me—to death!'

'Who?' queried Ben, suddenly aghast.

'The boys—and some of the men—too. They just—made my life—miserable.'

'Well! the lazy sons-of-guns!' ejaculated Ben. 'I'll fire the whole caboodle of them.'

'Oh, no, Ben. It's not so—so bad as that. They only hatched every pretense and excuse to approach me—just to make outrageous love.'

Ben's haw-haw mingled with Ina's scream of laughter. The high spirits of Ben and Ina and the certain evidence of her mother's improvement were sufficient to lift Hettie to the heights.

'What'd you bring me from Frisco?' she asked presently.

'Candy,' replied Ben, with a smile.

'A new spring dress and hat—oh, adorable,' replied Ina.

'I fetched you somethin' too,' added Mrs. Ide.

'I'm—I'm almost glad you went off and left me alone,' responded Hettie, gratefully.

Nothing was said during supper about the main object of the journey to San Francisco. Later, when Mrs. Ide had retired, Ben took Hettie into Ina's room, where the ecstatic Blaine gloated over his new toys.

'Well, Hettie, your sending us off on this trip means a great change in our lives,' began Ben, gravely.

'Oh—Ben!' faltered Hettie.

Here Ina interposed to reprove Ben for his abruptness. She added, 'Hettie, it's nothing to frighten you.'

'Winter and spring are too damp and cold for mother,' continued Ben. 'To keep her here longer will endanger her life.'

'Then we certainly won't keep her,' replied Hettie.

'Exactly. Ina and I got that far, anyway, in our decision.'

'Will mother—be all right in some other climate?'

'She'll get well,' answered Ben. 'She needs a mild, dry, climate in winter and a high, dry, climate in summer.'

'Where can we find them?'

'Easy enough. But the thing that stumps Ina and me is how to decide what's best to do.'

'That's easy enough,' returned Hettie. 'I will go with mother and live with her.'

'Sure you will. But that doesn't solve the problem.'

'Surely we can afford it, Ben?'

'I reckon. However, the point is I don't want to be separated from mother and you. Neither does Ina. That much is settled. We won't be separated.'

'Ben, you can't imagine how happy you make me,' said Hettie, feelingly. 'I have only mother and you and yours to live for. . . .'

'We've sure got to go with you,' interrupted Ben, forcibly. 'But what to do is sure a sticker.'

'Sell—out!' said Hettie, huskily.

'But we've lived here all our lives. This land has made us prosperous. It's home.'

'Ben, it'd not be home without mother.'

'No. And it wouldn't be the same if we were all separated. But I'd hate to sacrifice the land just to get a quick sale. And we'll need money, wherever we go.'

'Ben, I can sell this lake property of ours for two hundred thousand,' declared Hettie.

Her brother stared. At length he spoke: 'Hettie, don't make statements like that. It's hard enough to make decisions.'

'I can sell for that *to-morrow*,' grandly added Hettie.

'Now I know she's crazy,' wailed Ben, turning to his wife.

'Bennie boy, you're only a wild-horse hunter. Hettie and I have the business brains.'

'By George!' cried Ben, leaping up. 'You're right. But I can't believe we could sell for that.'

'It's true, Ben. Listen,' said Hettie, and then briefly told about the offer of the Klamath Falls syndicate.

'Horses not included in the deal? Not

California Red?' queried Ben, beginning to manifest signs of extreme excitement.

'Their offer embraced land and buildings on this ranch, and all the Ide cattle. But no horses.'

'Girls, it's settled!' cried Ben. He kissed Ina and hugged Hettie.

'Ben, aren't you ashamed? All that show of gladness over selling our home!' exclaimed Ina, reproachfully.

'Forgive me and try to understand,' he said. 'It is home and I reckon I love it, but not as you. Father was hard on me for years. He made me an outcast. For years more I lived over there across the sage hills, hunting wild horses, lonely and wretched. Then Nevada dropped into my life. Then, Ina, you came, too. . . . And so between you I was brought home again. But despite all, there has been something lacking. . . . This ranch country is too populated for me. The sage hills and the valleys are now ranches and farms. I'd be happier in a new country—say in Arizona, where the ranges are vast and ranches few. I'd do better, working as I used to. . . . That's why I'm glad to sell out here, to take mother where she'll get strong again, where you all will be the happier because of these things.'

'Arizona? Ben, you didn't tell me you'd decided,' expostulated Ina.

'I hadn't until now. Hettie settled it, bless her heart.'

'Arizona!' murmured Hettie, thoughtfully. 'We know so little about Arizona. Isn't it very wild?'

'Wild? I reckon,' replied Ben. 'Arizona is everything northern California used to be. It is a wonderful country for the pioneer.'

'Hettie,' added Ina, 'we met an Arizonian in Frisco, a grizzled old fellow. I wish you could have seen him. He surely was full of Arizona. But Ben didn't tell you all.'

'What'd I forget?' inquired Ben, lamely.

'About the bad crews who live off the ranchers. That worries me, Ben, if you must go there.'

'It'd worry me, too, if I thought I'd fall into such company as the old Arizonian bragged about. But he was only blowing. . . . At that, though, I think I could stand a few wild cowboys. Couldn't you, Hettie?'

Hettie tried to smile, but her effort was a

71

wan one. There had seemed to come a knocking at her heart.

'I'll keep Forlorn River Ranch and Mule Deer Flat,' mused Ben, pacing the room. 'I'd never part with them. We own them, Nevada and I, share and share alike. . . . Some day I'll come back to see them, and who knows?'

Hettie could not tell whether she wanted to weep or rejoice. Ben's revelation had not been such a surprise, though the violence of his feelings dismayed her. How he had welcomed this opportunity to get away from Tule Lake!

Ben was late at breakfast next morning. No one had to tell Hettie and Ina that he had been out to the corrals. He strode in more like his old self than for months, keen-eyed, virile, with the spring of a rider in his step.

'Say, girls, what do you think?' he declared, radiantly. 'Red came to me this morning. He did, and it sure tickled me. And I said to him, "Old boy, you're going back to the unfenced ranges." He understood me, too. . . . Oh, Ina—Hettie, I'm another man this mawnin'!'

'You look it, Bennie,' replied Ina.

'But you and Hettie look as if you'd lain awake and cried all night.'

'That's a way women have, sometimes,' said Ina. 'It's a break, of course. But we're happy for you, and, thank God, we've found the way to restore mother.'

Mrs. Ide came in at the moment.

'Nana, we's doan Ar-zoonie,' chirped up little Blaine, with great importance.

Mrs. Ide had not until that moment been given any inkling of the secret.

'Land's sake!' she ejaculated. 'So that's the mystery. ... Ben Ide, you ain't goin' back to chasin' wild hosses? Your father would turn over in his grave.'

Ben Ide was not noted for deception or beating round the bush. Despite warning glances from Hettie and a kick under the table from Ina he told his mother that he was thinking of selling out and moving to Arizona. Mrs. Ide declared she would never go or permit Hettie to leave home. Ben tried to expostulate with her and, failing that, tried to laugh it off. But when his mother asked him a deliberate question

73

he maintained silence. Whereupon she rose from the table and, weeping, left the room.

'It was a shock, Ben,' said Ina. 'You were so abrupt. But she'll come round to it all right.'

'Leave mother to us,' added Hettie.

They talked it over, and at the conclusion of breakfast both Ina and Hettie urged Ben, now that he had made the great decision, to proceed at once towards its fulfillment.

'There's something sort of tough about this deal,' said Ben. 'Yet it's great, too. . . . I'll go to Klamath Falls to-day. Reckon the papers will require your signature, Hettie. Say, what're you going to do with all that money?'

'What money?' queried Hettie, blankly.

'Why, ninny, your share in the Ide property!'

'Goodness! I never thought of that in money. Ben, I'll want the same share in your Arizona ranch.'

'Good. You're one sister in a million. I'll leave you to talk some sense into mother, and you, Ina, to do the same by your folks. Reckon that'll be leaving you a job, because you and Marvie have all the sense in the Blaine family.'

CHAPTER 7

THREE days later the Ides stood on their front porch. Ben held a certified check in his hand, for which he had signed away the broad fertile acres of Tule Lake Ranch. He had also agreed to turn over the property before the first of September.

'By George! it happened quick!' he exclaimed, breathing hard. 'Ina—Hettie—we're homeless.'

'Ben, if it hurts you to lose this ranch, how will you ever give up Forlorn River?' asked Hettie, wonderingly.

'I'm keeping Forlorn River,' declared Ben. 'That reminds me, I'll have to ride out there.'

'I'll go with you,' said Hettie.

'Me, too,' added Ina.

'Honest, girls, I'd rather go alone,' returned Ben.

'We won't intrude on your grief, Bennie dear,' smiled Ina.

The morning of departure came.

A string of horses led the cavalcade up the long hill road. They were in the charge of three of Ben's best riders. Next came the chuck wagon, and after it the one containing extra supplies, both of which were drawn by four horses. Ben's wagon came third, and Hettie's last. Late in the afternoon a halt was made for the first camp.

When Hettie retired to her wagon that night she had a clearer realization of the tremendous task of travel Ben had set himself. Almost it daunted her. But there came a strengthening and enduring memory.

Her little tent room was as cozy and comfortable as she could have wished. Hettie prepared herself for bed, put out the lamp, and slipped into her blankets. She lay wide-eyed, staring at the flickering shadows on the canvas. After a while the low voices of the men ceased and the firelight faded.

Ben's cheery call seemed to rend Hettie's slumbers. To her dismay, she saw the sunlight gilding the canvas. Hettie made such haste that she was not late for breakfast.

It was a wonderful moment when the horses came trooping in behind the yelling riders. After that all seemed action and noise, color and life. Breakfast over, Hettie helped in what few tasks she could find, then made her bed and was ready for the long day's ride.

Then followed days that held increasing interest for Hettie. They expected to reach Lineville in time to pitch camp early, but sunset had come and gone before they rode into a wide street lined by strange old houses, which constituted the border town. Presently Ben poked his head between the curtains at the back of the wagon and said: 'There's a hotel here, but I reckon we'll dodge it. It was a terrible dive once, an' it's pretty raw yet. But there's a woman has a nice place near the edge of town. We can drive in her yard and get our supper there. It'll be a little change and save waiting. The men will go on to a farm outside town and make camp.'

The driver called, 'Getdap' and again the wagon rolled on.

Darkness had fallen when again Ben

called: 'Come, mother and Hettie. Supper is ready. And I'll bet it'll be good, for I was in the kitchen. The woman's name is Mrs. Wood. She's a Westerner, all right, and likes to talk.'

Ina was beside Ben, and he held the sleepy Blaine in his arms. Ben led the way round to the side, where a bright light shone. They were ushered into a clean, warm kitchen, where in the light Hettie saw a woman who appeared most kind. She had keen eyes that did not miss anything. Hettie liked her, particularly her solicitude for the weary little Blaine, who did not thoroughly awake until he was being fed.

CHAPTER 8

THE days multiplied until Hettie no longer could keep account of them. Endless leagues of Nevada, wastes of barren ground, plains of green, valleys between bleak ranges, ridge and upland ever heaving higher, lay back along the winding, rolling road.

On the Ide caravan traveled, down into the dim-hazed marvelous region of canyons. Kanab was a lonesome Mormon settlement close to the Arizona line. Its white church stood out against the green background: orchards and fields encompassed log cabins and stone houses. The sun smiled upon the fertile spot.

Arizona at last! Early the next morning Hettie heard that pealing slogan from Ben's lusty throat. One long breathless look won Hettie Ide forever. After all the weeks of travel, the training of eye, the judgment of color and distance, she was confounded here on the border of Arizona.

At sunset the riders halted to camp in the edge of the pines, far above the valley which it had taken all day to cross. It had to be a dry camp, but the horses had been watered below. Hettie stood under the last pines and faced the west. After so many camps on the desert, how wonderful this stand in the forest!

'Supper,' sang out Mrs. Ide, cheerily.

That night Hettie sought her bed early.

CHAPTER 9

IT was late July and the long wagon-train journey had ended. The Ides were comfortably camped on a running brook in a grove of cottonwoods outside the little Arizona hamlet of Sunshine.

Forty miles from Sunshine lay the town Winthrop. The Ides had stopped there long enough to ascertain that there were a number of good stores, two banks, a huge sawmill, workmen available, and a sprinkling of solid prosperous Westerners.

After an absence of three days Ben returned to camp like a whirlwind.

Hettie called out to Ina: 'It's Ben. And you can bet we're settled now.'

They ran out to find him surrounded by his men, from whom, as Ina eagerly called, he broke away.

'I've bought my ranch,' he said, with solemn finality.

'Where?' asked Ina.

'About a hundred miles from here. A thousand acres. Fine grazing all round. No other ranches near. Ten thousand head of cattle. Forty thousand dollars! Isn't that a bargain? But listen. I'll tell you all about it. . . . Day before yesterday I rode back to Winthrop after a hard trip to half a dozen ranches. I was pretty discouraged and was coming back here pronto. Some horsemen rode up to the hotel where I was sitting out in front. They got off, tied up to the hitching-rail—went in to drink. Presently some one touched me on the shoulder. I turned round to see one of the riders. "Excuse me, sir," he said. "Are you the Californian who's lookin' for a ranch hereabouts?"

'"Yes. My name's Ide," I replied, "I'm not having luck."

'"They tell me you're hard to please. Just what kind of a ranch you want to buy?"

'So I told him just what I was looking for. He said: "My name's Burridge. I've got exactly what you want. Somewheres around ten thousand head. Lots of unbranded calves an' yearlin's. Cabins an' corrals not worth speakin' of. But water, grass, timber, an' range can't be beat in Arizona. It suits me to sell for cash. That's what they call me—Cash Burridge. Suppose you get a lawyer an' come over to the city hall an' see my title. Then if it strikes you right, I'll take you out to my ranch." Well, Mr. Cash Burridge hit me about right. I liked his blunt way of putting the deal, and knew he didn't care a rap whether he sold or not. I consulted a lawyer recommended by the hotel man, and we met Burridge at the town hall. The title was clear. So I told Burridge I'd like a look at his property. We started right out in a buckboard behind a team of fast horses, I'll tell you. For thirty miles or more the road was good. Then we pitched off into what he called the brakes. Briefly, that part of the road was a terror. It was only a trail, up and down, narrow and rough. Burridge said there was a better way in, but longer. We reached his ranch before sunset. I'm only going to tell you that it was the most beautiful and wildest place I ever saw in my life. If I don't miss my guess, you'll all fall in love with it as quickly as I did.'

'Ben, am I in on this ranch deal with you?' asked Hettie.

'That's for you to say, my dear sister,'

replied Ben. 'But I believe I'd rather you didn't come in, for it is a risk.'

'Then I'll take the risk.'

'So will I. We'll share the risk, and together make a grand success of it,' added Ina, happily.

Next morning the travelers rode into rough forest land, where the main grade was uphill. Travel was exasperatingly slow. Only fifteen miles were covered that day, and everybody was wearied and glad to make camp. Before sleep came to Hettie she heard a blood-curdling cry of a wild beast unknown to her. It seemed a deep far-away moan, so sad and uncanny that she shuddered. Next morning Ben told her the cry had come from a timber wolf, a beast the guide called a lofer and said was plentiful in those parts.

Tedious travel began into an ever-increasingly wild and wonderful woodland. The trees hid any possible view of the country beyond. The air grew clearer, less oppressive, and the heat no longer made the shade desirable. Massed foliage, like green lace, dark-brown seamed boles of pines, patches of sunlight on the white grass, the red of a tufted flower, like a stiff brush dipped in paint, and golden aisles of needles up and down the forest, held for Hettie a never-failing delight.

About the middle of the afternoon the travelers rode to the edge of open light forest.

'We're here,' shouted Ben, leaping down. 'California to Arizona! ... Ina— mother—Blaine—Hettie, get down and come in, as these Arizonians say.'

'Gee! I see turkeys!' cried Marvie, leaping off his horse and tearing his rifle from the saddle sheath.

'Indian!' called Ben, after him.

The Ides, imbued with Ben's spirit, set earnestly to work to wrest a beautiful home from this wilderness.

Those were busy days. One hot midday, during the noon rest hour, a rider appeared on the road. Arriving at the camp quarters, he dismounted and hailed the riders in a booming voice.

'I'm Tom Day an' I'm wantin' to meet Mr. Ide.'

Raidy led him up to Ben.

'Howdy, sir!' said the visitor. 'Are you Mr. Ide?'

'Yes, and I'm glad to meet you, Mr. Day,' replied Ben.

'I'm your nearest neighbor,' said Day. 'My ranch is over heah ten miles or so. Reckon I'm a little late in callin'. Shore we're pretty slow folks in Arizona.'

'Better late than never,' returned Ben, with his frank smile. 'Meet my family, Mr. Day. . . . This is Ina, my wife . . . and this my mother. . . . Hettie, my sister. . . . And this is my son Blaine, who's destined to be an Arizona rancher.'

'Wal, now I'm shore glad to meet you-all,' drawled the visitor. 'Reckon I'd like you to show me aboot,' said Day to Ben.

'I'll be glad to,' replied Ben. Then he turned to Hettie. 'Sis, have Hank fix us up something to eat.'

They strolled away in earnest conversation and did not return for an hour. Whereupon Hettie set lunch for them on the table under the fly; after which she repaired to her wagon-tent close by.

CHAPTER 10

SOME eighteen or twenty miles from Tom Day's ranch, Judge Franklidge maintained the last outpost of his extensive cattle range. The hundred and sixty acres which comprised the ranch lay in a strip along the rim of Chevelon Canyon. Cabins and corrals, built of logs, showed the weathering of years of storm and heat. The main cabin stood on the rim, and the wide porch ran to the edge of the gray rock wall. On this mid-August afternoon the porch was a shady and cool place to lounge and rest.

Judge Franklidge had just arrived on one of his rare visits to this margin of his vast cattle interests. The ride out from Winthrop had tired him, and with a great sigh of content he sank into one of the comfortable seats on the porch.

'Jack,' he said to the cowboy who had driven him out, 'I'm to meet Day here. Put the horses up. I'll stay all night. Then find Day if he's arrived, and come back yourself.'

'Yes, sir. An' how aboot Stewart?' replied the cowboy.

'Stewart? Tell him I'll send word when I want him,' returned the judge, somewhat impatiently.

'All right, sir,' said Jack, and slapping the reins he drove away toward the barn.

'Humph! I'd forgotten about that foreman,' muttered Judge Franklidge. 'Damn the cattle business, anyway. . . . I'd like to forget it and enjoy the peace of this place.'

This ranch was a favorite with Franklidge, owing to its wild beauty and solitude and the abundance of deer and turkey that ranged the forests. Every fall he came there for a few days of hunting.

'I'll invite young Ide to hunt with me in October,' he soliloquized, 'Fine chap that. Too bad about the rotten deal he fell into here. It sure doesn't speak well for Arizona. And what a lovely girl that sister of his! . . . If I were younger now . . .'

The judge fell into a daydream that amused as well as made him sigh. Presently a jangle of spurs and thud of footsteps interrupted his reverie, and he looked up to see Tom Day and the cowboy approaching. Day had his hand on the younger man's shoulder and was talking earnestly. That reminded the judge of the strong friendship Day had always evinced for this young man the range called Texas Jack. How good to see two men he could swear by!

'Howdy, Judge! I'm shore glad to see you,' said Day, as he heavily mounted the porch with beaming smile and extended hand.

'How are you, Tom? Pull up that bench. We're in for a good long talk.'

'Wal, it's aboot time,' returned Day, as he deposited his huge bulk on a seat, with back to the porch rail. He threw his sombrero to the floor.

The judge laughed, and then glanced sharply at the cowboy waiting at the step.

'Jack, you've got something on your mind,' he said.

'Yes, sir, but it can wait. No hurry, sir,' replied the cowboy hastily.

'Wal, Judge, if you'll take a hunch from me you'll not wait too long,' interposed Day.

'Come up and sit in with us, Jack,' was Franklidge's reply.

The cowboy did as he was bidden, but he made no reply. He sat near the porch rail and leaned over to gaze down into the green canyon. The judge's appraising eyes took stock of the lithe figure, the service-worn garb, the lean bearded face that was half hidden under the wide sombrero.

'Stewart was in town last night, drunk,' spoke Franklidge, casually. 'Is he here to-day?'

'Yes, sir—an' he's all right now,' rejoined the cowboy.

'Judge, your foreman *may* be all right, as Texas Jack says, but I've my doubts,' put in Day. 'I cain't find anythin' ag'in' him, 'cept the drinkin'. But I've just come to distrust the man. Mebbe I'm wrong. It shore is a distrustful time.'

'Mr. Franklidge, I hunted up Stewart, an' found him an' Dillon off under a cedar, talkin' deep an' quiet,' said Texas Jack.

'Dillon? Who's he? That name's familiar.'

'Dillon is young Ben Ide's foreman,' replied Day, with interest. 'He's held jobs all over the range the last two years. Fine cowman. Engagin' sort of chap. Everybody likes him. I shore do.'

'Which ought to be recommendation enough for Ide or even me, sore old cattleman that I am. . . . Well, Tom, have you considered the offer I made you some time ago?'

'Reckon I have, Judge, an' I'm acceptin' with thanks. I know I'm getting the best of the deal,' returned Day, heartily.

'We're not agreed on that. You're counting only the relative value of your ranch compared with this one. But I count your friendship and help. . . . It's a deal, then.'

'Heah's my hand, Judge,' said Day, reaching out his huge paw.

'We're partners, then,' replied Franklidge, as he shook the proffered hand. 'We'll throw these ranches and all the stock together. I'll have papers made out when I get back to town. . . . Now get what's troubling you off your chest.'

'Wal, boss, the situation heah has grown from bad to wuss,' returned Day, seriously.

'Where do you mean by here?' demanded Franklidge.

'All this range thet haids along the wild

brakes of the Mogollons. Say, fifty miles in a straight line.'

'Yes?'

'Reckon it takes in a good many ranches, countin' everybody, an' mebbe two hundred thousand haid of cattle. But Ben Ide's range an' this one of yours an' mine have come in fer the wust of the rustlin' this last month.'

'We've always had rustlers to deal with. We always will have. What's the difference between say a year or five years ago and now?'

'Wal, Judge, fer a big cattleman you're shore poor informed.'

'Tom, you know most of my holdings lie along the railroad and north in the open country. I know next to nothing about what goes on in this backwoods. That's why I wanted you for a partner.'

'The difference you asked aboot I'd calkilate off-hand to stand you an' me an' Ben Ide around ten thousand haid.'

The judge's boots came down off the porch rail with a crash.

'What?' he demanded, incredulously.

'Boss, I said ten thousand, an' mebbe thet's conservative. Shore most of this rustled stock belongs to Ide. But we've lost a good deal, an' stand to lose more or all unless somethin' is done. You see, Ide proved an easy mark. He bought out Burridge, who had some stock, nobody knows how much. Wal, young Ide's cow outfit was green an' raw for Arizona. I gave him two of my best riders. One of them, Sam Tull, was found daid in the woods. Shot! We've never found out aboot it. The other cowboy, Rang Jones, had a quarrel with Dillon an' quit. I cain't see thet Dillon has changed matters fer the better. But I reckon no one man could at this stage of the game.'

'So they've hit young Ide hard,' muttered Franklidge, indignantly. 'Funny he didn't complain to me. I've seen something of him lately.'

'Ide's not thet kind, Judge,' replied Day, warmly. 'He's as game as they come. An' his sister—say, she's a thoroughbred. She stands to lose 'most as much as Ide.'

The two men, warming to the subject, might have been alone for all the notice they took of Texas Jack. He leaned far over the porch rail, his face hidden, his long lithe form strung like a whipcord. It was the strained position of a listening deer.

'Tom, I admire Miss Ide very much indeed, and her brother, too,' responded the judge. 'I regret exceedingly the reception Arizona has given these two fine young people. I am ashamed. We all ought to be ashamed. We must end this damned wholesale cattle-stealing.'

'Ahuh! . . . Boss, I reckon I feel it more than you, as I've come to be friends with the Ides. Why, he paid Burridge's debt to me. Four thousand! An' then I'm a son-of-a-gun if he didn't send for Elam Hatt an' pay the lien he had on Burridge. Don't know how much. But the Hatts were drunk fer a week.'

'Well!' ejaculated Franklidge.

'Ever since then the rustlers have been bolder than I ever seen them yet in Arizonie.'

'Who are these rustlers, Tom?'

'Huh! If I said what I think it'd be old to you. But I reckon there is a new leader workin' now. Shore they're all working'. But there's some big chief who's keen as a wolf.'

'Where are these stolen cattle driven?'

asked the judge, wonderingly. 'I've been twenty years in this business. Yet this beats me.'

'Reckon the stock gets drove everywhere,' replied Day.

'Not to the railroad?' queried Franklidge, aghast.

'Shore to the railroad. Not to Winthrop. But, man, there's other stations along the line. Then I had a Mexican sheepherder tell me he'd seen herds of cattle drove over the Rim, down into the Tonto. Thet's a wild country. Shore no cow outfits are followin' rustlers down into the Tonto.'

'Tom, the Hatts are a bad outfit,' rejoined the judge, thoughtfully. 'Some years ago I had trouble with Elam Hatt. The Stillwells are another. Surely these backwoodsmen run with these rustler outfits.'

'Shore they do,' snorted Day. 'But I reckon the Hatts ain't the ringleaders. Cedar Hatt is the wust of thet bad lot. He's dangerous. Bad *hombre* with guns! Ever' once in a while I heah of some shootin' scrape he's been in out there, among his own kind. The Mexican herders are afraid of Cedar. But they're close-mouthed. In the years I've lived heah I've known of several sheepherders bein' murdered.'

'Cedar Hatt?' mused the judge. 'Yes, I know of him. Bad name; gun-fighter. . . . How many Hatts in the family?'

'I know the whole outfit,' replied Day. 'Elam an' me always got along pretty good. But I've no use fer Cedar. He's the eldest son. Then there's Henny an' Tobe—packrats if I ever seen any in the woods. An' last there's a girl—Rose. Reckon she'll be about sixteen. Pretty slip of a lass, whose mother died when she was a baby.'

'What a pity! No mother. No decent home. No schooling. There are many such unfortunate girls in this wild country, alas! Why don't some cowboy take this Rose away and marry her? She might turn out a good woman.'

'Shore she might. An' so I've said often. But I ain't hit on any cowboy yet who cared to risk his skin down there in the brakes.'

'What has Ide done in regard to the raids on his stock?' asked the judge, curiously.

'Aboot all any man could,' replied Day,

admiringly. 'He has spent a lot of money hiring extra hands to trail stock. He took over this Dillon at a high salary. An' I reckon he puts a good deal of confidence in Dillon. Funny about Ben Ide, though. He gets sore when the rustlers make a raid. But he really don't care a damn aboot the cattle. He's shore afraid fer his horses, though, specially thet California Red. There's a grand hoss, Judge. I'll bet if the rustlers got thet stallion Ben Ide would hit the trail himself. Strikes me he's seen some wild life. He shore is a rider. Strange, wonderful sort of chap Ben Ide is. I'm just gettin' acquainted with him. He always struck me as a rancher whose heart wasn't in his ranch. There's somethin' he wants. But he worships his wife an' kid an' thet handsome sister. It ain't thet. I cain't explain what I don't savvy. But I've a hunch young Ide has been hurt. Mebbe he killed some one over in California an' had to get out. I've often wondered if thet could be it. Then it might be he's *lookin'* fer some man. Like a Texan, you know, who he never *forgot*.'

Before the judge could reply to Day's

earnest statement the cowboy, Texas Jack, whirled round with a silent wrestling violence that indicated a suppressed and poignant passion. Under the shadow of his broad sombrero his eyes gleamed like clear coals of fire.

'I'm—heahin'—all—you say!' he burst out, pantingly.

'Suppose you are, Jack?' queried the judge, in kindly surprise. 'If I'd minded about being overheard I'd have sent you away.'

Tom Day stared, and it was evident he was not so surprised as expectant. He had lived with cowboys all his life.

'Wal, what the hell ails you son?' he growled.

Jack whirled away in the same sudden violent action with which he had faced them, only now it seemed there was added a fierce struggle of mind over body. He bent over the rail. He sprang up erect and rigid. In a moment more he turned toward the men again, to present a remarkably transformed front.

'I'm shore beggin' pardon, Mr. Franklidge, an' of you too, Tom,' he drawled, in slow, cool, easy speech. 'I couldn't help heahin' all you said, an'— wal, it knocked me off my balance.'

'No offense, Jack,' replied the judge, kindly. 'I think Tom's talk sort of locoed me, too.'

'Wal, see heah, you long, lean, hungry-eyed Texan,' spoke up Day, forcefully, 'jest *why* did I knock you off your balance?'

'Tom, I reckon I happened to hit on a way to fix the rustlers,' replied Jack, nonchalantly.

'The hell you did!' ejaculated Day. He accepted the statement without doubt or ridicule. He was pondering deeply. His sharp light-blue glance was riveted on the shadowy, half-concealed eyes of the cowboy.

Judge Franklidge sat up with a jerk, but his smile robbed his action of a convincing sincerity.

'Jack, we'd be grateful for any suggestions from one as well proven as you on the range.'

'Wal, what is this heah idee you hit on?' added Day, sharply.

'Shore it's as simple as a-b-c,' rejoined the cowboy, blandly. 'Somebody has got to ride down into the brakes an' get thick with the rustlers.'

'Oh-ho! I see!' quoth Day, almost derisively.

The cowboy's mild manner changed subtly, in a way to impress his listeners, though they could not have told how.

'Somebody has got to shoot up the Hatts an' mebbe the Stillwells. An' kill some of that Pine Tree outfit—in particular the *hombre* who's at the haid of it.'

'Shore it'd be hard enough,' admitted Texas Jack, who refused to see the ridicule.

'Hard! Fly, cowboy, you're loco!' exploded the other. 'Shore you hit on the way to fix the rustlers. Shore! But who'n hell's goin' to do it? Was you figurin' on us hirin' some fancy gunslingers to do the little job? Kingfisher from Texas, huh? An' Wes Hardin? Or mebbe you had in mind some new Billy the Kid or Pat Garret? Or more like, perhaps, Jim Lacy, who they say has been hidin' quiet in Arizonie for a long time!'

Texas Jack's tan appeared to become a shade less brown. He grew tense, steely-eyed.

'Tom Day, how long have you known me?' he demanded, in a voice that rang.

'Two years an' more, son,' replied Day, surrendering to something compelling.

'Would you trust me?'

'I shore would. With my stock, my money, my reputation ... with my life— so help me Gawd!'

'Judge Franklidge, how long have I worked for you?' queried the cowboy, turning to the other.

'About a year and a half, as I remember.'

'An' what is your opinion of me—as a man?' flashed the cowboy, growing more piercing of eye and voice.

'Jack, you're the squarest and best man, the finest hand who ever worked for me!' responded the judge, feelingly.

'Thank you. Reckon you can have no idee what that means to me,' returned the cowboy. 'An' you'd trust me?'

'As well as I would my own flesh and blood.'

Texas Jack removed his sombrero and sailed it against the wall. His brow was broad and pale, his clear light eyes seemed to burn with a steady flame; there were white hairs in the long locks smoothed back above his ears; under the thin bronze beard, cheeks and lips set hard.

'Wal, then, it's my job to fix the rustlers,' he said, deliberately.

'You! Nonsense!' declared the judge. 'You wouldn't tackle that alone?'

'It's got to be done alone.'

'Nonsense! I say.'

'Judge,' interposed Tom Day, 'it shore does look thet way. But wait. This cowboy has got somethin' up his sleeve. I always knowed it. ... Come heah, Texas Jack. Spring it.'

What shrewd, hard, comprehending yet wondering light flashed from the old rancher's eyes!

'Listen,' went on Jack, bending to his hearers. 'To serve Arizona an' you an' your good friends I've got to become a rustler. I may have to go a long way to find the leader of this heah Pine Tree outfit. I'll have to drink an' steal an' kill. Shore I may lose my life finishin' the job. An' I want my secret kept till it's ended. Then if I come back alive I want my name cleared.'

'Who'n hell *are* you?' asked Tom Day, in low and husky voice.

'Man, you're forcing me against my will,' said the judge, rising to his feet. 'I don't want you to attempt this thing alone. It's a wild cowboy idea. You'd only be killed. But I admire you, Jack.'

'Dead or alive, I want my name cleared!' exclaimed the cowboy.

'Of what?'

'Of the stealin' an' lyin' I'll have to do.'

'Man, I have power to make you a deputy sheriff right here and now. And I'd do it.'

'No. Shore I'll never be an officer of the law. What I want is this. Your word of honor to keep my secret, an', if I come back alive, to clear my name.'

'Jack, are you going to persist in this mad plan?' demanded the judge.

'Reckon I shore will, whether you stand by me or not,' returned the other, grimly. 'It's too late now. I've got a reason, Judge. But it'd only be fair for you to uphold me—to tell in court, if necessary, that you an' Tom Day were parties to the job I undertook.'

'Jack, you misunderstand,' replied Franklidge, hastily. 'Don't make me ashamed. I will give you any support and authority right here and now. In writing, if you want.'

'Only your word, Judge.'

'There! You have it. And here's my hand.'

Texas Jack broke from that strong, earnest handclasp to make the same proffer to the other rancher.

'Tom, will you stand by me—when I come back?'

'Hell, yes,' boomed Day as he pumped the cowboy's arm up and down.

Abruptly, then, with sharp husky expulsion of breath, Jack wrenched clear of the vigorous grasp and wheeled to a post of the porch, against which he leaned and clutched hard. Something long buried was being resurrected. Ignominy loomed out of the past to stain an honest name. There was sacrifice here, far greater than appeared plain to the two grave and expectant, on-lookers. Whatever the strife was, it passed as swiftly as it had come. Then the cowboy turned again, somehow different, so that the judge and Day had awe added to their surprise.

'Gentlemen, I shore hate to give myself away,' he drawled. A smile outshone the strange, steely light in his eyes, 'But I reckon it's got to be done.'

'Wal now, who'n hell are you, anyhow?' queried Day as the other paused.

'Tom Day, the starved cowboy you once took pity on, happens to be Jim Lacy!'

CHAPTER 11

IT was Sunday, and that hour of the afternoon when all the men off duty at the Franklidge Ranch would be anywhere except round the bunkhouse. The cowboy, Texas Jack, striding in, was relieved to find himself alone. He made for his bunk for the purpose of hurriedly packing his few belongings. An old pair of black chaps worn thin hung at the head of his bed, with a belt and gun. An instinct prompted him to throw out his hand. There, as if by magic, the gun whirled in the air.

'Reckon it was fate,' he muttered as he sheathed the gun. 'Somethin' never let me stop practisin' that old draw. Wal, wal!'

In a few moments he had tied his belongings into a small roll to fit behind a saddle. His movements were swift, but made as if he were in a trance. He rose from his knees to gaze around; then strode out into the rude yet comfortable living room. Something prompted him to step before the mirror.

'Wal, so long, Texas Jack,' he said to the image reflected there. 'Reckon I been almost happy with you. A shave an' haircut will shore say *adios* to you forever. . . . An' then there'll be men who'll recognize you as Jim Lacy.'

A quarter of an hour later he rode briskly down a trail that led into the cedars. He had taken his own saddle, but the horse he bestrode was one long discarded by the boys at the ranch. Once under cover of the cedars, the rider pulled his mount to a walk. It was nineteen miles to Sunshine, and he wanted to reach that station after dark and board a night train without being seen.

A melancholy resignation had no power to cramp the slow-mounting exaltation in Jim Lacy's breast. Once free of the need to hurry, his mind reverted to the cause of this extraordinary adventure he had voluntarily accepted. Facts were cold, hard things. He had hidden his real identity; he had buried the past; he had risen on stepping-stones of his dead self to honest useful service; he had earned peace and victory, if not real happiness; and then, like a thunderbolt from heaven, an inevitable, irresistible fate had confronted him. What he had suffered during the moments when Tom Day had talked to Judge Franklidge about Ben and Hettie Ide! The old wound had not healed. The old love lived in his heart, stronger for the years of denial and repression. Jim Lacy rocked in his saddle. No eyes but those of hawks and prairie-dogs and perhaps a skulking coyote could see him surrender to his emotion. The old horse walked slowly down the trail; the west wind blew hot desert fragrance in the rider's face; the dust arose and the heat beat down.

'Aw, I shore knew it—all these weeks I knew,' whispered Jim, huskily. 'Ben come to Arizona to find me! . . . Didn't he comb California—didn't he send men to all the ranges in the West? . . . Didn't Tom Day tell me no more'n a month ago—how Ben Ide wanted to know if he'd ever met a cowboy called Nevada? . . . That was it—the name Ben gave me—*Nevada!* . . . He never forgot. An' at last he come to this wild land. He's married an' got a baby, they say. Old Amos Ide must have died an' left Ben rich. Shore it was Ina he married. Yet all that didn't hold him back.'

How terrible sweet and soul-satisfying that knowledge, and yet somehow bitter! In one tremendous moment of decision it had flung him back into the past, once more to own an infamous name. It had destroyed all he had built up. Only through the power of his dreaded name could he ever bring to successful issue the task he had set himself. What irony of fate that the fame he hated must be his open sesame to the rendezvous of the rustlers who were ruining Ben Ide!

'Like as not in the long-run I'll stop a bullet,' he muttered, harsh in his agitation. 'But hardly before I get the job 'most done. . . . An' shore that's be better so. Ben would never know I am Jim Lacy. An' Hettie—*she* would never know. . . . But I reckon that's not my kind of luck. Like as not I'll run plumb into Ben before it's over. An' Hettie, too! . . . O my God! How sweet an' terrible!'

He rode on through the hot waning afternoon, absorbed with the strife of his soul. A storm, passing in gray-black pall at a distance, cooled and cleared the atmosphere. Sunset came, a glorious gold and purple pageant in the west, where it vied with the wonder of a rainbow, receding with the storm. But Jim Lacy scarcely took note of these physical manifestations around him.

When darkness fell he had reached the outskirts of Sunshine, and he halted under a clump of cottonwoods. Here, removing saddle and bridle from the horse, he turned it loose. That act seemed to sever the last thread which bound him to the ranching life he had followed for long. It had, too, a singular effect upon the emotions which had beset him. The hour had come when he must plan his return to the old life. Wherefore he sat down beside his saddle and pack, and with bowed head and rending of his spirit, he slipped, as into a long-unused garment, back into the old personality. And it seemed that the instant this transformation was consummated his plan for the perilous adventure at hand was simple and complete. He had only to be Jim Lacy.

The whistle of an approaching freight train inspired him with an idea more satisfactory than the one of waiting for the passenger train. He would steal a ride on the freight, thus obviating any risk of being recognized at the station. To this end he shouldered his pack and saddle and, hurrying to the railroad track, which was only a few hundred paces away, he waited beside the slowly halting train, peering through the gloom for an empty car. At length it reached him, just as the train stopped. Jim threw pack and saddle aboard and climbed in.

Daylight found him across the Territory line, in New Mexico. When the train stopped outside of a town at a water tank, he threw his baggage out, down over a grassy embankment, and got off. He had some money, beside the considerable sum Judge Franklidge had forced him to take. And it was with something of an old familiar zest that he strolled into the town.

Before encountering any riders or cattlemen Jim entered a barber shop, from which he emerged a changed man. Next he purchased a complete new outfit of rider's apparel, the costliest he could find. Jim Lacy, he remembered, had once affected something near to dandyism. He retained only his gun and chaps, which were things more intimate than clothes and were not to be discarded.

His next move was to buy a good horse. This turned out to be easier than he had anticipated, and was accomplished without exciting any particular attention. Lastly he led the horse out of town, found his saddle and pack, and soon he was riding back across the line into Arizona.

Traveling leisurely, and stopping at ranches and stations convenient to the day's travel, Jim Lacy in due time arrived in Winthrop.

The day was a Friday, toward the close of afternoon. He made his way to Beacham's corrals, where overnight visitors to town usually left their horses to be cared for. The first corral appeared to be a little too crowded for Jim, so he led his animal out to another and smaller one. Several rangy, dusty-garbed riders had just ridden in, evidently behind a dilapidated old wagon drawn by a shaggy gaunt team. The driver, a lanky man, dark of face and bearded, clambered down with the cramped movements of one more at home in the saddle. Jim had seen him before, but could not place him. There was a young girl sitting on the driver's seat, and she appeared quite pretty in a wild-rose way. Jim's quick eye also took in the stock of a rifle projecting from the side of the seat.

Jim led his horse somewhat closer to the wagon, and choosing one of the covered stalls adjoining the fence, he leisurely began to remove the saddle, while his eyes roved elsewhere. He noted presently, when the girl jumped down, that her slim brown legs were bare, that she wore beaded moccasins, and the rest of her apparel showed further indications of the backwoods. As she passed out of the corral with the bearded man, Jim had a closer scrutiny.

'Shore, I'll bet that'll be Elam Hatt an' his daughter Rose,' muttered Jim. 'An' if so, those three riders are the other Hatts. . . . Reckon the ball is openin' *pronto*.'

By the time Jim had turned his horse over to the Mexican stable-boy the Hatts had gone into town. Jim got out just in time to see them turn a corner. He followed very slowly, not reluctantly in any sense, but ponderingly. Familiar as he was with Winthrop, it did not seem the same town. Turning into the broad main street, he strolled along, seeing everything while not appearing to be interested in anything. He passed several persons whom he knew well. They did not give him a second glance. The restaurant-keeper, standing in a doorway, did not recognize Jim. A cowboy came along on his horse, evidently going home. It was Jerry Smith from Franklidge Ranch. He saw Jim, yet did not look twice.

'Jerry! An' the son-of-a-gun didn't know me,' soliloquized Jim, elated. 'He owes me money I'll never get now. Wal, could I surprise him?'

The later afternoon hours were the busy ones in the stores of Winthrop, owing to the heat of midday. The saloons were always busy, all day and all night. Jim had never entered a saloon in Winthrop. He would break that record presently, but not just yet.

At the next corner he came abreast of three cowboys sitting on a stone step of a saloon.

'Look, Bill, do you see the same as

me— something' awful pretty?' asked one.

'By josh! I do,' was the jocular reply.

'Boys, anybody'd know there was a dance on to-night—huh?' said the other.

'Hey, stranger, yore sure steppin' high, wide an' handsome,' spoke up the third.

Jim wheeled round to face them, with amusement difficult to hide. These fine-spirited cowboys were far from being harmless, but it was only their way to extract fun out of every incident.

'Wal, are you boys lookin' for a fight or a drink?' he asked, smiling.

'Since you ask us, stranger, it sure must have been a drink,' replied the first speaker.

Jim waved them into the saloon, followed them, threw money on the bar, and said: 'On me, boys. Sorry I ain't drinkin' today. I just buried my grandma an' feel bad.'

Loud guffaws greeted his sally, and as he walked out through the swinging doors one of the cowboys yelled, 'You're all right, stranger.'

Jim crossed the side street and went on down toward the center of the main block.

He idled along, halting to gaze into windows, leaned against doorways here and there, watching the people. Presently he came to the entrance of a store and espied the girl he had taken for Rose Hatt standing in the door. She had a package under her arm and was evidently waiting for some one.

'Excuse me, miss,' said Jim, doffing his sombrero and stepping up to her. 'Don't I know you?'

She looked up at him with big hazel eyes that had not been long free of tears.

'You might, mister, but I sure don't know you,' she replied.

Jim decided she was more than pretty and not such a child as he had first supposed. She had wavy brown hair, rather rebellious, red lips, and tanned rose-tinted cheeks.

'Aren't you Rose Hatt?' he asked.

'Sure.'

Jim leaned easily against the doorpost, smiling down upon her. 'Reckon I thought so. Shore there's not many girls as pretty as you in these parts.'

'Put your hat back on, mister,' she replied, tartly. 'Standin' bareheaded don't go with such taffy. Besides, I ain't used to it.'

'All right,' returned Jim, good-humoredly. 'Bad habit of mine. I'll get sunstruck some day,'

'Say, you'll ketch worse if my dad comes along,' she said, laughing. 'Onless you tell me *pronto* who you are.'

'Wal, Rose, I might be Samuel Snoozegazzer,' drawled Jim.

'Only you ain't,' she added, with interest, and she looked Jim over from boots to sombrero. She was not bold, but she certainly did not show embarrassment or shyness. Jim gathered that she was used to men.

'I'll tell you my name if I drop in on the dance tonight,' he said.

'Mister, I knowed that was comin',' she returned. 'An' I'll bet you never met me before.'

'Wal, to be honest, I never did.'

'Reckon it ain't no difference. But I'm afeared I can't promise to dance with you.'

'Why not?'

'Dad says I can go, but Cedar—he's my brother—he says no. An' Cedar is boss of our outfit.'

'Wal, if your dad's willin',' why, go ahaid. He's your father.'

'Say, mister, I reckon you ain't acquainted with Cedar Hatt,' declared the girl, almost with scorn. 'You're sure a stranger in these parts.'

'Yes, I am, sorry to say,' replied Jim, thoughtfully. 'But what's so bad aboot your brother?'

'Cedar's just plain cactus an' side-winder rattlesnake mixed up with hell.'

'Aw, that's a terrible thing to call a brother,' rejoined Jim.

'He's only a half brother, same as Henny an' Tobe.'

'Oh, I see! Your dad was married twice an' your ma was the second.'

The girl's eyes grew somber and her red lips curled with bitterness.

'There're some folks out in the brakes who say my dad wasn't never married no second time.'

'Shore he was, lass. Don't believe gossip of low-down people. An' don't be so hard on your brother Cedar.'

'I hate him,' she burst out, with passion.

'Wal! Why do you hate your own kin, little girl? Shore it's not natural,' went on

119

Jim, in his slow persuasive drawl, so full of interest and sympathy.

'Reason enough,' she retorted. 'It was his fault that Clan Dillon took to runnin' after me.'

'*Dillon!*' flashed Jim, in an amaze too swift and deep to hide.

His tone, his look betrayed to the simple passionate girl that she had allowed her tongue too much freedom.

'Say, mister, here I am talkin' like an old woman,' she cried, almost in affright. 'I'm beggin' you to keep mum that slip of my tongue. Cedar would half kill me.'

'Shore I will,' returned Jim, in his former kindly tone. 'Rose, you just happened to run into a man you can trust.'

'You look it, mister. I like you,' she replied, with relief.

'Thanks. I'm shore the lucky *hombre*. But I reckon now you're engaged to marry this Clan Dillon.'

'Marry, hell!' she exclaimed, suddenly almost fierce again. 'I wouldn't marry *him* to save his life, the handsome, smilin'-faced liar. Not even if he wanted to, which he sure don't. I'd be only a sheepskin rug to Clan Dillon.'

Jim dropped his head, conscious of an inward shrinking of tingling nerves, to the coldness of ice. It had come again—that thing which had not frozen within his breast for years. How life tracked him down! Then he looked once more at the girl. She was recovering composure. Manifestly she was a primitive little girl, as much like a wildcat as a wild rose. Jim felt intuitively that she was good. The flame left her hazel eyes and the hardness around her lips softened. Jim did not need to be told more about her life.

'Rose, have you any friends?' he asked, earnestly. 'Shore I mean women-folks who could advise a young girl like you.'

'Me? Why, mister, didn't I tell you I lived down in the brakes?'

'Haven't you a man friend, then, or even a boy—who's good?'

'No. But I was makin' one fast enough,' she replied, both with resentment and mischievousness in face and voice. 'A boy from California! Say, he was nice. But Cedar caught me with him.'

'Too bad. What'd Cedar do, now?' queried Jim, much concerned.

'Not much, for Cedar,' replied the girl,

demurely. 'He drove my boy friend off into the woods, dodgin' bullets! An' he kicked me till I couldn't set down for days.'

'Wal! . . . Look heah, girl, you're old enough an' you've sense enough to know a friend when you meet him, aren't you?'

'Mister, I think so. But I—I'm afraid to trust myself,' she faltered, swayed by his earnestness.

'Wal, you needn't be in my case. I'm going to trust you.'

'How?' she asked, wonderingly.

'I'll tell you presently. I don't want you to run off scared before I say all I want to. . . . Now who's this California boy your brother caught you with?'

'Swear you'll never tell?' she returned, impulsively, drawn by his potent sympathy.

'Rose, I'll shore keep your secret, an' more. I'll help you to *make* a friend of him.'

'Oh, mister, if that could be!' she cried rapturously.

'Hurry. I see your dad comin' down the street.'

'His name is Marvie Blaine,' she whispered.

Jim Lacy drew a sharp swift breath that seemed to cut him like a knife as it swelled his breast. He leaned down to the girl.

'Listen,' he whispered. 'I will be your friend—an' this boy's—if you'll keep your mouth shut.'

'Lord, mister, you needn't be afeared of *me*,' replied the girl. 'I wouldn't dare. Sure I don't know why I ever talked to you. But you're different. An' oh! how I need some one to talk to!'

'Shore you've found some one. Me! I'll be goin' down into the brakes.'

'But who are you, mister?' she queried, aghast at his assertion.

'Did you ever heah of Jim Lacy?'

Her red lips parted to let out a little gasp and her brown face paled. 'My Heavens—are you him?'

'Yes.'

'Hear of you, Mister Jim Lacy!' she ejaculated, her eyes dilating. 'Ever since I can remember I've heerd of you. Many men ride to my Dad's ranch, an' none but they speak your name. Some of them had seen you, an' two of them at least knowed you once.'

'Rose, I'll tell you their names—Hardy Rue an' Cash Burridge.'

'Yes—yes. Oh, you *are* Jim Lacy. An'—an' I'm not scared a bit,' she whispered. 'Why, it ain't so long ago that I heered Cash Burridge tell of seein' you call out an' kill a man for beatin' a girl. . . . Oh, Mister Lacy, no one ever taught me about God, but I've prayed—prayed night after night—for some one to come an'—'

'That your Dad right heah?' interrupted Jim.

'Oh yes. . . . What'll I say?'

'Nothin', lass. He hasn't seen us. Don't forget. Keep mum. Good-by.'

Jim strode out as if he were just leaving the store, and he passed Elam Hatt so close he might have touched him. Hatt was walking with a man as rough in garb and hard of face as he was himself. Neither appeared to notice him. After a few steps Jim glanced back. The girl had disappeared and the men were passing on.

'Good!' said Jim, to himself. 'That lass is game, but she's only a kid, an' I reckon it's better her dad didn't see her with me. Wal, wal! The old luck of Jim Lacy! Half an hour in Winthrop an' I'm on a hot trail.'

Marvie Blaine! Marvie—the boy who had worshipped him and Ben Ide in those wonderful Forlorn River days! Jim had found the boy way over here in Arizona. Marvie would be eighteen now—quite a man as cowboys were rated on the ranges. But then Ben and his family had only arrived at Cedar Springs in July.

'Tall, freckled-faced, tow-haided kid, Marvie was,' went on Jim. 'Shore he's straddlin' mean hosses an' packin' a gun. . . . Reckon it's not the best country for a boy like him. But Ben could hold him in. . . . By golly! I'm forgettin' Rose Hatt. Shore as shootin' Marvie has fallen in love with her. No wonder. Reckon I would, too, if my heart hadn't been eaten up long ago. Wal, wal! A girl an' a boy I hadn't reckoned on. . . . How queer things come! Rose said it was Cedar's fault that Clan Dillon . . . Poor kid! She shore called Dillon. Handsome, smilin'-faced liar! An' she knows, if I ever saw truth. Wal now, I wonder, just *what* kind of a *hombre* is Ben

Ide's foreman. Tom Day liked him. So does everybody I've ever heard speak of him, except this Hatt girl. . . . It's a hunch. I'll be damned if I don't back her against all of them.'

Jim strolled the length of the main street, and crossing, sauntered back again, talking to himself in an undertone, and with his apparent casual observance taking cognizance of all visible persons. He had the pleasure of meeting Judge Franklidge face to face in front of the hotel. The rancher saw Jim only as a passer-by. It would have been the opposite of pleasure, however, for Jim to have encountered Ben Ide face to face; and that was one reason Jim's keen eyes sighted every man first. But accidents could happen. It would be well for Jim, while in Winthrop, to keep under cover of the saloons or places not likely to be frequented by Ben Ide. At most, Jim's hours in town would be few and far between.

He went to a side-street restaurant to get his supper and engage lodgings for the night. As darkness came on he ventured into a store, where he made a few purchases, and then he returned to the corral for his pack. This he carried to his room.

'Reckon that'll be aboot all,' he soliloquized, as he stood gazing around the dingy bare room.

He was thinking that he had walked the streets of Winthrop about the last time as an unknown man whom few people had noticed. Those swift moments—an hour or so at most—had seemed singularly sweet to Jim.

'Wal, I'm shore ready to pay all it'll take.'

The small mirror showed his eyes piercing and light, like points of daggers gleaming out of shadow. He stood an instant longer, motionless in the chill lonely silence of the room. He knew that when he went forth again it must be into the raw, evil life of outlaws, gamblers, murderers—all that riffraff of the South-west, which like a murky tide, had rolled into Arizona. He calculated coldly that he must be all he had ever been, all that his name had ever meant. He must add to these the intelligence which had shar-pened in the years of peace. He seemed fitted for this task, and his motive had the strength of love and passion and the sanction of right.

'Reckon I ought to thank God,' he said, to his pale image in the mirror. 'Shore I never had no chance to do somethin' worth while. An' now I can use my evil gifts to a good end. For Ben—an' that means for *her*—an' then Franklidge an' all the honest people who're tryin' to civilize this wild country. Reckon, after all, they need such men as Jim Lacy. . . . I see clear now. Even if I'm killed, Ben an' Hettie will know the truth some day. It's got to come out, an' I reckon I'm glad.'

Then before the mirror, with a grim smile on his face, he came at last to the practical business of the matter. Though the success of this enterprise depended upon his cunning and his knowledge of the outlawed men with whom he must throw his lot—and the more of such qualities he exercised the surer his chances—the cold hard fact was that all hung upon the deadliness of his skill with a gun. This job had to do with death. Such was the wildness of the time and the evil code of outlaws, that he could kill this one and that one, any number of them, and only add to his fame, only give himself greater standing among them. True, by so doing he must make bitter and relentless enemies; he must face the strange paradox that many an incipient gunman, or notoriety-seeking desperado, or drunken cowboy would seek to kill him just because he was Jim Lacy.

Whereupon, with deliberation he treated himself to a tense exhibition of his swiftness of eye and hand. In secret he had practiced all through these peaceful months while engaged in honest labor. An impelling force had exacted this of him. He understood it now. And with a dark satisfaction he realized that he had gained in speed, in sureness of hand. Beyond these he had in large measure the gift peculiar to all gunmen who survived long in the Southwest—and that gift was to read his opponent's mind.

'Reckon I might have bit off more'n I can chew,' soliloquized Jim, as he sheathed his gun. 'But from the minute I step out this heah door I shore won't be makin' many mistakes.'

The Lincoln County war in New Mexico had ended recently. It had been the blackest and bloodiest fight between rustlers and cattlemen and many others who had been drawn into the vortex, that had ever been recorded in the frontier history of the Southwest. As such it had possessed an absorbing, even a morbid, interest for Jim Lacy. He had never lost an opportunity to hear or read something about this war. And once he had ridden into New Mexico on a cattle mission for Franklidge, during which trip he had seen at first hand some of the places and men who were later to become notorious. That war had in its beginning something analogous to the present situation here in Arizona. Jim did not believe there could ever again be such a fight as the Lincoln County war. But there was no telling. Arizona had vaster ranges and more cattle. Some of the characters prominent in the Lincoln County war had not been killed. They had disappeared. It was not unreasonable to suppose that one or more of them had drifted into Arizona. 'No two-bit of a rustler is headin' that Pine Tree outfit!' ejaculated Jim, voicing aloud one of his thoughts. To be sure, Billy the Kid, the deadliest of all the real desperadoes of the Southwest, had fallen in the Lincoln fight, along with the worst of his gang. But they had not all bitten the bloody dust of New Mexico.

'Shore I'll run into some one from over there,' muttered Jim. 'When I do I'll shoot first an' ask questions after.'

With that he opened the door, to step out into the dark, oppressive August night.

CHAPTER 12

WINTHROP, the same as many other Western towns of the period, supported more saloons than all other kinds of business houses combined. It had a vast area of range land to draw from; and if there were a thousand cowboys and cattlemen in this section, there were probably an equal number of parasites who lived off them, from the diamond-shirted saloon-keeper and frock-coated gambler with all their motley associates, down to the rustler who hid in the brakes and the homesteader who branded as many calves not his own as he raised from his stock.

Once a month, if not oftener, the men of the range could be depended upon to visit town, 'to paint it red' and 'buck the tiger.' These customs were carried out as regularly as the work of punching cows.

During the early evening hours Jim Lacy visited some of the main-street saloons, steering clear of the Ace High and others of prominence. He lounged about the bars and tables, agreeable and friendly to anyone who wanted to talk, willing to buy cigars and drinks, while he made some excuse or other for not indulging at the time. Cowboys were all friendly folk, except now and then one whom drink made mean. Gamblers and hangers-on, Mexicans and Indians, attracted by Jim's liberality and presence, added their little to the sum of information he was gathering.

'I'm lookin' for a pard,' Jim would say to most everyone he met. 'A cowboy who broke jail over in New Mexico.' And then he went on with more of such fabrication, always to conclude with questions. Cowboys under the influence of a few strong drinks soon acquainted him with range gossip he had not heard. Several *habitués* of these dives accepted Jim's advances without telling him anything. These, of course, were the men who knew most and required cultivation. But they only eyed him covertly. Bartenders were mostly procurers for this or that gambling house, and from them he amassed much information. At length he left the last resort, intending to hunt up the dance hall.

'Shore, that wasn't so bad for a start,' mused Jim as he summed up and sifted the bits of talk in which he found significance. 'Cash Burridge, sold out an' gamblin' his fortune away, spends half his time heah in town. Thick with some Spanish girl. Same old Cash! ... Clan Dillon one grand *hombre*, eh? Wal, wal! The Ides rich Californians who're bein' rustled an' sheeped off their range. Tom Day just as liable to be boss of the Pine Tree outfit as any one. That'll shore tickle Tom. The Hatt outfit, except Cedar, just no-good home-steaders, low-down enough for anythin' not really big an' dangerous. Cedar Hatt, though, is a plumb bad man. Not the even-break kind, but crafty as a redskin, treacherous as a Greaser. The Stillwells hardest nuts down in the brakes. Never come to town! Now that's shore worth rememberin'. Last an' perhaps meanin' most to me—what that half-drunk sheepherder told me. Strange riders often seen by herders passin' through the Mogollons. Wal, most of all this sounds familiar, as I think back. But now it comes close.'

Jim, by following in the footsteps of hurrying young people, soon found where the dance was being held. It was out a side street, almost at the edge of town, in a low wide adobe building, very picturesque now with its hanging coloured lanterns, its trailing vines over archways. Outside there was a crowd of Mexicans, Indians, white men in rough garb, noisy boys, all looking in through the archway at the couples walking down the long patio and the dancers inside, swaying to and fro with the music. There was something of the spirit of a *fiesta* in the air.

Upon entering the place Jim was aware that he came under the scrutiny of men who evidently were conducting the dance, or at least overseeing those who entered. One of these individuals was Macklin, the sheriff of Winthrop, an officer who arrested cowboys sometimes, and Indians and Mexicans, but who never had been known to jail a gambler or one of the more dangerous characters. Jim, however, was not questioned. He strolled up the wide steps to watch the dancers, and then moving from one vantage point to another, amused and pleased with the scene, he at length found a place that suited him, where he sat down to watch and listen.

Jim Lacy, in the old Texas and Idaho, even the Nevada days, had enjoyed dancing, but since his advent in Arizona he had never attended a dance. This had been one of the peculiar things about Jim that had puzzled his cowboy associates of the Franklidge Ranch. Failing to persuade him, they called him a woman-hater.

It did not take Jim long to appreciate that this dance was conducted on proper lines. He understood now why he had been so closely scrutinized at the entrance. There was no drinking permitted on this occasion, nor any obstreperous behavior. The cowboys and other young men present did not show any evidence of the bottle. Among the dancers, and promenaders in the patio, there were a number of dark-haired, flower-decorated Mexican girls, very bright and pretty in their festal array. It was indeed a gala occasion, full of color and life, and soft laughter and Spanish music. Jim had to admit that his calculations had fallen awry in this case. Rose Hatt might be in attendance, but it was a safe wager that Cedar Hatt would not be admitted, nor any of the men Jim wanted to watch, unless it might be Dillon. He, surely, would not only be welcome, but very probably the lion of the dance.

Presently Jim believed he had caught a glimpse of little Rose Hatt at the far end of the patio. So he arose to walk in that direction, and found it rather a running of the gauntlet, for as the music started up couples began gayly to hasten to the dancing floor. More than one pretty girl bumped into Jim's right side where his gun hung low. Finally another, dodging around a couple she evidently wanted to get ahead of, plumped into Jim's arms.

'Oh, goodness! Excuse me,' she giggled, recovering her balance.

'See heah, lady, are you shore you didn't mean that?' drawled Jim, with a smile.

She could not very well have grown redder of face, so Jim could not tell whether or not she blushed. There was, however, a hint of coquetry in her merry eyes. Then a tall cowboy, very young in years, loomed over her and glowered at Jim.

'Hey, you dressed-up quirt!' he said. 'You say "lady," but you don't know one when you see her. I've a notion to slap your smart-alec face.'

'I'd hate to be slapped, so I beg pardon, sonny,' replied Jim, and walked away.

The momentary halt had caused him to lose track of the dark curly head he had believed to be Rose Hatt's. At the end of the patio he turned, to espy the girl just stepping out upon the floor. It was indeed Rose, and a transformed little girl, too. She had on a gaudy, cheap, flimsy dress, with shoes and stockings to match, but these did not detract from her prettiness. She was young and radiant. Her partner was a cowboy not much older than herself. They stood a moment, holding to each other, self-conscious and awkward, before they began to dance. Rose did not know how to waltz, but she made a valiant effort.

Jim watched the couple until they were lost in the whirl of dancers. This end of the patio opened into a garden or yard where a walk wound between clumps of shrubbery. There were benches here and there, and some of these were over-shadowed by vines. Jim watched the dancers, hoping to see Rose again, and perhaps catch her eye. But he missed her in the whirling throng, and when the dance ended he retreated to a seat on the adobe wall. Then again the dancers tripped to and fro, hurrying for refreshments and seats, and the wide aisle was filled with murmuring voices.

This scene roused in Jim Lacy a strange regret. The pleasure and life manifested here were things he had missed. 'I can't see that it was my fault, either,' he muttered. Young couples passed near, excited and gay, thoughtless, enchanted with the moment. There were older people, some with gray hair, and they did not seem beyond the magic of the hour. Jim's envy was short-lived. Happiness had eluded him. But it was not given to many men to serve as he could now.

Presently a couple approached out of the shadow. As they reached a point beyond, yet near where Jim sat, half concealed, the girl halted.

'Please—let's go outside,' begged the man.

His voice prompted Jim to turn so that he could see better. The fellow had the build of a rider, lithe, tall, wide in the shoulders. He wore a dark suit and had a flower in the lapel of his coat. His face had a compelling attraction. But Jim, in his quick glance, could not decide whether it drew him because it was a handsome, unusual face, or for some other reason difficult to grasp at the moment.

Jim started so violently that he almost fell off the adobe wall. That voice! He would have known it among a thousand voices. His cool curiosity vanished in a rushing tide of emotion. His glance leaped from the man to his companion. She stood full in the soft rose light of one of the colored lanterns. Hettie Ide! His heart bounded, then seemed to become locked with a terrible pang. It was Hettie, grown into a woman. The face that had haunted Jim's camp fires in the lonely watches of the nights! The same rippling fair hair, the deep earnest eyes, the rich clear complexion that spoke of contact with the open, the strong full lips, more hauntingly sweet than ever for the sadness which had come!

So rapt, so agonizing was Jim's attention that he lost something of the words which passed between the two. It was the name Dillon that roused Jim from his trance.

'Mr. Dillon,' she was saying, 'the reason I can't marry you is that I don't love you.'

'But, Hettie, you will—you must love me in time,' he returned, passionately, seizing her hand and trying to pull her into the shadow. She resisted, broke away from him.

'I never will,' she said, with eyes and cheeks flaming. 'What kind of a man are you—that you persist so rudely? I liked you—even admired you until you forced such attentions as these on me. I've overlooked them because my brother Ben thinks so much of you. But no more, Mr. Dillon.'

Her dignified yet spirited reply might as well not have been spoken, for all the effect it had to restrain Dillon. He burst into low impassioned appeal, and he backed her under the overhanging vines against the wall. Dillon was no young cowboy, mad with love. He appeared to be a man, masterful, adept at making love, absolutely indifferent to anything but his own desires. The way he confronted her in her several attempts to pass him, and without laying a hand on her crowded her back to the wall, proved how he was thinking about what he was doing.

'I—I thought you were a gentleman,' she burst out.

'No man thinks of bein' over-gentle when he's in love,' retorted Dillon. 'I tried that with you. And to tell you the truth, I wasn't so natural then as I am now. I've plumb lost my head. I tell you I love you an' I'm goin' to have you. What do you say to that?'

'I say this, Mr. Dillon, we've all got you figured wrong,' she retorted.

'Sure you have,' he rejoined, with an exultant laugh. 'An' here's how!' With that he attempted to seize her in his arms. But he had evidently cornered the wrong girl. Supple and strong, she wrestled free in an instant and wheeled away from the wall.

'What do you—think—Ben will do—when I tell him—you've insulted me?' she panted, backing into the aisle.

'If you've got any sense you won't tell

him,' replied Dillon, in a flash changing from an ardent lover to something almost menacing. 'Ben Ide's in bad here. Arizona isn't California. There are rustlers here an' you can bet some of them are the ranchers he thinks his friends. I know this cattle game. I know these men. He's lost most of his stock. If he buys in more he'll lose that too. Hettie, I'm the only cowman in Arizona who can save him from ruin.'

'Indeed! Are your aware that I have a share in the Ide ranch?' retorted Hettie, sarcastically.

'I've heard so, but I didn't believe.'

'Well, it's true.'

'Ahuh! What do you mean by share?' he queried, curiously.

'I own one third of the land and the stock. Besides, I have my own house apart from Ben.'

'That's news to me,' said Dillon. 'But it sure makes my case stronger. What ruins Ben Ide will ruin you.'

'The loss of a few thousand cattle won't hurt either my brother or me,' she returned, almost flippantly, studying his face with steady, penetrating eyes. She was seeing the man as if he had suddenly unmasked.

'You must be pretty rich to talk like that,' replied Dillon.

'Quite well off, thank you. I often wondered if that didn't interest you, and now I know.'

He laughed in a way that would have been a revelation to an older woman, well versed in the life of the frontier. But Hettie did not grasp what seemed as plain as print to Jim Lacy, crouching like a tiger under the shadow.

'Thanks, you're very smart,' he said. 'But I'd be crazy about you if you were as poor as Rose Hatt. I tell you I love you—want you—need you so terribly that if I fail to get you it'll make a devil out of me.'

'I'm beginning to imagine the process of *making* has progressed very far already.'

'You've got cat in you—same as other women,' he retorted. 'Listen, we're wastin' talk. If you'll marry me I'll save Ben Ide. If you won't I'll quit him an' use my influence all over the range. I'll make ranchin' impossible for him in this country. An' I'll get *you* in the bargain.'

Hettie Ide turned so pale that her eyes shone black.

'Mr. Clan Dillon! Popular fellow! Splendid cattleman! Best and squarest foreman in Arizona!' she exclaimed, with amazed and infinite scorn.

Dillon, whose back was now turned toward Jim, made a deprecatory gesture in reply.

'Mr. Dillon, weeks ago when you first came to us and began your—your attentions to me, I thought there was something queer about you,' went on Hettie, deliberately. 'You were too good to be true, as old Raidy said. Well, I think you're as bad as you seemed good. I think you're a contemptible, conceited ass. I think you're a deep, cunning scoundrel. . . . You need not return to Cedar Springs to-morrow. Marvie Blaine will drive me home.'

'What do you mean?' demanded Dillon.

'You'll not get a chance to quit Ben. Right here and now you're discharged.'

'Me! What? Who's dischargin' me?'

'I am.'

'Bah! You're loco, girl. Ben Ide wouldn't listen to you. He can't run that ranch without me. Haven't you sense enough to see it?'

Hettie Ide abruptly turned her back upon Dillon and walked away, to disappear in the crowd of dancers returning to the floor.

'—damn the luck!' muttered Dillon. He lighted a cigarette and stood thoughtfully inhaling and expelling smoke.

Jim Lacy strode out from under the vines and the shadow.

'Howdy, Dillon!' he said, as he confronted the foreman.

A lightning-swift glance took Jim in from head to feet and back again.

'Howdy, yourself. Reckon you've got the best of me,' returned Dillon gruffly.

'Shore, I reckon I have,' drawled Jim, with cool significance.

'Who are you?' queried Dillon, sharply.

'I might be Peter Punkins—only I ain't.'

'Pretty smart, aren't you?' rejoined Dillon, feeling his way. He knew men; he knew the West. 'Reckon you're more Simple Simon than Peter Punkins. I don't care. But I'm curious about where you just sprung from.'

'Wal, I hail from New Mexico,' returned Jim.

'The hell you do!' flashed Dillon. 'That's nothin' to me. But where'd you come from just now?'

'Dillon, you're figuring quick,' returned Jim, in slow deliberation. 'Wal, I was settin' right heah on the adobe wall.'

Jim pointed to the spot in the shadow, but he did not take his gaze off Dillon.

The man cursed under his breath and flung his cigarette down so hard that the sparks flew from the stone pavement.

'You set there watchin'—listenin'?' he demanded, with sudden and powerful self-control.

'Shore did,' drawled Jim.

'Stranger, where I come from men got shot for such offense.'

'I reckon. That's why I'm not apologizin'.'

Dillon seemed to accept this as confirmation of the suspicion which had evidently been growing with his thoughts. Abruptly his bullying manner changed. The swift retreat of his personality was almost as remarkable as the new one which took its place. He stood unmasked, as far as his pretense was concerned. Cautious, steady, cold, and hard he stood a moment, his strange green eyes trying to pierce Jim's mind. He was searching more for Jim's intent than for other knowledge of him.

As for Jim, he measured Dillon to be a Westerner vastly different from the character he enjoyed in that section of Arizona. He judged Dillon without recourse to the words of Rose Hatt. Jim did not recognize a kindred spirit, but he read in Dillon the depth, the courage, the desperate experience of a man used to the rawest and deadliest of frontier life.

'Ha! I see you pack a gun, stranger,' coolly remarked Dillon, as he lighted another cigarette.

'Yes. I got sort of used to it.'

'Reckon you see I don't?'

'Shore. I seen first off you didn't an' then just now I read it in your eyes.'

'Mind-reader, eh? Well, it's a helpin' trait for some men.'

'Are you meanin' any particular breed?' queried Jim, dryly.

'Yes. Spies, gamblers, thieves, gun-throwers, an' the like.'

'Thanks. I'm shore appreciatin' the way you speak. An' not wantin' to be outdone in compliments, I'll just repeat what Miss Hettie Ide called you—a conceited ass! A deep, cunnin' scoundrel!'

'You heard all she said?' snarled Dillon. Deep and crafty as he was, he could not help the risk of passion, though he controlled it.

'Shore. An' I never heard a low-down man called more proper. Tickled me more because only to-day some one called you a handsome, smilin'-faced liar.'

'Aho! You happened to hear a good deal, now didn't you, stranger?' returned Dillon. 'Well, I don't care a damn.'

'Shore you don't. A skunk stinks so bad that nothin' but bullets can get to his hide.'

'You're a brave man, stranger, shoutin' that way above your gun. But I'm tired listenin'. Are you from New Mexico?'

'No. I was lyin'.'

'Ahuh? An' you've got a hunch that's where I come from?'

'I reckon.'

'You see I don't deny it. What do I care what you know or think or do? You pose

149

for a dandy cowboy. But you're not ridin' for any outfit around Winthrop. You excite a little suspicion yourself, mister, considerin' this country is full of outlaws an' rustlers.'

'It shore is. That's why I come over,' returned Jim, meaningly.

For the first time the dark red showed in Dillon's face.

'I'll have you put out of here,' he said. 'And I'll tip Macklin off that you need watchin'.'

'Wal,' drawled Jim, with his glance cold and set, 'go ahaid, but be sure to tip him off that I'm Jim Lacy.'

Dillon's stalwart frame jerked with a perceptible tremor. A slow pale shade began to blot out the brown of his face.

'Jim Lacy, eh! Say, I've had that dodge worked on me before. Paradin' under a dead man's name! It's an old trick of four-flushers.'

But Dillon was not so cocksure as his bluster was intended to indicate. His iron nerve had been pierced. Here was a name to conjure with. For a moment the revelation of it unmasked him as had nothing else. Honest men seldom had anything to fear from Jim Lacy or any other of his class. It was only a sudden, instinctive fear at that, a weakening at once controlled. Dillon might have been afraid of a name, but not of any man.

'You expect me to believe you're Jim Lacy?' he demanded, hoarsely.

'Wal, I'm tellin' you, but it's nothin' to me what you believe,' returned Jim, icily. This interview was about to conclude.

'All right,' went on Dillon, breathing hard. 'But I still figure you a liar.'

Jim sprang forward and knocked Dillon down.

'Wal, shore it may take more'n that,' he said, in slow accents. 'But I told you who I am. An' that's somethin' you didn't tell me.'

Dillon cautiously arose on his hand, lifting a dark face to his assailant. But he made no response.

Jim, wheeling away to go, found himself confronted by Rose Hatt. The girl had seen at least the last of Jim's encounter with Dillon.

'Oh—mister!' she cried, in a comprehension bounded by fear.

The dancers were trooping off the floor.

A tall youth, with features strangely familiar to Jim, appeared behind Rose. She clasped his arm, while she stared from Jim to Dillon, who had not attempted to get up. Without a word Jim hurried on.

'My—God! Who was that?' called out some one Jim took to be the youth with Rose. The voice added to the stirring of Jim Lacy's memory. It also urged him faster through the throng of dancers and out into the street.

'That was Marvie Blaine, God bless him!' whispered Jim, as he gained the darkness. 'Shore a close shave for me.'

It was eleven o'clock when Jim Lacy entered the Ace High Saloon, at the period one of the noted gambling hells of the southwest.

John Brennan, its proprietor, had two unique characteristics that stood in his favor. He had the reputation of being a square gambler and he would not have a woman about the place. Consequently he was not so prosperous as most men of his business and his house was without costly and gaudy fittings. He did not bar any man from his tables, so long as that man played fairly. More than one crooked gambler had been carried out of the Ace High, feet first. This fact was reported to have had its effect upon the intent-eyed, still-faced sharps who frequented the rooms.

Jim Lacy bolted into the barroom like a man who was being pursued. He was, indeed, though not by any visible thing.

'Cowboy, what you runnin' from?' queried a tall man. He happened to be standing nearest to the door, his back to the bar, his high hat tipped back, to expose a weatherbeaten face. A brass shield, with letters printed upon it, stood out prominently on his vest.

Jim recognized this individual almost instantly.

'Howdy, Macklin!' he said, nonchalantly. 'I was just runnin' from a sheriff.'

'Wal, you run right into another,' growled Macklin, surprised and annoyed. 'Who air you?'

'I'm foreman of the Coffee Pot outfit,' drawled Jim.

'What's your handle, smarty? It jest

happens there ain't any Coffee Pot outfit at this particular time. . . . I've a notion to clap you into the jug. You look kinda pale round the gills. What have you been up to an' who air you?'

'None of your damn business,' returned Jim, with abrupt change of tone and manner. 'But if you hang around I reckon somebody'll tell you.'

'Hyar, you come right along with—'

'*Lookout, Mack!*' interrupted some one behind Jim. A glass went crash on the floor, and the rasp of heavy boots followed. Then a man strode in front of the sheriff, facing Jim. 'Excuse me, stranger, but I believe I know you. If I'm wrong, say so.'

'Howdy, Cash!' returned Jim, extending his hand.

Cash Burridge looked a full ten years older than when Jim had last seen him. Drink and hard life and evil passion had broken the man. His lined dark visage lost its set expression of uncertainty, almost alarm, and worked convulsively into a broad smile.

'Jumpin' steers!' he ejaculated, grasping Jim's hand in both his and wagging it vigorously. His smile kept on expanding. His eyes lighted. 'If it ain't you!'

'Shore is, Cash. Just got in, an' am lookin' for trouble.'

'No! *Who*?' queried Burridge, with a sudden check to his almost boisterous welcome. He had bent forward and lowered his voice.

'Wal, nobody in particular, Cash. I just feel mean.'

'I'm a son-of-a-gun! It's you—changed a lot. Most in disposition—if it's true. You're *lookin'* for trouble.'

Here the sheriff interposed by placing an ungentle hand on Burridge's shoulder and turning him somewhat.

'Friend of yours, hey? Thet's no guarantee to keep him out of jail.'

'Hell!' exploded Burridge. 'I'm tryin' to keep *you* out of the boneyard. My Gawd! if I told you who this man is you'd sweat blood.'

Macklin's jaw dropped and he swayed back against the bar, dominated by Burridge's fierce sincerity. Then Burridge drew Jim aside from the gaping, grinning bystanders at the bar and the gamesters at the tables.

'It's you—really *you*, Jim?' he whispered, huskily.

'Shore, Cash. Cain't you see?'

'But we heard you were dead.'

'That was terrible exaggerated, Cash.'

'Dropped from the sky! Jim Lacy, just down from heaven, huh? Well, I'm damned! . . . An' I never was so glad to see a man in my life. Honest, Jim.'

'Wal, I'm glad to see you, Cash, though we was never very thick.'

'Where you been, Jim, since you left Lineville? Lord! I never forgot that night you shot Link Cawthorne's eye out.'

'Wal, Cash, never mind where I've been.'

'Sure, that doesn't matter, only I always had my idea, an' I was curious. I had a hunch you went to New Mexico an' got mixed up in that Lincoln County war. *Some* of those *hombres* got out of that fight alive. I know one of them did. Close pard of Billy the Kid.'

'Who?' queried Jim.

'I'm not givin' any man away, Jim. Sure wouldn't have said as much as that to anyone else. When'd you drift in?'

'To-day.'

'You'll be recognized here.'

'Shore. I expect to be an' I'm not carin'.'

'Lord! Jim, have you grown reckless with the years? You look older, but fine, healthy, an' prosperous.'

'Who's goin' to recognize me, Cash?'

'You remember Ace Black? He's the gambler we knowed at the Gold Mine back in Lineville.'

'Shore I remember Black.'

'He's upstairs playing faro. Reckon Black will know you, but he'd never give you away. Hardy Rue, though, he will. He never cottoned to you. Always had a hunch you'd killed Less Setter. Rue has dogged me all these years. An' I'm layin' it to him that I'm down on my luck now.'

'Wal, what come of your ranchin' deal heah, Cash?'

'Jim, you had me figured. I couldn't stand prosperity,' returned Burridge, heavily. 'But I swear I went straight till I got in need of money. I'd made poor deals. I could steal cattle an' make money, but not by tradin' or ranchin'. I began to borrow. Then I had a chance to sell out to Ben Ide, a Californian. I did him dirt, an'

I've lived to be sorry. There's a man, Jim.
. . . Well, when I was flush again I began to
drink an' buck the tiger.'

'An' now you're aboot broke. Who got
all that money, Cash?'

'Aw, everybody. Brennan some, but
then I don't begrudge it to him. Hardy
Rue beat me out of most of it. I fell in love
with a Spanish girl here. She an' Rue
double-crossed me. Got my pile!'

'Wal, why didn't you kill him?'

'I couldn't try an even break with Rue.
An' I never had a chance to shoot him in
the back.'

'Is Rue heah now?' asked Jim.

'Reckon he's with that black-eyed
hussy. It's a little early for him to drop in.
Lord! it'll tickle me to have him see you
with me. Rue was afraid of you, Jim, an'
you need to watch him.'

'Where do you hang out, Cash?'

'I've been most here in town,' replied
Burridge. 'I've a cabin down in the
brakes.'

'Are you acquainted down there?'

'Sure am, Jim. Know everybody except
the newcomers. An' I'm givin' you a
hunch there's some hard customers

driftin' in. It's a hell of a rough country an' big as all outdoors. I sure learned to love Arizona.'

'Wal, Cash, when you was rich an' high-handed I didn't have much use for you,' said Jim, with a smile. 'But now you're broke an' down on your luck, I reckon I'll chip in with you.'

'Jim Lacy! You always was a queer one,' returned Burridge, feelingly. 'Reckon I know you've got somethin' up yore sleeve, an' whatever it is, I'm sure with you.'

'All right, Cash. Suppose you tote me round to look 'em over.'

CHAPTER 13

HETTIE IDE had attended the dance at Winthrop as a guest of Alice Franklidge, a girl of nineteen, daughter of the judge's second wife. She was a frank, breezy, Western girl to whom Hettie took a liking, and they were on the way to becoming real friends.

They left the dance before midnight, to be driven out to the Franklidge house by Alice's escort. The night was cold and clear, with myriads of blinking stars overhead. Hettie removed her hat to let the cool wind blow her hair.

'Did you enjoy your first dance in Arizona?' asked the young rancher.

'Yes indeed I did, Mr. Van Horn—in spite of a—a rather unpleasant incident,' replied Hettie.

'Sure, we're awful glad. Sorry, too, somethin' annoyed you. But, honest, the dances now are Sunday-school affairs to what they once was. Isn't that so, Alice?'

'It is. I used to be afraid to go,' replied the girl. 'Fights were common. One for each dance! They're really nice now. Dad and some of the town men have seen to that. ... Hettie, it mortifies me that you were annoyed by—by Clan Dillon. I know it was he. You danced with him—then came back to us all flushed and nervous.'

'Yes, it was Mr. Dillon. He—he insulted me.'

Van Horn cracked his whip over the horses in rather abrupt and forceful action.

'I'm not surprised,' returned Alice, thoughtfully. 'Dillon is a handsome, fascinating man. Very agreeable, winning. But I always thought him a little common and bold.'

'Who was the pretty girl Marvie paid so much attention to?' asked Hettie.

'I didn't notice her. But I saw he was having a grand time.'

'He had her with him just before we left,' went on Hettie. 'She wore a white muslin dress, cotton stockings, cheap slippers too large for her feet. She hung back as Marvie came up to me. I think she was afraid to meet us. I thought her very pretty. Big staring dark eyes. Red lips. Curly brown hair.'

'That was Rose Hatt,' replied Van Horn.

'Rose Hatt? She couldn't belong to that notorious Hatt family we hear about?' asked Alice.

'There's only one family of Hatts, Alice, an' Rose is the only girl,' explained the young rancher. 'I'd seen her before. Charley Moss danced with her. Pretty kid. An' she seemed modest an' quiet. Young Blaine sure acted smitten with her.'

'Indeed he did,' corroborated Hettie, seriously. 'Marvie is such a fine boy. But he's going a little wild. I've remonstrated with Ben, who lets Marvie run around too freely.'

'Hettie, love affairs in Arizona go like fire in the dry desert grass,' said Alice, with a little laugh. '*You* want to watch out, doesn't she, Frank?'

'Sure won't do her any good to watch out,' returned Van Horn, gayly. 'One of our Arizona lads is goin' to get her.'

'Mr. Van Horn, that's the second time to-night I've heard such prediction,' replied Hettie, pleasantly. 'I'm sure I feel flattered.'

Soon they arrived at the Franklidge

home, which stood on a bench of high ground, among stately pine trees. The girls went in to find Judge Franklidge smoking beside an open fireplace. He greeted Hettie warmly.

'Did you meet your brother?' he asked, as he placed a chair for her.

'No. Did he come in after all?'

'Yes. He was here for an hour,' replied the judge. 'Came in to talk over a cattle deal. I advised him not to buy more stock just now.'

'Was Ina with Ben?' asked Hettie.

'Sure was, and she looked powerful handsome. I wanted them to stay here overnight. But Ben said he'd rather go to the hotel, so he could be in town early. Left word if he didn't see you at the dance that you were to meet him tomorrow at noon sharp. At Brydon's.'

'Goodness! I'm glad we got away from the dance before Ben arrived,' exclaimed Hettie, with a rather unmirthful laugh.

'Well now, you don't say?' queried the judge, lowering his head to gaze at her over his glasses.

'I'm afraid it's going to be embarrassing

163

for me when I see Ben. I'll have to tell him I—I discharged Dillon.'

'Dillon! Clan Dillon? Did you fire *him*?' asked the judge, sitting up abruptly.

'I sure did,' rejoined Hettie.

'I'll be darned. What for, lass?'

'I had reason enough, though I'm afraid Ben may not see it that way. He swears by Dillon. In fact he trusts Dillon implicitly and entertains a very high opinion of him. Well, Mr. Dillon has made it rather hard for me out at the ranch. He waylays me whenever I go outdoors. At first he didn't do me the honor to offer marriage. But finally he got that far along, and despite my refusals he kept at it. I did not know he was to be at the dance to-night, or I wouldn't have gone. But I danced with him, and walked with him, on the terrace—and—well, to make it short he insulted me.'

'Dad, I'm not surprised. I never liked Dillon,' interposed Alice.

At that juncture Frank Van Horn entered.

'Lass, now just how did Dillon insult you?' asked Judge Franklidge, with fire in his eye.

'He declared he was going to have me whether I wanted it or not, and I had to fight him!'

'You don't mean he dared to lay a hand on you?' demanded the old rancher.

'Both hands, and arms, too,' laughed Hettie, though she blushed as she admitted it. 'In fact, he was a ruffian. I imagine Dillon has had his way with a certain kind of women. I think he expected me to squeal, or beg—then flop into his arms. But I'm strong and I broke away from him.'

'Damned hound! Somebody ought to use a quirt on him,' ejaculated the judge, growing red in the face.

'I'd suggest a gun,' added Van Horn, with a compression of his lips.

Hettie held back a revelation of Dillon's threat to ruin Ben and herself. Upon cool reflection she had not been sure of how Ben would react to her taking upon herself the authority to discharge Dillon. Unfortunately, Ben was used to Hettie's complaints about the attentions his men bestowed up her, and he had come to take them with a grain of salt.

'So I discharged Dillon,' concluded Hettie.

'You did right, lass, but how in the devil is Ben going to take that?' queried Franklidge, seriously. 'He thinks a heap of this Dillon. Only to-night he was bragging about Dillon's recovery of a bunch of cattle that'd just been rustled off into the brakes. . . . Still, come to squint at the offense, Ben can't overlook it. He's bound to stand by your dismissal of this foreman.'

'You don't know my brother very well yet,' returned Hettie, shaking her head. 'If he had *seen* Dillon insult me he'd have horsewhipped him. But Ben scouts my statements. He's tired of hearing about these lovelorn cowboys who annoy me. He thinks I'm—well, a little too sensitive. Once he said, "If I was that cowboy I'd throw you on a horse and ride off with you." And another time when I went to him in distress he said: "Of course he tried to kiss you. Why shouldn't he? You were made to be loved and kissed." . . . Sometimes I believe Ben is only in fun. He doesn't mean that as it sounds. But he hasn't so much patience with me as he used to have. I declare I don't know how he will take this Dillon affair.'

'I'll tell you, lass, now that you've expounded the situation,' replied the judge. 'He'll not uphold you. Dillon will get to him first and soften his offense, and Ben will keep him on.'

'That would be dreadful,' said Hettie. 'I'll actually be afraid of Dillon.'

'Well, the only solution to your problem, Hettie Ide, is to fall in love with some fine Arizona lad,' declared Judge Franklidge, with both kindly conviction and teasing good humor.

'Indeed!' returned Hettie, trying in vain to look haughty. Then she thought it might be just as well to drop a hint to these new friends. 'I'd take your advice, Judge Franklidge—if it wasn't for an insurmountable obstacle. . . . I can't fall in love with a fine Arizona lad, because I'm already in love with a fine—*Nevada* lad!'

As the beloved name sounded off her lips Hettie felt the swift blood rise to tighten and heat her face.

The judge laughed heartily, but Alice, intuitively grasping the import beneath Hettie's rather flippant speech, crossed over to Hettie and put an arm around her.

'Dad is as bad as Ben, dear. Come, it's late. Let's go to bed,' she said.

'Well, Hettie,' added the judge, in the same mirthful vein, 'if I were forty years younger I'd contest this mysterious Nevadian's right. Where is the confounded lucky jackass?'

Hettie looked back from the doorway, through which Alice was leading her.

'I do not know,' she replied, sadly.

When the door closed she heard the judge burst out: 'Did you hear that, Van? It explains a lot. . . . Well, doggone me for a thick-headed fool! And I'll gamble Ben Ide is the same.'

At breakfast next morning Judge Franklidge seemed to have undergone a subtle change. His interest in Hettie had increased, and he dispensed with the mischievous bantering. Hettie felt that in his estimation she had grown into a woman overnight, and that she had found a friend in him.

'Hettie, I'm going to be sort of a dad to you,' he said, at parting. 'I'm ashamed of the way Arizona has treated you and Ben.

But listen, lass. Have faith in us and this grand country. Have patience with your brother. Try to persuade him not to spend more money just now. We may have a year or two, or more, of hard times. But take the word of an old cattleman who has been through more than one rustler war. We will come out of it. These outlaws destroy themselves. I've a hunch some hard-shootin' gunman will come along and do for the ringleaders. It's happened here before. It happened lately in New Mexico. So do not lose your nerve and come to hate this beautiful country. We want you Ides to love it. We need such fine people. We are pioneers, Hettie. I've lost a million on cattle. But it'll come back. And so will your losses. Likewise your happiness.'

'Judge Franklidge,' answered Hettie, smiling through her tears, 'despite my weakness for *Nevada*—I reckon I'm Arizona's for life.'

'Whoopee! That's the game lass! . . . Come to see us often, Hettie. *Adios*.'

One of the Franklidge stable hands drove Hettie into town, so that she had time for thinking how best to approach Ben. It had not occurred to her that Ben might get a warped version of the affair from Dillon. She felt grateful to Judge Franklidge for his kindly counsel and advice. Indeed, she had felt, too, with a woman's keenness, something in regard to the judge's attitude toward Dillon—something he did not confide. Yet she sensed his friendship. He would very likely take her side, if the issue came to an argument. She decided to wait and see if Dillon had approached Ben.

Hettie, upon arriving in town, went about buying the supplies usually ordered twice a month. She and her mother had preferred to keep house in their own little cabin, a proceeding that Ina and Ben had opposed. But Mrs. Ide vowed she would never be a mother-in-law to anybody.

After she had finished her ordering, Hettie passed on down street, presently to encounter Ben. He did not look in a very good humor. There was a dark shade on his face which Hettie had learned to regret, long ago back at Tule Lake Ranch. Her heart sank a little, despite her fortitude. What if she had offended Ben?

'Ina is at the dressmaker's,' he said,

after greeting her. 'Reckon it's a good time for you to go to the bank with me.'

'Bank. What for?' she queried, as she yielded to his hand and turned back up the street.

'I'm having a certified check made out for your interest in the ranch.'

'Ben!' she cried, in amazed reproach.

'Yes, Ben,' he returned a little testily. 'Hettie, I can't have you doing things without my knowledge. Besides, to be honest with you, I don't want to see you lose that money. And I'm pretty certain I'll lose all I put in cattle.'

'But, Ben, it was an investment. I played to win or lose with you,' she protested.

'I know, dear, an' you sure are a thoroughbred. But this was a crazy deal of mine. I don't regret it,' he added, hastily. 'But I can't feel right to have you in with me. Maybe some day, when these bad times are over.'

'Ben, something has happened since I saw you,' said Hettie, quickly.

'Reckon it has,' returned Ben, dropping his head so she could not meet his eyes. 'California Red is gone!'

'Gone? Oh no, Ben!' she cried poignantly.

He nodded disconsolately. She saw his lips quiver.

'Stolen?'

'We don't know. He disappeared from the pasture. Raidy swears Red was stolen, that he couldn't jump the fence. I know he could jump over the moon if he took a notion. Dillon agrees with me that Red just got away.'

'But you don't *know*?' queried Hettie, sharply.

'That's the rub, Hettie. We don't. And there isn't a man in my outfit who could track Red. Sure disgusted me. I tried to track him myself. Had to give up. . . .Reckon there never was but one horse hunter who *could* have done it.'

'Ben, you'll get Red back,' replied Hettie, earnestly, and forthwith she launched into an eloquent speech, drawing upon the judge's advice and optimism, and adding considerable of her own hopeful and persistent opinions as to their ultimate success and happiness in the future.

'You're game, Hettie,' he returned, squeezing her arm. 'With you and Ina and the kid I can an' will beat this rotten deal. Reckon it'll help some if you consent to withdraw from it.'

'I'll consent to anything that will relieve or help you.'

They reached the bank, where presently Hettie received a certified check for her share in the transaction. She immediately deposited it to her account.

'For the time being I'll leave it there,' she said.

'Yes, do. I might have to borrow from you,' he laughed, then with serious brow he drew her to a seat and said in a low voice, 'Dillon just told me you'd discharged him.'

'Yes?' queried Hettie, lifting her chin, while the tingle and heat of battle ran along her nerves.

'Hettie, I had to countermand your order,' he went on, gravely. 'Now we won't argue about it. Dillon is the best man available. I can't get along without him. He knows it, too. I had some trouble conciliatin' him.'

'Oh, indeed!' retorted Hettie, biting her lips. 'May I ask what Mr. Dillon told you.'

'Not much. He was sore, but he laughed, at that. Said he loved you an' had been coaxin' you to look upon him favorably. Then last night—at the dance—he asked you to marry him. Said you weren't very encouragin'. Then he tried to kiss you, an' you made a fuss an' took it upon yourself to fire him.'

'If you believe him, Ben, why, there's no need in my bothering you with my side of the story,' rejoined Hettie, finding her self-control.

'Reckon there's no call to think Dillon's a liar,' went on Ben. 'The truth is, Hettie, you're a little of a man-hater. Oh, I know—I remember, an' I sure don't blame you for bein' true to—to *him*. . . . But you're hard on all these poor devils who fall in love with you. That's the way I see it.'

'Ben Ide, I am not a man-hater,' protested Hettie.

'We won't argue the question,' said Ben, wearily. 'You an' Ina always beat me. But please don't misunderstand. I don't want you to marry Dillon. He seems a fine fellow who'll make a big man in Arizona some day. Just the same, I'd want to know him better before I'd let him have you.'

'Thank you, Ben. I can forgive you now,' murmured Hettie.

'I'd like to ask you somethin',' went on Ben, with both concern and mirth in his look. 'Did you strike Dillon last night—when he tried to kiss you?'

'Strike him? No, I certainly did not,' declared Hettie, vehemently. 'I wouldn't soil my hands on—But why do you ask that?'

'Well, he had a beautiful black eye,' replied Ben, ponderingly. 'He told me he had stumbled in the dark—in his room—an' hit a chair. Sure it could have happened. But it looked to me like a beautiful black eye that had come from a good swing an' a hard fist. I've been wonderin' if he lied to me.'

'Well, I'm wondering who gave him just what he deserved. But, Ben, if you have such faith in this Dillon, why did you wonder at all?'

'I happened to run into Dillon talkin' to Stewart, who is Tom Day's foreman,' replied Ben. 'I heard Dillon say somethin' about bumpin' into a chair. Then Stewart, who'd been drinkin', gave Dillon the horse laugh. Struck me funny, that's all.'

'Brother dear, I hope you won't be struck by anything funnier,' said Hettie, as she arose. 'I've got more shopping to do, and time flies. You wished me to meet you at twelve?'

'You bet; *pronto*, too,' he returned. 'It's a long drive home, you know. I've got a lot of things to see to. But reckon I'll make it.'

'How about Marvie?'

'He'll be there. Marvie hunted me up an' asked for money. I'd just given him some, before we left. The kid was intoxicated, all right.'

'Ben! You don't mean he was drunk?' burst out Hettie, in horror.

'No, I was goin' to tell you he was intoxicated over some girl. Wanted to buy her candy an' presents. But, by George! I forgot I promised not to give him away. Don't you dare give *me* away. . . . So long, till twelve. I'll pick you up at Brydon's store.'

'What a fright you gave me!' complained Hettie. 'You should choose your words more carefully. As to Marvie—I think he's in love. I saw the girl. Tell you more later.'

Hettie's thoughts reverted to Marvie and lingered dreamily and anxiously around him until she reached the dry-goods store, where she forgot everything except the important shopping at hand.

It lacked five minutes to twelve when she labored to the front of the store, burdened by bundles, and vastly satisfied with herself that she had finished in time to meet Ben. He was punctuality itself and appreciated the same in anyone. Hettie deposited her bundles on a window seat beside the door, and looked out for Ben. He had not yet arrived.

Suddenly a man, hatless and coatless, dashed by, yelling, '*Keep off the street!*'

'What's the matter with him?' asked Hettie, amused.

Several clerks came hurriedly to peep out.

'Looks like another fight,' said one of them, excitedly.

Shouting and trampling of feet followed. Across the street pedestrians hurriedly ran into the first open doorway they happened upon. The noise ceased. Then a man entered the door where Hettie stood transfixed and thrilling.

'Hello, Matt! What's doin'?' queried the clerk.

'Darned if I know,' replied the man. 'I seen people run off the street, so I ducked in here. Just before I heard Jim Lacy was in town.'

'Who?' shouted his questioner.

'Jim Lacy. Don't know how true it is. But somebody's in town, you can gamble on that.'

Faces appeared at all doors and windows. Some peeped down the street, then jerked back. How ridiculous it seemed to Hettie! Yet there she stood likewise, her heart throbbing, her whole being in a state of suspense.

A shot pealed out, deep and ringing. Then *bang*! Another followed, almost like an echo. Silence ensued, palpitating, stifling to Hettie. What had happened? A fight! Guns! A single shout came from far down the street.

The man beside Hettie peeped out.

'By Gawd!' he ejaculated, in husky accents.

The clerk, frightened as he was, also had to look. He jerked in his head, with pale face and eyes staring, and he began to jabber.

Hettie obeyed an irresistible instinct! She peeped out. The street appeared empty. No, there was a man lying face down, not fifty feet from the door. His arms were outstretched.

'It's Jim Lacy. I never saw him, but I know them who has,' said the man beside Hettie.

'Oh—how dreadful! . . . the dead man—there in the road—Jim Lacy?' whispered Hettie, beginning to shake and grow sick.

'No. Jim Lacy is the one comin' up the street. . . . See his gun. It's smokin'!'

Then Hettie, looking farther, espied a man in rider's garb, gun in hand, stalking toward his victim. He passed him, with only a downward glance. He sheathed the gun. He strode toward the sidewalk.

His walk! His shape! A terrible piercing sensation attacked Hettie. Had she been horrified out of her senses? Was she mad? What flashed so swiftly in memory? But this man—this Jim Lacy! He was coming. He would pass the door.

Hettie drew back with the last of failing strength. She reeled. Her mind had halted. The quivering of her body ceased as if paralysis had set in. Cold, numb, awful suspense held her up-right, waiting, as if for death itself.

The man in rider's garb passed the doorway, erect, stone-faced, with eyes of lightning set ahead.

Nevada! Hettie's faculties leaped out of terror and stupefaction to recognize him. Nevada! Jim Lacy? . . . *Nevada!*

She had a sense of sinking down. All went blank—then slipped into black oblivion.

CHAPTER 14

HETTIE recovered consciousness before she had strength enough to open her eyes. She was lying down, with some one supporting her head. Cold water had been dashed in her face. She felt it trickling down her neck.

'It's Miss Ide,' said some one. 'She fainted. . . . Fell right down!'

'No wonder!' returned another speaker, evidently a woman. 'I'm sort of sickish an' weak myself. Hadn't you better call a doctor?'

Whereupon Hettie opened her eyes, to whisper weakly, 'I'll be—all right.'

She lay on the window seat, with her head supported by the young clerk. Several persons, one a woman, stood around sympathetically.

'There! She's come to.'

A bewildering complexity and whirling of thought suddenly left Hettie with her mind clear.

'Is my brother here?' she asked, trying to sit up. With the aid of the young man she managed it, and slipped her feet to the floor.

'No,' was the reply.

'First time—in my life—I ever fainted,' said Hettie.

'Better set still a little, miss. You're awful white yet,' said the woman kindly. 'Let me help you put on your hat. It was here on the floor. You must have had a tumble.'

The clerk smiled and got up. 'No. She just sank. Like a limp sack. So she couldn't have hurt herself.'

'Indeed, I'm not hurt,' returned Hettie. 'You're all very kind. . . . It was silly of me to—to keel over like that.'

While she talked there seemed to be an awful question hammering at her consciousness. When Ben and Marvie entered, at that moment, she understood what the question was. Neither of them knew what she knew. Her relief was so great that it overcame her, and when she tried to rise she only sank back again.

'Why, Hettie!' cried Ben, in sharp concern, as he sat down to grasp her. Then Marvie knelt on the seat at her other side. Hettie smiled wanly at them and closed her eyes. She felt dizzy, and then feared to look at them.

'It's nothin' serious, Mr. Ide,' spoke up the clerk, hastily. 'She just fainted. It was the shootin'. She peeped out—an' then when I seen her again, there she lay on the floor.'

'Whew, Hettie! You gave me a scare,' said Ben, as he hugged her and shook her a little. 'But you're all right. It was only you went flooy over a street duel. Why, I'm surprised at you. Anyone would think you'd never heard a gun back in California. . . . Come, brace up, Hettie.'

'Take me home,' replied Hettie, opening her eyes again. 'I—I want to get out of this town.'

'Wal, I should smile! Me, too,' joined in Marvie, squeezing her hand. Hettie had never seen the lad look quite as he did then. The freckles stood out on his pale wet face. His eyes held a bright stare. She did not dare ask him if he had seen the participants of the street duel. She feared he had.

'Marvie, you fetch these bundles,' requested Ben, as he lifted Hettie to her feet. He had to support her, or she could not have walked just yet. He swore under his breath, then, scornfully, 'This Arizona's a nice place for women! ... Never mind, honey; maybe we'll get over it. I'm thankin' my stars Ina didn't see.'

Ben helped her into the back seat of the buckboard. 'There, you're all right. ... Marvie, put the bundles under the seats. Then get in beside Hettie an' hang on to her. I've got some drivin' to do. Soon as I pick up Ina, I'll sure leave this town in a cloud of dust.'

Hettie did not look to right or left, yet she saw and heard the excited people passing, talking down the street. Ben drove rapidly. Soon the center of town lay behind. The streets were quiet. Hettie lost the cold dread of seeing a lithe stone-faced man in rider's garb. Ben halted the horses before a house set well back in a green yard, and as he leaped to the ground Ina appeared.

'Hello, you-all!' she called, merrily. 'See, Ben, I'm right on the dot. Now, sir.' As she reached the buckboard she suddenly halted aghast. 'Why, Hettie! ... You look terrible. Are you ill? Oh, what has happened?'

'Ina, I'm a poor pioneer,' said Hettie, with rueful smile.

'Nothin' to upset you, wife,' replied Ben. 'Hettie had a scare. There was a shootin' fray downtown, an' she fainted. Climb up, an' we'll be off *pronto*. These ponies are sure rarin' to go.'

As soon as Ina had climbed up she turned solicitously to Hettie and reached for her hand. 'You poor dear! I never saw you look like this. Fainted! That's strange. You never fainted in your life.'

'I did this time, all right,' returned Hettie.

'Why? What happened? Did you see a fight?' queried Ina, excitedly.

'No, I didn't see—the fight,' replied Hettie, shutting her eyes tight. 'But I heard it. . . . Then I peeped out—to see a—a dead man lying in the street.'

'How dreadful? Oh, this wild Arizona! It's worse than Forlorn River when we were girls.'

'Worse?' laughed Ben, grimly. 'Say, Ina, California in our day could never hold a candle to Arizona.'

'Did you see this fight?'

'No. I missed it.'

'Did you, Marvie? Oh, I hope you didn't.'

'All I saw of it was the dead man. I walked by him. He had a bloody hole in the top—'

'Shut up, you infant gun-slinger,' interrupted Ben.

'Did you know the fighters, Ben?' went on Ina, curiously.

'No. Some one told me Jim Lacy had come to town, lookin' for trouble. He gave a rustler named Hardy Rue choice of leavin' town or throwin' a gun. Rue chose to stick, an' it cost him his life. Had no chance on earth, some one said. They met in the street. Even break, of course, as these Arizonians call a fair fight. But Rue was fallin' when his gun went off.'

'Terrible,' said his wife, shuddering. 'But a rustler cannot be a very great loss to the community.'

'Ina, I sure hope Mr. Jim Lacy sticks around for a while,' replied Ben, laconically. 'Tom Day told me Hardy Rue might be the leader of the rustlers who've been pinchin' me so hard. But Dillon scouted the idea.'

During this conversation Hettie was

glad to have the support of Marvie's arm and shoulder. She had not opened her eyes. But her ears rang acutely with the words she heard.

'Ben, I reckon you an' sis might shut up, yourselves,' declared Marvie, significantly, 'or talk about somethin' else.'

'Sure, sonny,' agreed Ben. 'It's no pleasant subject.'

The spirited team drew the light buckboard at a rapid pace over the smooth, hard road. The breeze stirred by this pace was cool and pleasant to Hettie's throbbing brow. After a long rest, she opened her eyes and sat up again. Already the dark line of cedars was in sight, and beyond them the uneven timbered ridges that ran up to the black frowning Mogollons. How vast and wild that range! Hettie's heart seemed to come to life again. It had been locked, clamped, frozen. What was it that had stricken her, almost unto death? If she were only alone in her room, so that she could face the catastrophe, so that she could give way to her agony! But many miles and hours lay between her and seclusion. She essayed to make conversation with Marvie.

'Your girl is very pretty, Marvie,' she said, close to his ear.

Marvie actually blushed and squirmed in his seat, and gripped Hettie's arm so hard under the robe that it hurt.

'You had met her before last night,' whispered Hettie.

'Ahuh!' he replied.

'Marvie, you are no longer a boy. You're a young man with prospects. And she—forgive me—she belongs to that notorious Hatt family. I don't blame you for—for admiring her; she's like a wild rose. But say it's not serious.'

'I wish I could,' whispered Marvie, swallowing hard.

'Marvie! Tell me.'

'Not now. I can't, Hettie,' he said, huskily. 'But I will when we get home.'

'I'm on your side, Marvie,' concluded Hettie, pressing his arm.

For a while she was able to concentrate her thoughts upon this lad and the girl, Rose Hatt, and the unhappiness that might accrue for both. Marvie was under probation. Yet it would not be long until he was of age and his own master. It seemed altogether unlikely that he would ever return to Califonia. The rich acres of Hart Blaine had no hold upon Marvie.

Soon Hettie's will succumbed to the tremendous pressure of recurring thoughts and emotion. She gave up. She had to let herself go. Then while her gaze strained out over the yellow and green prairieland, and the rolling ridges with their slopes of sage, and the miles of white grass where herds of cattle grazed, and on and on, and ever upward to the purple ranges lost in the rosy pearly clouds of hot afternoon, while she saw these beautiful characteristics of Arizona, she was confronting herself with the staggering truth.

She had seen Nevada. She could not torture herself with a thought of doubt— that she might have been mistaken. Sight and heart and mind, her whole being had recognized him in one terrible instant. He was in Winthrop. He was Jim Lacy. Jim Lacy, whom range rumor had long made mysterious, famous, ruthless. Jim Lacy was Nevada. Back in those Forlorn River days, when she and Ben and Ina and Marvie had loved him as Nevada, even then he had been Jim Lacy. Why was she stunned? Ever since Nevada had killed

Setter and ridden away never to be heard of again Hettie had realized he had borne a name he could not endure for her or Ben to know. That was not so astounding. Nevada might have been any one of the noted desperadoes of the West. The overwhelming thing was that Nevada was here in Arizona, alive, virile, stone-faced as she had seen him but once, here in Winthrop, close to the home she and Ben had chosen almost solely in the hope that they might find him some day.

What if she had seen him? A sickening helpless impotence assailed her. All the longing of years wasted! All the hope and prayer and faith wasted! Vain oblations. Nevada had been false to her, false to the best she had helped to raise in him, false to the blessed conviction she had always entertained—that whoever he was and whatever he had done, out of love for her and assurance of her faith, he would go on to disappear from the evil roads of the West and turn to an honest life. Hettie would have gambled her soul on that. And now the soul she would have staked grew sick with horror and revulsion. Nevada was a consort of rustlers, a bloodthirsty killer, a terrible engine of destruction.

But perhaps he had only killed another man! A bad man—a thief—even as Less Setter had been! The insidious small voice beat at the gate of her consciousness of faithlessness. And she listened, she clutched at it with the hope of a drowning woman, she hugged it to that soul which seemed to be freezing. So with unseeing eyes on the rolling, darkening desert, she admitted more and keener anguish into this strife of love and faith. How could she be faithless in hope, in trust? Had she not sworn, with her lips close to his, that she would die before she ever failed him? What if he had used his deadly gun again? He had killed, as before, perhaps more than once in his life, a worthless wicked man, whose death must serve some good purpose. Nevada had once saved Ben and Ina and her, all of them, from grief and misery. Who could tell what the killing of Hardy Rue might be to some one? No! Nevada had not sunk to the companionship of evil men and women, to drinking, gambling, rustling, to the vile dregs of this wild West.

Over and over again this stream of consciousness eddied through Hettie's mind, like conflicting tides, now rushing, again receding, now full and devastating.

Through the waning afternoon, sunset, twilight, dusk, on into the night Hettie acquired deeper insight into the gulf which yawned beneath her.

The swift horses had swung into the home stretch, over the short-cut road that had been one of Ben's achievements. How the night wind moaned in the lofty pines! It seemed the moan of the world. The fragrance of sage filled the air. Down through the pale aisles of the forest moved shadows, unreal, grotesque, things as strange as shadows of the mind.

Marvie now leaned against Hettie's shoulder, sound asleep. Ina had not spoken for hours. Ben, tireless and silent, kept the horses at a steady clip-clop, clip-clop. He always took pride in driving to town in eight hours and home in nine. A good road, a stanch fast team, a light vehicle, had conquered the one draw-back to Ben's wilderness ranch.

When at last they arrived Hettie crept exhausted to her room, and falling upon her bed, she lay quiet, wanting to rest and think before she undressed. But she fell asleep.

When she awakened the sun was shining gold in at her window, and the fresh sweet cool fragrance of the forest blew over her. Instead of being beautiful they seemed dreadful. She dreaded wakefulness, the daylight, the many duties to be met, the imperative need of action, the facing of her family and of life. But she could not keep them back. And with the truth there surged over her the catastrophe that had fallen.

'Maybe it's not a catastrophe,' she whispered to the faithful, waiting silence of her room.

Hettie sensed then that her greatest trial was yet to come, and a faint intimation of what it might be appalled her. It roused her to battle. Dragging her aching body off the bed, she undressed, and bathed her hot face, and brushed out her tangled hair, and put on her outdoor clothes.

Then she slipped out without awakening her mother in the adjoining room. What was it that she must do? Find him, save him, or perish! All that she faced in the golden morning light seemed to mingle in one subtle whisper. There was no deceit, no blindness, no vacillation in the nature that spoke to her.

Only the birds and the wild game, and the calves in the pasture, the roosters in the barnyard, the burros out on the range shared with Hettie those perfect uplifting, clarifying moments of the sunrise.

Golden gleams of light crossed the brown boles of the stately pines; low down through the foliage shone patches of pink sky; to the north and west opened the vast slant down to the desert, illimitable and magnificent in the rosy, shadowy soft dawn. Deer and antelope grazed with the cows in the pasture. Squirrels barked from the trees, hawks sent down their shrill piercing cries, wild turkeys gobbled from over the ridge. Joy of life, radiance of creation, peace and solitude, wholesomeness and sweetness of nature, the exquisite beauty of woodland and wasteland at the break of day, and a marvellous, inscrutable, divine will pervaded that wilderness scene.

Hettie absorbed it. She lifted up her

head to the one black dome of the Mogollons. The misery of the night faded away like a nightmare. She had been a coward. She had failed to be grateful for the very thing that had been the beginning and end of her prayers. Could she be so slight and shallow a woman as to succumb to heartbreak? A terrible ordeal faced her, the outcome of which she could not divine. She could only endure and fight whatever fate had in store.

'Oh, if I can cling to this blessed strength!' she cried. 'To hold it fast when I'm distracted! To have it in hours of gloom!'

That day Hettie did not cross the picturesque log bridge that spanned the brook between her cabin and the beautiful rambling residence of her brother. She plunged into her work, which consisted of the housekeeping she shared with her mother, her dressmaking and other personal tasks, and all the bookkeeping necessary to the running of a large expensive ranch.

She did not see Ben all day. Late in the afternoon, when she went out to walk a little in the open air, she espied Marvie sitting on the porch, a most abject-looking lad.

'Hello, Marv, old pard! Come and walk with me,' she said, brightly.

'Aw, I want to die!' replied Marvie.

'Goodness gracious! Well, don't do that on my porch. It'd be a perpetual reminder of you.'

She dragged him to his feet and locking an arm with his led him off into the woods, until they were out of sight of anyone at the house. Then Hetty bade him sit with her under an old pine where the fragrant brown needle mat looked so inviting.

'Now, Marv, I'm through teasing,' she said, with gravity that suited his mood. 'What's the trouble?'

'I had a run-in with Ben,' replied the lad. 'First one we ever had.'

'You did? Well, I've had a thousand. When Ben gets sulky and cross a good run-in clears him up, as a thunderstorm does a sultry day. Where did Ben go to-day?'

'He finally rode off to a deserted homestead over here, five miles or so. Some one found tracks of Califonia Red, and that news upset Ben. Then he waited round hours for Dillon, who didn't come. Raidy, who's on the outs with Dillon, said some things that made Ben sorer. You know Raidy. Well, dog-gone it, Ben pretty soon pitched into me.'

'What for?' queried Hettie, practically.

'Nothin'. Not a darned thing. 'Cept I moped along at a job he gave me. Fixin' fence. If there's any job I hate it's that. He swore at me. Then I told him to go to the devil—I'd quit and go home.'

'What did Ben say?' asked Hettie.

'He said, "Go ahead, you bull-headed, lop-eared little jack-ass." . . . So I rode off home. And I reckon I'll quit. I'm goin' to be a rustler.'

'All right. You want to become a rustler,' returned Hettie, accepting the statement. 'What for?'

Marvie did not reply for a long while, during which his head sank lower.

'Hettie, I'm turrible—in love,' he said at last, with an effort.

'Rose Hatt?'

'Yes. It couldn't be nobody else.'

'Does Rose love you?' asked Hettie, softly, her hand going to Marvie's.

'I thought she did, at first,' replied the

boy, writhing. 'She let me kiss her—kissed me back. But last night, when I asked her to meet me again, she said no. I got mad. But she stuck to it. When I accused her of flirtin', and me dead in earnest, she said: "Marvie, I've a bad name. I belong to the Hatts. You've a lovely sister" (she'd seen *you*) "and a proud family. I'm only a backwoods girl. It won't do. I'll not see you no more." She ran away from me then an' I couldn't find her. She'd hidden or left the dance. In the mornin' I tried again. No luck.'

'Marvie, I admire Rose for that,' said Hettie, earnestly. 'I think she's a square girl, even if she is a Hatt.'

'Now, Hettie, don't you go talkin' like dad or mother,' burst out Marvie, warningly.

'Oh, Marvie, I won't,' declared Hettie, ashamed of the fact that she had been about to do so. By Marvie's warning she estimated his regard for her.

'I don't care a damn about myself—even when I do love her turrible,' went on Marvie, passionately. 'But what's to become of Rose?'

In the sincerity and inevitableness of

youth he had hit upon the thing that mattered most.

'I understand, Marvie,' said Hettie, gravely. 'You make me ashamed. Rose is not to blame for her family, for her surroundings, for—anything.'

'Now you're talkin' like Hettie Ide,' returned Marvie, fervently. 'And I'm givin' you a hunch. If Rose really loves me I'll stick to her. In spite of dad or Ben or anyone!'

Hettie dropped her head. Here was a problem. What should she say? Marvie's confidence in her suddenly meant more than ever before. He needed something from her.

'What knocks me flat is—I'm afraid she doesn't love me,' went on the lad. 'I'm goin' to find out though, if I have to ride right under Cedar Hatt's nose. . . . Last night I believed she didn't. This mornin' I thought she did. If not—if she was only a little hussy—why'd she say she had a bad name and wouldn't meet me no more?'

Hettie had no quick reply to his passionate query. Owing to her own stress of emotion during the last twenty-four hours, she was far from being her old logical self. But she was fighting a conviction that Rose Hatt had shown nobility and sacrifice in her attiude towards Marvie's advances. If those attributes did not spring from love, Hettie did not know what to call it.

'Tell me, Hettie,' begged Marvie, with soul-searching eyes that hurt her, 'don't you think Rose cared really? Wasn't that good in her—givin' me up? Wasn't it because she—she liked me too well to go on with what she thought might disgrace me an' you an' Ben?'

'Marv, I can't be sure, but I think so.'

'Thanks—Hettie,' choked the lad, sitting up straight and facing ahead. A light crossed his somber youthful face. 'You hit me right here.' And he put his hand to his breast. 'Sure I couldn't tell nobody else but you. It's helped a lot.'

'Marvie, how in the world did all this come about?' asked Hettie, in wondering sympathy.

'Like a story, Hettie. I met Rose over a month ago. Went huntin' on Sunday. Rode a long way, then walked. I got after some turkeys. They were awful wild. I followed them a long ways, down into a big grassy canyon where a stream ran. Most beautiful place. Deer, elk, beaver all along. But I wanted one of them big old gobblers. So I kept on. And I run plump into a girl. She was cryin'. I spoke to her— sat down with her. After a while she began to talk. First she was sore an' hot at her brother, Cedar Hatt, who beat her. Showed me black-and-blue marks on her bare legs. I said somebody like Jim Lacy ought to come along and kill him. Funny, wasn't it—me sayin' that? Well, we got real friendly. She said she'd meet me again, but farther away. That place was too near home. So she told me where a trail ran and how I could find it. I never told her who I was that time. Forgot. Anyway, I kept the day she set, and sure enough she came. . . . It was different that day. I reckon I fell in love then—not the first day. And she— but never mind. . . . I met her three times more. And last time, night before last at the dance. That's all.'

'It's quite enough isn't it, Marvie?' said Hettie.

'It sure is. I forgot to tell you. At the dance, when she said first she wouldn't meet me no more, I said I was goin' to our place Wednesday at the same time as before. I'm goin', too.'

'Marv, if what I know of girls holds true—if she really cares—she'll come. Rose is too young to stick to a hard decision like that, if her heart's involved.'

'Hettie, you're a comfort,' cried Marvie, gratefully, almost hugging her. 'I'll hope she'll come. I'll believe it. Maybe that'll let me eat and sleep.'

'You'll tell me everything?' asked Hettie, earnestly.

'You bet I will. Now I'll go and crawl to Ben.'

Several days passed. Hettie took to horseback-riding again, venturing perhaps farther away from the ranch than Ben would have allowed, had he known. But Hettie seemed driven. On Wednesday she rode with Marvie for five miles back into the forest toward the brakes, and that was the greatest ride she ever enjoyed. Ridge and canyon, the aspen thickets, the wonderful swales where the turkeys and elk lived, the beaver dams and bee trees, the first coloring of vines and sumach in the open spots, the deep dark thickets where the horses scented bear and reared to turn back, the roar of water over boulders and the wind through the pine tops—these things enchanted Hettie and won her more than ever to the wilderness of Arizona.

On the last stretch back home, where the trail was fairly level and open, she urged her horse to his best speed. That race satisfied, for the time being, a restlessness and need of violence. Her blood danced hot; wind and sun burned her cheeks; the tang of the woods acted like wine. Thus she rode down into the clearing and on to the barn and corrals. And she ran pell-mell into Ben, Raidy, Dillon, and Tom Day, scattering them like quail.

'Hey there, you Indian!' yelled Ben, and he climbed a corral fence, the better to tease her.

Hettie reined her mount and, wheeling him, trotted back, and slid from the saddle.

'He's a—fine horse, Ben,' she declared, patting the wet neck.

'Wal, he suits you, lass,' said Tom Day, admiringly, as he took her in from boots to sombrero.

'Miss Hettie, strikes me this hyar Arizonie has got into your blood,' added old Raidy, shaking his head dubiously. 'Reckon I don't like it. Day says it ain't safe for you to ride out alone. So does Dillon.'

'What do *you* say, Ben?' queried Hettie, archly.

'Not a darn thing. I quit long ago tryin' to run you,' returned Ben.

Dillon leaned against the corral, in the background, without entering into the conversation. The discoloration round his eye had not wholly disappeared.

'Miss, can't you be happy ridin' on the ranch, without headin' off into the woods?' asked Raidy.

'Do you think I'd ride inside a fence? Not much.'

'Wal, Hettie Ide. I sure know what you need,' declared Tom Day.

'To be spanked, I suppose,' laughed Hettie. 'But seriously, what's the danger?'

'Wal, lass, mebbe there ain't any real danger,' replied Day, thoughtfully. 'But we're sort of locoed these days. Reckon it's far-fetched to think hoss-thieves an' rustlers might take a notion to steal you.'

'Kidnap me for ransom?' queried Hettie, incredulously.

'Wal, yes, an' for other reasons, too,' rejoined the old cattleman, significantly. 'You don't 'pear to know it, but you're a mighty handsome girl.'

'Thank you, Uncle Tom. That's a fine compliment. But it's not scaring me.'

'Hettie, look here,' interposed Ben, gravely, stepping to her with a piece of paper in his hand. 'Read this.'

Hettie took the coarse dirty paper and read:

Ben Ide.

Sir.

Fire your foreman Dillon or dig a grave for him.

X.

Without a word Hettie returned the slip to her brother.

'We found that nailed on the bunkhouse door,' he said, angrily. 'It's a threat. Dillon recovered another bunch of my cattle yesterday. Only a few head, but enough to make these rustlers sore. To-day we found where they'd been camping in an old cabin, on my own land. Of all the nerve! I've been reasonable about this cattle-stealing. I expected it. But when these thieves grab my best horse and camp right under my nose—it's time for me to get sore.'

'See, Miss Hettie,' added Raidy. 'That's why it ain't safe for you to ride out so far.'

'I'll be careful hereafter,' replied Hettie, soberly, handing her horse over to Raidy. 'Mr. Day, won't you stay for supper?'

'Sorry, lass, but I've got to be goin' home.'

'Good-by then. Come soon again,' said Hettie, turning away. She was proceeding up the lane, revolving in mind that threatening note Ben had showed her, when he caught up with her and fell into her step.

'Hettie, on the square now—did you write this note and stick it up on the bunkhouse?' he asked.

'Ben Ide! Are you crazy?' Hettie cried, incredulously. Then she burst out laughing. 'Of all things! . . . Brother, I fear the loss of your cattle and California Red has caused you to lose your head.'

'Forgive me, Hettie,' returned Ben, contritely. 'I imagined you might have done that, just to plague me. And honest, I wish you had.'

'Ben, why in the world can you wish such a thing as that?'

'Because if you had I wouldn't worry. I hoped you'd done it. Reckon I am loco, as these riders say. But, Hettie, I don't like this situation I'm in.'

'Neither do I, Ben,' retorted Hettie. 'But nobody can tell you anything.'

'Aw now, Hettie, that's not nice of you,' said Ben, reproachfully. 'I told Ina about your affair with Dillon—*your* side of it, mind you. She pitched into me like sixty. I can't stand havin' both of you against me.'

'We're not against you, Ben,' returned Hettie, earnestly.

'Yes, you are,' he said, doggedly. 'An' I'm getting sore at everybody. I'm going against your advice and Ina's, even Tom Day's. I've offered a reward of one thousand dollars for the return of California Red. Posted notices along the trails. Tom didn't like that. Said some one would bring the horse back, then steal him again.'

'What did Dillon say?' asked Hettie, curiously.

'He approved my offering the reward. You know Dillon said he could get Red back. And he was away two days, after he returned from Winthrop. I don't know where he went. He's worked with most of these outfits along the Mogollons. He knows them all, anyway, and no doubt some of them are clanny with the horse and cattle thieves. That's the worst of this country. You really don't know who is honest. Well, Dillon came back and said he couldn't find out anything about Red. So I decided to offer a reward. And Dillon himself took the notices out on the range.'

'You'll get Red back,' returned Hettie, hopefully.

'I've got another idea,' he went on. 'I want to send for several well-known sheriffs and put them on the track of these rustlers. Pat Garrett, of New Mexico. If I could get him, and a couple from Phoenix, and hire a gang of hard-shooting cowboys, I'll bet they'd clean out the rustlers. But Tom Day yelled murder at the very idea. And Dillon, he hit the roof. Swore they'd burn me out instead of just rustling a few cattle. Few? By George! I'd like to know what Dillon would call a lot of cattle.'

'Ben, you should listen to Tom Day, at least,' replied Hettie. 'He knows the country.'

'I'm listening, Hettie. But I want some action,' he retorted. 'If I don't get Red back inside of ten days there'll be hell to pay by somebody.'

Marvie did not return to the ranch till late. Hettie sat up waiting for him, trying to read, but mostly gazing into the wood fire with dreamy, sad eyes. She heard his swift step on the porch, and a jingle of spurs, then a quick knock.

'Come in, Marvie,' she called expectantly.

In he rushed, like the wind, but quietly, and he startled her with his pale face crossed by black smudges, and his piercing, radiant eyes. He carried a rifle and quirt and gloves in his hands; and altogether he appeared a striking, thrilling figure. Hettie knew before he spoke what had happened.

'She was there!' he whispered, dramatically.

'Marv, I knew that the instant you entered,' said Hettie, with a smile. There was a contagion in his spirit.

'Hettie, I'm sure the happiest an' miserablest man in the world,' he added.

'Sit down, Marvie, and tell me all about it.'

'Not a great deal to tell, but what there is of it is turrible,' he returned, coming to the seat beside her. Then in a low voice, full of suppressed emotion, he went on: 'Rose was there. She'd been there for hours, waitin', cryin', fearin' I wouldn't come. She said her heart broke. She'd found out she loved me. I was the only one who'd ever cared for her—been good to her. She said she could give me up—to save me disgrace—but she'd have to kill herself. I swore I'd stick to her—marry her. I talked an' talked. An' then I told her I'd fetch you down the trail next Wednesday. She was turrible scared at that. But I told her you'd help us. An' finally she agreed. She's to ride down a trail we know, till we meet her. . . . That's all, Hettie. An' for God's sake—'

Marvie broke off huskily, his voice failing.

Hettie impulsively kissed him. 'Marvie, I think you're pretty much of a man,' she said. 'I'll go. And I'll find some way to solve your problem.'

He mumbled something incoherent and rushed out of the room, neglecting to close the door. Hettie watched him stalk away in the moonlight, then shutting the door she drew her chair nearer the fire and fell into grave and sympathetic pondering over Marvie's love affair.

CHAPTER 15

HETTIE, early riser as she was, outdid herself on this Wednesday morning, which was the day on which she had agreed to ride into the brakes with Marvie.

There were tasks to see to, some of which she performed before her mother called her to breakfast. Hettie was still at the table when whoops outside alarmed her. Then she recognized Mavie's 'Whoopee!'

'Gracious! Is the poor kid celebrating the arrival of this day?' ejaculated Hettie, mirthfully.

Nevertheless, she ran out on the porch, followed by her mother.

'For the land's sake!' cried Mrs. Ide. 'Has Marvie gone daffy!'

They saw him running wildly bareheaded, up the walk toward Ben's house. Once up on the ridge, Marvie espied Hettie, and waving to her he yelled:

'Look down in the pasture!'

Hettie did so, at least toward the near

pasture, but as her view was mostly obscured by pine trees she did not see anything unusual.

'*Whoopee!*' yelled Marvie again. 'Hey, Ben!'

Hettie realized now that something was up, so she started to run across the lodge bridge. When she got halfway she saw Ben rush out on the porch, in his shirt sleeves, rifle in hand.

'What's the matter, Marv?' he shouted.

'CALIFORNIA RED'S BACK!' bellowed Marvie, coming to a halt.

Hettie saw Ben start as if struck. Then he ran to meet Marvie. Hettie lost little time getting over the bridge and across the grassy bench. Breathless and excited she arrived in time to see Ben sink down on a log, as if overcome. Ina came running in her dressing-gown.

'Oh, Ben—who—what is it?' she cried, in alarm.

'Glory be! Ina, Red is back.'

'That all? I thought we were attacked by rustlers. Marvie, you can yell like a demon.'

'Ben, I'm—so glad,' panted Hettie.

'Boy, you're not playin' a trick on me—

213

because I was sore on you?' implored Ben of Marvie.

'Nope, I saw him sure. An' I was tickled to death.'

'Aw! . . . Reckon Dillon fetched him back,' sighed Ben in unutterable gratitude.

'Dillon, hell!' exclaimed Marvie, evidently provoked out of his radiant pleasure of being the first to inform his boss about the return of his beloved favorite. 'Dillon is in bed. There's nobody up but me.'

'Ahuh! By George! Did you see anyone?'

'Not a soul,'

'Well! That beats me. Let's go down. Ina, get some clothes on if you're comin'. Tell the kid. This'll sure tickle him.'

Ben and Marvie, with Hettie trying to keep beside them, stalked down off the ridge, into the lane, through the courtyard, and on to the corrals. Three times during that swift walk Ben asked the same question and three times Marvie made the same reply. Raidy appeared on the bunkhouse porch and he carried a rifle.

'Boss, what's the bellarin' about?' he queried, as he joined the trio. Marvie led the way through two corrals, and then across the wide square to a high pasture fence, up which he scrambled like a squirrel.

'There!' he shouted, pointing.

Ben surmounted the fence ahead of Hettie, and his wondering exultant cry prepared her.

California Red stood not far distant, down along the fence. Nervously he jerked up at Ben's cry, and wheeled with head high, ears up, eyes wild. How sensitive, splendid he looked to Hettie!

Ben whistled and began to call: 'Red—Red, old boy, come here, Red!'

The stallion lost his alarm, and laying down his ears he approached slowly, step by step. Ben kept calling. Red knew the voice and showed increasing gladness. He whinnied. Then he trotted straight to where Ben straddled the fence. He looked the worse for his absence. Ragged, scratched, muddy, somewhat thinner, he showed the effect of hard travel and probably harsh treatment.

'Ben, somebody's been mean to him, else he wouldn't come hankerin' to you thet way,' declared Raidy.

'By Heaven! if that's true!' cried Ben,

fiercely, and reaching out his hand he called again. 'Come, Red. Come, old boy. Don't you know your boss?'

But Red would not come all the way. He halted uncertain, pawing the ground. His dark eyes shone softly. Again he whinnied. Ben guardedly got down off the fence, speaking all the time, and slowly went up to Red, finally encircling the noble neck with his arm. Then he buried his face in the red mane.

Hettie's thoughts went back to the Forlorn River days when California Red had roamed the sage hills, free and proud, when Ben had been a lonely, outcast, wild-horse hunter, and when Nevada had come so mysteriously into their lives. Hettie's eyes dimmed. She could not understand Ben's great and passionate love for that grand horse, but she felt sympathy for him and rejoiced in his happiness.

Meanwhile the cowboys had arrived on the scene. Raidy had opened the pasture gate. Presently Ben led the stallion through to the square.

'Look him over Raidy,' said Ben.

While the cowboys crowded around and Hettie still stayed on the fence, the better to see, the old horseman walked round Red, feeling him, examining him, lifting his hoofs one after the other.

'Wal, boss, he's as sound as a bullet,' declared Raidy, gladly. 'Ganted up a little an' got a couple of bad cuts. An' he's lost a show. Nervous an' skittish. But you can bet he's glad to git home; an' far as I can see he's no wuss for bein' stolen.'

'Raidy do you still hang to that opinion?' inquired Ben.

'I sure do. They ain't anything else to it. Why, man, don't you know hosses? Can't you see he's been haltered an' hobbled?'

'Aw, no!' said Ben.

'Sure. Look thar. Use your eyes, boss. You got him back an' I reckon you'll keep him this time. But don't let your love for the hoss blind you to facts.'

Raidy kept running gentle, skillful hands over Red, ruffling up the silky hair, looking with the eyes of long experience to marks and signs by which he read something of what had happened to the horse.

'See for yourself,' went on Raidy, with vehemence. 'Look hyar! . . . My Gawd! he's been roped, too!'

At this point Hettie espied Dillon stalk around the corner of the high fence which had obscured the men and horse. Abruptly he halted. Swift amaze and consternation leaped across his expression of curiosity, blotting it out. Then as swiftly his face changed, smoothing to a smile. What a handsome, pleasant man! Hettie marveled at his consummate control and acting. But he could not fool her again. The return of Red was actually as startling to Dillon as it had been to anyone else there.

The circle of cowboys opened to admit Dillon.

'Ha! So, boss, what'd I tell you?' he broke out, and vigorously shook Ben's hand. It was strange for Hettie to see how much pleasure that gave Ben. But just then he was up in the skies. 'The old red son-of-a-gun has come back. Jumped the pasture fence goin' an' comin'. . . . Red, I take off my hat to you. But you never had me guessin'!'

'Dillon, I had it figured the same,' declared Ben.

Raidy snorted his disgust. 'An' you once a wild-hoss hunter! Say, if Red had *run* off he'd never have come back. I asked you to take a peep at them marks on him. But you keep huggin' the hoss an' you won't look.'

'Old-timer, I'm so happy to get him back that I don't want to do anythin' else. Besides, Raidy, on the square, I'd hate to have it proved he'd been stolen.'

'Stolen? That's nonsense, I tell you,' interposed Dillon, testily. 'Red took a little run an' come home. I've had many a hoss do it.'

'Not wild hosses, Mister Dillon,' snapped Raidy.

'What do you know about hosses, Raidy?'

'Wal, I reckon I've forgot more'n you ever knew,' retorted the older man. 'I ain't doubtin' you've *had* a lot of hosses, Dillon, but you didn't *raise* them—you didn't *catch* them—an' you didn't *keep* them long.'

This was pretty plain speaking, as was evinced by Ben's stepping between the men, and the dark flash that wiped out Dillon's geniality.

'What're you hintin' at?' he queried.

'I'm not hintin'. I'm tellin' you, that's all. An' you can like it or lump it.'

Ben raised a hand to silence Raidy. 'That'll do. You're both privileged to your opinions, but don't get nasty.'

'All right, boss,' replied Raidy, in an aggrieved tone. 'But my word is sort of ridiculed hyar. An' I'm askin' thet you look at these marks on Red. If you won't I reckon I'll take it as a slap at me, an' I'll quit you cold.'

'Raidy!' exclaimed Ben, astounded.

'You know me, boss,' returned the old horseman, sturdily.

Ben wavered. It was plain to Hettie that he hoped to keep peace between the old and new hands, so valuable to him now. But Raidy had thrown down his gage and looked formidable.

'Ben,' called Hettie, from the fence, 'you've known Raidy all your life. He taught you how to ride. It's only fair that you listen to him.'

'All right, Raidy, if you feel that bad about it,' replied Ben, resignedly.

Again the old horseman ran his gentle, skillful hands over Red's supple body, down to the wonderfully muscled legs. 'Look hyar,' said Raidy, as he stooped. 'He's been hobbled. See! He's been gone *ten* days. Thet mark was made no more'n yesterday.'

'Reckon you're right,' admitted Ben, as he slowly arose. 'I apologize.'

'No apology wanted,' said Raidy. 'All I want is for you to come out of your trance. . . . Now look hyar. Look at Red's nose. He's been roped.'

'By thunder! There's been a hackamore on him,' ejaculated Ben.

Dillon was not to be outwitted, and he had swiftly followed Ben's examination of the horse.

'Damn if Raidy isn't right, boss,' he exploded, evidently regretful. 'I hadn't even looked at Red. But there are the marks, plain as print. . . . I apologize, too, Raidy. My mistake.'

'Wal, Mister Dillon, I'm acceptin' your apology,' drawled Raidy, his keen old hawk eyes on the handsome foreman.

Hettie was riding beside Marvie, across the western end of the sage flat, toward the fence which marked the limit of Ben Ide's ranch land.

Marvie dismounted to open the gate for them, and when he vaulted to the saddle again he grinned. 'Nobody but Raidy saw us, an' he won't tell. But Ben would stand for anythin' to-day. Gee! how he loves that red horse!'

'He does indeed. Well, I love him. Gave me a hundred dollars, just for seein' Red first!'

'Early to bed, early to rise, makes a boy healthy, wealthy, and—'

'Gee! I do feel rich!' interrupted Marvie. 'An' I'd like to fly to town an' back. But it'll keep.'

'Marvie, were you looking at Dillon when he first came on us and saw Red?' inquired Hettie.

'No, I wasn't. Why?' returned Marvie, turning to eye her.

'He struck me as being more amazed than any of us, and *not* so happy.'

'Ahuh!' replied Marvie. It was evident that he chose to be noncommittal. Hettie, however, did not fail to catch the glint in his eye.

'Raidy and Dillon are at odds,' she continued. 'That's plain.'

'Wasn't Dillon the slick one, though, when he turned the tables on Raidy?' rejoined Marvie, as if impelled.

'Yes. He's too clever for men. It takes a woman to see through him.'

'I'll bet *daylight* will show through him—presently,' returned Marvie, in dark significance.

'Marv, you are absorbing a lot of Arizona.'

'Here's where we turn off, Hettie,' said Marvie, as he left the road. 'Narrow trail, but good. Look out for the brush an' duck the branches. Ride now!'

He spurred his horse into a lope and Hettie did likewise. Soon they entered the forest, where the shade was welcome and no dust arose. Hettie had been on this trail several times, though not to go very far. It led west, toward the brakes and the frowning dark notches of the Mogollons, dim and purple in the distance. Soon they passed the limit of Hettie's experience in that direction, a fact which gave her a thrill. She scarcely had a chance, however, to look at the scenery, for Marvie was making time, and she had to watch her horse and the low branches.

They rode perhaps five miles before the trail began to penetrate deeper into the forest and to ascend into rockier and rougher country. They climbed high, and Hettie had a glimpse now and then of the red desert far to the north, and the black slopes beneath her, falling away to the west. She soon gathered what the brakes of the Mogollons meant. The brakes were canyons, running like the ridges of a washboard, walled with brush and rock, choked with dense thickets, above which the lofty pines and spruces towered. Ridge after ridge Marvie climbed and descended, until coming to a deeper, clearer canyon he turned off to follow a willow-bordered stream.

As they progressed, again riding at a lope, the canyon widened and deepened, the walls grew rugged and unscalable, the fringe of pines on the rims lifted higher, and every aspect of the wilderness seemed likewise intensified. The time came when the horses had to walk again, down and down, under narrow gray shelves of stone, under the massed foliage of maple, oak, aspen, all beginning to show a tint of autumn, especially the fluttering aspens, just turning to gold. The stream grew larger, swifter, deeper, and its mellow roar filled the dreamy solitude.

At corners, where the trail turned, Marvie always exercised a caution which added more than romance to Hettie's feelings. This adventure grew with the miles. How dark, still, lonely some of the constrictions in this brake of the Mogollons!

Turkeys ran fleetly from the open grass patches into the thickets; deer walked up the steep wooded slopes; elk stopped their browsing on the willows to gaze at the disturbers of their solitude; beaver slipped off their muddy dams to make swirls in the still green pools; squirrels chattered; jays squawked; ravens croaked; hawks sailed across the blue strip of sky overhead.

'Somewhere along here we'll meet her,' whispered Marvie, fearfully. 'It always scares me. That Cedar Hatt might be prowlin' along the rim to spy us. Rose is cute, though. I've waited half a day before she came.'

They wound along the crooked trail, and if it were possible, Hettie imagined every vista wilder and more hauntingly beautiful than the last. The white bleached grass, the green willows, the amber rocks, the rushing foaming brook, the thickets of oak and aspen, russet and gold, the wonderful walls rising sheer, stained and mossy, gray and purple, up to the ragged fringed rims—all these aided the movement of leaves, the flash of birds, the fragrance of pine, the utter solitude, into working an enchantment upon Hettie's senses. No wonder Marvie had fallen in love with his wild Rose.

'I see her horse,' whispered Marvie, as he halted. 'She'll be near. We'll get off now. I'll hide our horses in the aspen thicket.'

Hettie got off to hand her bridle to him, and waited while he led their mounts out of sight. How noiselessly he moved! Marvie had become a woodsman. Soon he returned and led her off the trail into the grass.

'Anyone ridin' along behind us would sure see our tracks,' he whispered. 'But that's a slim chance. You see it's an old unused trail here. The Hatts live over in the next canyon.'

'She's a brave kid, to meet you this way. And you're not such a coward, Marvie, boy,' returned Hettie.

He led her up a gradual grassy slope,

into the protecting shelter of low pines and silver spruces. 'Look at the elk beds,' he whispered pointing to round places where grass and moss had been flattened.

Hettie espied a ragged red pony, without a saddle, haltered to a sapling. Then she saw a dark curly head rise above the tall grass. Next moment Marvie was speaking low: 'Hettie, this is Rose Hatt. . . . Rose, I've fetched her. This's Hettie Ide, my best friend an' sort of sister.'

As Hettie sank down, smiling, with hands outstretched, the girl rose to her knees, her eyes dilating, her face without color.

'Rose, I'm glad—to meet you,' whispered Hettie, pantingly, and she kissed the girl.

'Oh, Miss Ide—you're good to come,' faltered Rose. She was trembling all over. This child of the wilderness was nothing less than terrified at meeting one of Marvie's kin.

Marvie knelt beside Rose, and it was evident this was a torturing moment for him, too. The romance and excitement had passed. Ben Ide's sister was now face to face with the daughter of rustler and backwoodsman Elam Hatt, with the sister of notorious Cedar Hatt.

'Hettie, I reckon Rose won't be so scared an' shy if I leave you alone with her,' said Marvie. 'So I'll keep watch below. An' don't forget we haven't lots of time.'

Then with a bright and reassuring look at Rose he slipped off under the low-spreading trees. Hettie turned to the girl, trying to think of words to put her at ease. How like a woodland wild flower! Rose wore a buckskin blouse fringed and beaded, a ragged brown skirt, and boots without stockings. She held a sprig of tiny aspen leaves, turning gold.

'Rose, since Marvie loves you, I must love you, too,' said Hettie, speaking not what she had intended, but the words that welled from her heart. She did not need to be told that Rose Hatt had never had love of mother, sister, or friend. The girl gave a little gasping cry of wonder and pain, then fell into Hettie's arms, where she burst into tears.

This made the ordeal easier for Hettie, and she held the girl in silence until the paroxysms of weeping had subsided. Then she began to talk, kindly, soothingly, as if to a child, saying she hardly knew what, until the moment came when she felt she might venture a question. But before she could ask it Rose sat up, wiped her wet face, and smiled through her tears.

'Marvie was right,' she said. 'It's sure good to see you, hear you, now I'm over my scare. I'll never forget you till my dyin' day.'

'Rose, you love Marvie, very much?' said Hettie, venturing to open the serious interview.

'Yes,' replied the girl, simply. 'I couldn't help it. But I didn't know at first. Not till the dance.'

'Then you two have pledged your troth?'

'If you mean told our love, yes—Miss Ide. But I didn't promise to marry Marvie.'

'He asked you, of course?'

'He begged me to,' replied the girl, lifting her head with pride.

'Why did you refuse?'

'I love Marvie too well to hurt him with you an' all his family.'

'Do you mean you think you'd disgrace him and us because you're a Hatt?'

'Yes, an' a good deal more I haven't told Marvie,' she went on, steady of voice, though her round breast heaved. 'Cedar would come down on Marvie an' you an' your brother Ben for money. An' so would another man whose name I daren't tell. He—this man—has got a hold on Cedar— an' me. He'd ruin us all.'

'Rose, that's a strong statement,' said Hettie. 'But even if it isn't exaggerated it doesn't change the fact that you and Marvie ought to wait. You're both very young.'

'I'm not exaggeratin'. I could tell you more. An' about marryin'—Marvie's reason for hurry is to get me away from the life I live. It's turrible, Miss Ide. I have to cook, wash, scrub for an outfit of rustlers an' hoss-thieves. Look at my hands! Look at the black marks—here—an' there. I get kicked an' beat. Marvie knows an' he can't stand it any longer.'

'Could you not leave this home?' queried Hettie, earnestly.

'I've thought of that. Yes. I could. My dad wouldn't care. But I'd have to be a servant—or worse.'

'No, indeed. Rose, you could come to my home.'

'Oh, how—wonderful!' gasped the girl, rapturously clasping her hands. 'But that'd be 'most the same as marryin' Marvie, so far as Cedar an'— that other man are concerned. . . . No, it'd never do. But thank you—bless you!'

'Rose, we mustn't despair,' continued Hettie, touched to the heart by this girl's sincerity. 'Time will help us. If you could only escape this—this drudgery and shame.'

'That's the hope which keeps me up, Miss Ide. If I could only tide over a little time! Cedar is goin' to hell fast. He's rustlin', gamblin', drinkin' harder than ever. He's under the thumb of—the man I daren't squeal on.'

'But why daren't you?'

'Because if *he* didn't kill me, Cedar would. I'm the only one outside of this Pine Tree outfit who *knows*. An' my life ain't worth much.'

'Pine Tree outfit!' echoed Hettie, her

eyes lighting. 'That the mysterious gang of rustlers.'

'It sure is. I'm trustin' you with my life, Miss Hettie. But I daren't tell more. Nobody knows how secrets slip out. You might talk in your sleep.'

'Naturally. But I think you could risk it, considering I sleep alone,' said Hettie. 'Rose, this *is* a plot. We're all involved. Your people and mine. What a tangle! It must have been fate that brought you and Marvie together. Oh, if I only knew how best to advise you.'

'Reckon I wish so, too. But I've got a hunch. It's my job to stick home—to fool my people—to learn all I can—to fight that devil off who—who . . . I must see Marvie very seldom an' be sure we're never ketched. Somethin' will happen, Miss Ide. You've made me feel it. You made things different. Neither Cedar—nor *him*, can last long in this country. Not now. I heard my dad say so. . . . Oh, this is the second time my hopes have risen. Oh, I wish I could tell you of another friend I found lately. I forgot. . . . But he came to my house an' there was hell. I listened at night through the chinks of the logs. Cedar was wild. Cash Burridge was there. "We've got a big deal on," says Cash. An' that pleased all the gang except Cedar. They set to whisperin' an' I heard no more.'

'Rose—isn't your friend—Jim Lacy?' whispered Hettie, haltingly, with dry lips.

The girl caught her breath and drew back sharply, wonder the most predominant of her varying emotions.

'There, you have betrayed it,' continued Hettie, forcefully, trying to command her voice. 'Call Marvie now. We will plan another meeting, then hurry home. I've enough to think of—this time.'

Rose silently slipped away under the pines, and Hettie, staring at the green-walled foliage, seemed to see a ghost. 'Oh, my God!' she whispered in an agony. 'Nevada belongs to this thieving, vile crew!'

CHAPTER 16

FROST fell early in September on the high rims of the Mogollons. Soon after the sun set the rarefied air became cold and sharp, making a campfire something to draw the riders and hunters, and other men of the woodland.

A group of five dark-faced, dark-garbed campers sat around a beautiful opal-hearted cedar fire, at the wild edge of Black Butte, where it fell sheer into the brakes. Three of the men were playing cards, cross-legged in front of a saddle blanket, intensely intent on the greasy bits of colored pasteboard and the pile of gold coin and roll of greenbacks. They were gambling—the absorbing pastime of all dyed-in-the-wool rustlers.

The other two men occupied a position on the opposite side of the fire. One had his back and his outspread palms to the blaze, while the other sat against a log.

'Hell, Jim,' swore the standing man, flicking a hand toward the gamblers, 'they couldn't hear the crack of doom. They'll gamble there all night or till one of them has all the money. An' what difference would it make now—if they did hear what you say?'

'Wal, Cash, the fact is I'm not used to crowds,' replied the other. 'It takes long to get acquainted. An' you know I can never be shore of any man.'

'That's the price you pay for leadership. Reckon it's the same among honest business men in the world as among rustlers an' gunmen. But I didn't mean to split hairs over it. I was just complainin' because you're so close-mouthed.'

'What of it, Burridge?' queried Jim, somewhat acidly. 'I shore talk plenty to you, don't I, when we're alone?'

'Course you do, Jim,' answered Burridge. 'All I want to get at is this. If you'd loosen up a little more, drink an' gamble a little, especially when we run into other outfits, it'd facilitate our plans.'

'I reckon, Cash,' returned Jim, wearily. 'But how can I have a quick eye an' hand if I drink? I'll agree, though, to be more friendly an' set in a game now an' then.'

'Good! Reckon that'll do. Lord, Jim, don't get me wrong! Ever since you called

Hardy Rue out an' killed him I've been ready to crawl an' wear my finger nails off scratchin' for you. I mayn't have been your friend back in Lineville, but I sure love you now. You've put me on my feet again.'

'Wal, Cash, that's plain talk,' replied Jim. 'An' I don't mind sayin' I like you better than I used to. But I can't love any man or even be pards.'

'Sure, sure I understand,' returned Burridge, hastily. 'An' I'm damn glad for small favors. But you needn't tell that to our gang or any of these outfits we meet. They all think you were my pard back in California an' are yet. Burt Stillwell would have shot me, surer than the Lord made little apples. But he was afraid of you. He was undecided. He couldn't be himself, an' I'm tellin' you he was a bad *hombre*.'

'Aw, bad, yes, in a sense of dirty yellow behind-your-back viciousness,' agreed Jim, flashing a quick eloquent hand. 'I hate to throw a gun on such fodder. But he forced it. He kept still till he got a few drinks. Then he r'iled up aboot Ben Ide's red horse, an' he put in that ridiculous claim for his pard, Cedar Hatt. Wanted a share of the divvy for the cattle—for this Hatt fellow.'

'The hell he did! Well, I wondered what it was about. But I was so glad I didn't feel no curiosity,' returned Burridge; he turned round to kick the firelogs. Then again he faced his companion. 'Maybe you don't know it, Lacy, but you made a lot of friends by pluggin' Stillwell, an' one sure-enough enemy.'

'Who's that? This Cedar Hatt?'

'He's the bird. A red-tailed buzzard, an' no mistake. He's a backwoodsman, Jim, like an Indian, who knows the woods. Cedar wouldn't ever try you out, unless, like Burt, he'd been lookin' at the bottle. All the same you'll be in more danger from Cedar than from all the gun-throwers in Arizona. He's killed shepherds an' cow-boys enough, believe me. He'll trail you—ambush you in the woods.'

'Much obliged, Cash,' drawled Jim, yawning. 'Reckon I'd better look out for this heah Cedar Hatt.'

'I'm givin' you a hunch of hunches,' declared Burridge. 'I'm most damn honest an' selfish about it, too. I've other reasons beside affection not to want Jim Lacy killed. Cedar Hatt will be sore enough when he hears you put Stillwell over, but, say, when he learns you got that red stallion an' sent him back to Ide—my Gawd! brother, he'll be hell's fire!'

'How soon is he goin' to find out?' queried Lacy, with more interest. 'Stillwell cain't very wal tell. An' that pard of Stillwell's—Babe Morgan, some one called him—he'll be runnin' yet.'

'Cedar'll find out *pronto*,' declared Burridge. 'If not from some one outside our outfit, then from some one inside. For you were playin' a queer high hand, Jim, when you took the stallion away from Burt an' Babe an' sent it back to the Ide ranch. They'd stolen it. Your argument sounded good to me. Ben Ide would raise more hell over the loss of California Red than a hundred thousand head of stock.'

'Huh! I'll bet he would,' declared Lacy, dropping his head. The twig he had been twirling in his fingers snapped sharply.

'Well, to go on, your argument looked good to me. Now I've got brains, an' most of these rustlin' *hombres* haven't nothin' but spruce gum in their heads. That deal looked queer to all our outfit. Still, only

238

Hubrigg opened his trap to say so. Hubrigg likes you, though, an' I think you can gamble on him.'

Here Burridge leaned over toward Jim to whisper: 'If our gang seem a little standoffish yet, it's only your reputation. Since you helped us to steal cattle an' drive them an' sell them, why, they're sure you are one of us, even if you are Jim Lacy.'

'Reckon that ought to be aboot enough,' returned Lacy.

He turned his ear to the faint cold wind that breathed up out of the black void below.

'Hear anythin'!' queried Burridge.

'Rollin' stones. Might be deer on the trail.'

'Might be Stagg, too, an' I'll gamble it is. For he's overdue.'

'Listen,' rejoined Lacy, holding up a sensitive hand.

Both men turned their heads sidewise to the wind and waited. Fitfully the faint wind mourned through the forest. From far below floated up a soft murmur of tumbling stream. Solitude and silence seemed to be emphasized by these wilderness factors. The campfire cracked;

the gamblers slapped their cards and clinked their gold.

'Heah anythin'?' asked Lacy, suddenly relaxing.

'Sure. A lot of night sounds, includin' our gamblin' pards here, but no hoss,' returned Burridge.

'Wal, I heah a hoss,' said Lacy.

'Good! That'll be Stagg, unless it might be one of our hosses. I'll take a look an' then I'll unroll my bed.'

Burridge stalked away in the gloom of the forest, while Lacy, left alone, attended to the campfire. Once or twice he glanced at the absorbed gamesters, with something curious, strange, and menacing in his eyes. Then he fell to contemplation of the opal heart of the campfire. He watched it, the glow and sparkle and white shade and pearly red. And the moment arrived when he forgot the wild environment, the gambling rustlers, to become like a statue, cold-faced, with haunted eyes. He must have seen a ghost in the radiant embers, for not till a thud of hoofs sounded close at hand did he rouse out of his trance.

Presently two dark forms entered the

circle of light, and approached, talking low. Lacy got up to meet them.

'Howdy, Jim!' greeted the newcomer with Burridge. He was a swarthy-faced, beady-eyed white man with a strain of Indian or Mexican blood.

'Howdy, Stagg! Did you make a good job of it?' returned Lacy, with apparent carelessness.

'Wasn't no job a-tall,' said Stagg, reaching bare grimy hands toward the fire. 'Soon as you-all left, the red hoss quieted down, an' I coaxed him out of thet measly leetle corral. He din't like thet. An' after he found out I was leadin' him home he didn't make no more fuss. An' we made fast time. Reckon it was nigh on midnight when we got down on the sage. I tied up both hosses, pulled off my boots, put on my moccasins, an' led the stallion five miles through grass an' sage. When I run into Ide's fence I kept goin' along till I come to a gate. I opened it an' let him in.'

'Much obliged, Stagg. I—reckon it was no fool move of mine—though some think different,' replied Lacy, turning his face away from the fire.

'Lacy, it was the slickest piece of

headwork I ever seen on this range,' declared Stagg. 'I hadn't time to tell you I was at Burton's ranch the next day after Stillwell stole the stallion. Ide's cowmen came rarin' over the country. Thet Raidy, he's an old hand, an' he was mad as a hornet. An' to-day as I was climbin' the Hogback I run into a sheepherder I know. Greaser named Juan somethin'. He said Ide had plastered the trees along the trails, offerin' reward for Red.'

'There, Jim—you see, it was a wise move,' declared Burridge, with satisfaction. 'Young Ide would have spent a fortune gettin' back that stallion. Well, he sure was grand hoss-flesh. I only looked at him once. If I'd looked twice I'd been a hoss-thief, too.'

Lacy stared out into the gloom of the forest.

'Reckon you're hungry?' asked Burridge of the arrival.

'Had a bite at Hatt's to-day,' returned Stagg. 'But a chuck of deer meat an' a cup of coffee wouldn't go bad.'

'We got roast turkey. Young gobbler that Jim shot the head off as we was ridin' along.'

'Wal, friend Jim must pack a shotgun,' replied Stagg, with a attempt at facetiousness.

'Nope. Only that old six-shooter.'

Lacy turned from the darkness to the firelight. 'Stagg, did you see any of the Hatts?'

'Sure. They was all home, an' had company, too. Strangers to me.'

'Did you tell them about takin' Red back to the Ide ranch?'

'Sure. Thought it good idee. An' I rubbed it in, too. Elam's no hoss-thief. He said hoss-stealin' was a low-down bizness. But Cedar swore there was somethin' crooked about a gunman an' rustler who returned stolen property. Also he swore he'd steal the red stallion again, jest to spite you.'

'Ahuh. Wal, what did Cedar say when he heahed I'd shot his pard, Burt Stillwell?' inquired Jim, in a dry, caustic tone.

'What?' queried Stagg, with a start.

'You heahed me, man.'

'Sure. But it—I . . . An' you shot Burt?'

Lacy nodded coldly, eying the fire.

Stagg stiffened a little, and after a

stultified pause glanced from Burridge to Lacy, and then out into the forest. A silence ensued, broken only by the gamblers.

'Burt's dead—then—of course?' asked Stagg, presently, with an effort.

Cash Burridge broke the strange spell of the moment.

'Burt's under the sod an' the leaves, waitin' the Judgment Day. An' it was a damn good job, Stagg.'

'No arguin' ag'in' thet,' returned Stagg, recovering to grin. 'Wal, Lacy, fact is Cedar Hatt hadn't heerd no more'n me. But if you're curious, I can sure tell you— Cedar will be hoppin' mad.'

'I told Jim that,' said Burridge, impatiently. 'What's it amount to, anyhow? There'll be a Hatt less *pronto*.'

'Wal, pards, the population of this hyar Arizoni is sure deterioratin',' returned Stagg, with a guffaw.

One of the gamesters, disturbed by the loud laugh, looked up to say, 'Bill, shet your loud mouth, an' come set in this game. Hubrigg an' Brann ain't very much to stack up ag'in'.'

His bold face and rolling eyes expressed

exceeding gratification while he clinked his pile of gold.

'I'm on,' replied Stagg, eagerly. 'Wait till I swaller some grub.'

'How about you—Lacy?' inquired Brann, with marked hesitation. 'We ain't slightin' you. It's an open game.'

'Thanks, Brann,' drawled Lacy. 'I'd hate to win your pile. You see, I've got uncommon good eyes, an' it shore hurts my feelin' to see you men slippin' aces around. I'm a caird sharp. I'd break you. Like as not, then you'd get sore an' pull a gun—which would be bad for this outfit.'

Long and loud rolled the mirth of Burridge and Stagg down the aisles of the forest. Brann appeared a droll and good-humored rustler. He stared hard at Lacy, finally grinning.

'Jim, I'm recallin' thet invite for you to set in,' he said, meaningly.

'Gamble your heads off,' spoke up Burridge. 'We needn't break camp till late to-morrow. But I'm turnin' in.'

'Same for me,' said Lacy, and strode out of the lighted circle. Presently he had to feel his way to the black tent-like spruce tree under which he had spread his tarpaulin and blankets. Sitting down, he pulled off his boots. Then he sat motionless, peering back at the ruddy campfire. Presently he removed his coat and made a pillow of it. Next he unbuckled his gun belt, took it off, and laid the gun under the edge of his coat. After that he gazed a long time out into the spectral forest. The wind had risen, and sang through the pines. A deep wild bay of a wolf rang out. How lonely, hungry, mournful!

'Reckon that poor lofer is like me,' muttered Lacy, and rolled in his blankets.

The ring of a cold ax on hardwood awakened Jim Lacy from his slumbers.

There was a white frost on his tarpaulin and his boots and his sombrero, also his nose, from the feel of it. Hubrigg, who appeared to be an agreeable and helpful chap, was chopping wood for a campfire.

'Nifty mawnin', Hub,' said Jim, by the way of greeting. 'I'll pack some water.'

'Hullo! I reckon your conscience never lets you sleep,' said Hubrigg. 'Look at them stiffs there. Dead to the world. Now watch.'

With that he snatched up a bucket, pounded it with the ax handle, then tossed it to Lacy. The rustlers, rudely disturbed, leaped out of their beds, wild-eyed, hair on end, every one of them holding a gun or reaching for one.

'Haw! Haw! Haw!' roared Hubrigg. 'Wake up, you sour-dough eaters, an' help at the chores.'

All of his roused hearers, except Burridge, cursed him roundly, and Burridge, when he realized what had happened, said, 'Lord, I thought my day had come!'

Jim Lacy went down the trail for a pail of water.

Whenever such a duty as this, or other opportunity, afforded he always took advantage of it, seeking ever a moment away from the rustlers with whom he had cast his lot. That time, however short, was a blessed relief. He need not then be perpetually on the *qui vive*, watching, listening, reading the minds of his companions. In those stolen moments or hours he reverted to his old character,

Nevada, lover of the open, of desert and forest, of the life and color and mystery of nature.

The sun had not yet arisen. To the east the sky, over the long arms of the Mogollons, reaching, sweeping down black and wild, had begun to flush rosily. The forest seemed awakening from its slumber with the bark of squirrels and screech of jays, the bugle of bull elk, and the sweet, plaintive twittering of canaries. Rocks and grass showed the hoary coating of the frost. The air nipped, and the water at the spring felt like ice to his face. There was a thin edge of crystal ice along the margin of the little pool.

Upon climbing back to the rim he paused a moment to gaze down into that marvelous black basin called the brakes of the Mogollons. They were really not black, though black predominated over the rich gold of aspens, and the scarlet of maples, the russet of oaks, and the vivid cerise of vines for which he had no name. A ragged pine-speared slope fell almost perpendicularly to the ribbed and ridged lowland below, and here and there outcroppings of gray crags and yellow shafts added to the effect of an exceedingly broken country. His experienced eye wandered down to the brakes, over what from that height appeared undulating ridge and swale. Its vastness amazed Jim Lacy. Here was a wilderness country as large as the northern California he knew so well. And to increase the effect to one of staggering conception, there stretched the desert, grand and illimitable. He had a moment of silent ecstasy of appreciation, followed by a melancholy longing for a time when he might be free to love Arizona, to have a ranch of his own, a few horses and cattle, a home in the wilds where he could hunt and ride, free to live peacefully, dreaming of the past. Melancholy longing because he knew it could never come true!

Returning to the campfire, he arrived in time to hear Brann exclaim: 'What'n hell Columbia for do we want to bring the Hatts in on this deal?'

'Say, man, there's brains back of this deal,' replied Burridge, derisively.

'Meanin' yours, eh? Wal, all right, but I'm from Missouri.'

They ceased the argument at the approach of Jim Lacy.

'Somebody rustle the hosses,' called out Burridge.

An hour later the six men, with as many pack horses, started over the rim on the trail down into the brakes. It was a trail that would cause even the most expert and daring rider to hesitate before attempting it on horseback. Morever, it was seldom used. Lacy decided it must be a rear outlet from the rendezvous of desperate men. Many a time axes had to be brought into requisition to enable pack horses to pass down. Jumble of rocks, weathered slides, narrow slanting ledges, fallen trees and thick brush, made this Hatt trail one to remember.

But though very steep, it was not long. It let out into the head of a canyon where the stream gushed forth from under an amber-mossed cliff, and went singing down through a winding defile, surely the wildest and most beautiful that Jim Lacy's eyes had ever beheld.

'Cash, tell me,' said Lacy, at an opportune time, when they rode abreast, 'is Cedar Hatt the haid of this Pine Tree outfit?'

'Hell no!' ejaculated Burridge, in ridicule. Then as an afterthought he continued: 'But, Jim, I don't *know* he isn't. I mean I've sense enough to figure he couldn't be. There's a real man at the reins of that gang.'

'You're square now? You honestly don't know?'

'So help me Heaven!' returned Burridge, raising his gloved right hand. 'If I knew I'd tell you—even though the man was my pard. But I don't know. I never met a man who did. Of course no one is goin' to brag about that. The Pine Tree outfit is only three years old. It's got a brand, but sure no one ever seen it on a steer or a calf. I never seen it on anythin'. I hear it's cut on aspen trees. Sheepherders will tell you that.'

'Cedar Hatt might belong to it?' queried Lacy.

'Sure. But he'd be a bad *hombre* to trust, unless you had some hold on him. My idea of the Pine Tree outfit is this. Some slick rustler from other parts has ridden in here, either with a few choice men or picked

251

them carefully after he got here, an' he has the money an' the brains to control a small outfit. Some cowboy found a stray steer on the range. It had its brand painted out. Painted! That's new. But how the devil could they paint out the brands on a big bunch of wild steers?'

'Not very practical,' observed Jim, thoughtfully.

'It's no trick to steal cattle in this country, an' it's a heap sight easier to sell them,' declared Burridge. 'But to do it on a big scale an' not be found out—I call that brains.'

'How far to the Hatt ranch?'

'Round this next bend. Wonderful place to hole up, don't you think?'

'Shore is. Are all these canyons like this?'

'Like it? Yes, only rougher. Some of them are so thick you can't get a hoss through.'

When they rode around a high green corner Jim gave vent to an exclamation of utmost pleasure. The brake opened into an oval valley surrounded by gray-cliffed, green-thicketed walls, rising high. A level meadow, where horses and cows grazed in deep grass, ended in a low bench of land, upon which huge isolated pines and spruces towered halfway to the rim. Two log cabins stood picturesquely at the edge of this rise of ground. In the background a corral and a barn, with logs awry and roof caved in, showed half hidden in a blaze of golden aspens.

'Here's where the Hatts hang out,' remarked Burridge. 'It's like a fox den, with two holes. The one we just came down, an' a pass below where a couple of good shots could stave off all the cowboys in Arizona.'

'Beautiful!' ejaculated Jim, charmed out of his usual reserve.

'I've been here often. Once tried to buy the place from Hatt. Not much.'

'What do these Hatts live on?' queried Jim, gazing round.

'Meat an' beans an' corn meal. An' they make their own whiskey. If you take a swill of that it'll knock you flat.'

'How many women-folks?'

'Only the kid—Rose. There was a woman here, a while back, wife of one of the boys, I heard. But I never saw her. . . .

Well, old sharp-eyed Elam sees us already. He's comin' out with a gun.'

The riders in advance drove the pack horses up on the bench, and followed to dismount. Burridge arrived a little in advance of Jim. The old mountaineer, Hatt, stood shaggy-headed, with a smile of welcome on his craggy face.

'Howdy, Elam! Did you get word I was comin'?'

'Yep, but never expected you so soon.'

'Shake hands with Jim Lacy,' went on Burridge, laconically.

'Howdy, sir! Reckon you ain't no stranger, by name,' responded Hatt, offering his hand.

Lacy leaned off his horse to accept Hatt's advance. 'Shore glad to meet you, Elam,' he drawled. 'Reckon I fell in love with your homestead, heah. An' I'll hang around till you kick me out.'

'Welcome you air,' said Hatt, genially. 'We keep open house fer our friends. Git down an' come in.'

Burridge made no offer to introduce Jim to the other Hatts present, though he called them by name, Tobe and Henny.

Cedar Hatt did not put in an appearance, nor did Lacy's quick eye sight the girl—Rose.

'Throw yer packs back in the grove,' said Hatt. 'Jest turn your hosses loose. Never yit had a hoss leave hyar.'

While pack and saddle horses were led back toward the aspen grove Elam Hatt walked with Burridge, while the two sons followed. Lacy did not need more than a casual glance at Elam to define his status. He was a rough, sturdy backwoodsman who had, no doubt, lived by hunting until an easier vocation had presented with the ranging of cattle along the Mogollons. The two sons, however, exhibited nothing to impress favorably. They were uncouth, unshaven louts with bad teeth and pale eyes, and faces that indicated very low mentality. Lacy's advent manifestly did not cause them either apprehension or interest. Tobe was barefooted. Henny leaned on a short carbine, worn shiny from long service.

'Where's Cedar?' inquired Burridge, casually.

'He's hyarabouts somewhere,' replied Elam. 'He seen you fust.'

'Hope Cedar won't take exception to our comin'.'

'No tellin' what Cedar'll take,' replied Hatt, with a grin. 'But I'm right glad to see you. I'm wantin' news. Make yourself to home. I'll go an' see about grub. . . . Tobe, whar's your sister?'

'I dunno,' replied the son.

'Find her, you terbaccer-chewin' cub,' returned Hatt, and strode away toward the cabins.

Tobe Hatt might never have heard his father, for all the attention he paid to the order. Instead he gravitated toward Lacy.

'Got any smokin'?' he asked.

'Shore. Help yourself there in my saddlebag,' replied Lacy.

The other young Hatt, Henny, now moved out of his tracks, and dragging the rifle butt over the ground, he joined Tobe in a search of Lacy's saddlebag. Finding the tobacco, they availed themselves of Lacy's offer. They took it all.

'Cash, where you goin' to bunk?' asked Lacy, presently.

'Right here in the aspens. Good a place as any. Elam will offer the loft of the big cabin, but I'd just as lief be out.'

'Wal, I'd a good deal rather,' drawled Jim. 'Cabin lofts are full of dirt, spiders, centipedes an' smoke. I'll throw my outfit somewhere aboot.'

'Make it within call, Jim,' replied Burridge, not without significance.

Jim sat down, ostensibly to mend one of his stirrups, but as a matter of fact he did not care to pick out his bed site under the pale eyes of these degenerate Hatt boys. He could peer through the eyes of men to their minds. Either Tobe or Henny would commit murder for a sack of tobacco. Jim decided he would carry his bed to a secluded place in the brush and change that place every night. With covert glances he watched the Hatt boys and also kept a lookout for Rose.

'Wal, fellars, what about goin' on with our little game?' inquired Hubrigg.

'Sure,' replied Brann.

'I should smile,' added Stagg, cheerfully.

Cash Burridge shook his head dubiously, but did not voice his opinion until the Hatt boys had ambled off out of hearing.

'Say, men, I don't want to be a kill-joy,

but honest I question the sense of showin'
all that money here.'

'Why not?' asked Hubrigg.

'It might not be safe. We don't belong to
this Hatt outfit. They could have this
canyon 'most full of backwoodsmen in no
time. There's only six of us.'

'Wal, listen to him!' ejaculated Brann.
'You got it wrong, Cash. There's five of
us, an' Jim Lacy!'

'I just don't think it's wise,' added
Burridge, stubbornly, ignoring the sarcasm.

'We may have to hang around here for a
week or more,' spoke up Stagg. 'What'll
we do? If we can't gamble we might as well
not have any money.'

'Jim, what do you say?' asked Burridge,
in perplexity.

'Wal, seen' that money changes hands
so often, I reckon nobody'd miss it if the
Hatts did get it,' chuckled Jim.

'Haw! Haw!' roared Cash, slapping his
knee.

'Miss it!' ejaculated Brann, evidently
affronted with catastrophe. 'Say, I look on
thet pile as mine.'

'Jim, you seem a nice fellar, with fun in

your talk, but I'm sort of doubtful about you,' said Hubrigg, dubiously.

'How so?' queried Jim pleasantly.

'Wal, I can't exactly explain. But when you talk lazy an' easy, like all you darn Texans, an' look some other way, I always feel queer.'

'Right you are. Our new member makes me feel like a fellar who's runnin' like hell an' knows sure he's goin' to get the seat of his pants slung full of buckshot.'

This from Brann indicated the slow progress of the rustlers toward amity with Jim. They all laughed uproariously.

'Shore I must be a likeable cuss to have round,' declared Jim, presently. 'I've a notion to get sore.'

'Wal, for Gawd's sake, don't,' burst out Brann. 'Be a good fellar an' set in the game with us.'

'I'd like to, for pastime, anyhow. But suppose I catch one of you manipulatin' the cairds?'

'Huh! Manip-oo-latin'? What's thet?'

'Brann, our friend Jim means slippin' aces off the bottom, holdin' out, stackin' the deck, an' a few other tricks gamblers have.'

259

'Aw, I see. Wal, Jim has a right to holler when he ketches us, same as we when we ketch him doin' the same.'

That sally elicited a yell from Brann's comrades.

'Jest so he hollers only with his mouth,' shouted Stagg.

'All right, I'll set in a few hands,' said Jim, good-naturedly. 'Anyway, till I'm broke.'

'Jim, your credit is good in this outfit,' interposed Cash Burridge. 'An', anyway, you'll have a gunny sack full of money before long.'

Whereupon the rustlers, in high spirits, owing to being well fed and flush with money, repaired to the shade of a pine in front of Elam's cabin, and squatting round a blanket, emptied their pockets of coin and bills. Jim joined them, choosing a seat from which he could watch the cabins and the approach of anyone.

Bantering ceased abruptly the instant gambling began. And the cares of rustlers, if they had any, vanished as if by magic.

The game was draw-poker, the stakes any amount a player chose to wager, provided he produced it. Jim knew he could hold his own with these gamblers, but he preferred to lose the ill-gotten gains Burridge had forced upon him as his share of their first rustling deal together. So Jim played recklessly, making his losses more than discount the ridiculously lucky cards he held at times. His apparently casual glances at the cabin, however, were not few and far between.

The Hatt boys came to watch the game, soon growing equally absorbed with the gamblers; and it was noticeable to Jim that they gravitated round the circle of players, wherever the gold coin went. Old Elam came presently, and likewise fell to the attraction of the game, but it seemed the playing itself rather than the sums of money lost and won, that held charm for him.

Elam Hatt's house was one of the picturesque double-cabined structures under one roof, with wide porch space between. The logs had been peeled. They were old and brown, rotting in places; the sloping roof of split shingles had a covering of green moss and pine needles; the rude stone chimney, built on the outside of the right-hand cabin, had been repaired many times with yellow clay and red adobe mud. The porch ran all along the front of both cabins, and one end was littered with saddles and packs. Deer and elk antlers on the walls supported rifles and bridles. A bearskin hide, not yet dried, hung nailed flesh side out, on the wall of the left cabin. This was smaller than the other, evidently consisting of only one room. The window, without glass or shutter, opened toward Jim, who had been quick to see a face peer from the darkness and draw back again.

When he caught sight of it again he knew at once that it belonged to Rose Hatt and that she had espied him. She stood far back in the gloom of the cabin, her face only a vague oval, but with staring eyes like black holes.

'Elam, do you know draw-poker?' asked Jim, presently.

'Tolerable. I wisht I hed stake enough to set in this hyar game. I'd bust somebody,' replied old Hatt, to the amusement of the gamesters.

'Play a few hands for me,' said Jim, rising. 'Change my luck, maybe. I want a drink.'

'Whiskey?'

'No. Water. Where'll I get it?'

'Thar inside the kitchen door at the end of the porch,' replied Hatt, rising with alacrity to take Jim's place. 'My girl jest fetched some fresh from the spring. Snow water, an' thar's none better.'

As Jim neared the porch, Rose came out of the cabin where he had seen her, and crossed to enter the other. She wore buckskin. He caught the flash of brown bare legs and feet. Jim went down the porch and entered the door mentioned by Hatt. As he expected, he encountered Rose. Despite excitement manifest in her face, he thought she looked clearer of eye and skin, somehow prettier.

'Howdy, Rose! You see I've come,' he said.

'I saw you first thing,' she replied.

'I want a drink, please.'

She filled a dipper from a pail and handed it to him. Facing her and standing in the door, Jim drank thirstily. It was good water.

'Will it be all right if I talk to you?' asked Jim.

'Sure. 'Cept when Cedar's around.'

'Where is he?'

'Reckon he's hidin' somewhere, watchin' you-all. So we can't talk now. . . . But, oh! I've so much to tell you!'

'Yes? Tell me a little—quick,' said Jim.

'Marvie's to fetch Hettie Ide—to meet me,' whispered the girl, fearfully, yet with eyes full of glad light. 'Oh, she must be an angel! He says she will give me a home—if I can ever get away from here.'

'Wall, now, that's fine,' sympathized Jim, vibrating to this news. '*Three* friends now—Marvie an' Hettie Ide an' me. Lucky girl!'

'I can't thank God enough,' she breathed from a full breast.

'Keep on thankin' an' fightin',' said Jim, with ring of voice and meaning smile. Then he set down the dipper on the bench and backed out of the door, eyes still intent on Rose. She was flushed of face now, eager, hopeful, yet still fearful.

'I will. They can't stop me now—unless they kill me,' she answered, resolutely, with a wonderful blaze in her eyes.

'Who're they, Rose?'

'Cedar, for one. I told you,' she replied, haltingly. But there seemed to be tremendous impelling power working on her—greater, Jim sensed, than could come through him just then.

'Tell me the other man.'

'Oh, I daren't—I daren't,' she faltered, losing courage.

'If you love Marvie—an' if *she* will stand by you—you can dare,' he shot at her, relentlessly.

She showed then a struggle over fear that had outlived childish years.

'Rose, that other man is Clan Dillon?'

'Yes—yes,' she whispered, in unutterable relief, as if she had been spared betraying him. 'Are—are you to be here long?'

'Days, maybe weeks.'

'Keep watch,' begged the girl, finding courage. 'Cedar will drag me off in the woods—to meet Dillon. If he does—follow us, for God's sake.'

'I shore will, Rose. Don't lose your nerve.'

'But be *careful*, Cedar's an Indian in the woods.'

Jim Lacy leisurely turned, and with glance on the ground, apparently idle and lax, he strolled back to the gamesters.

'How comes the luck, Elam?' he asked.

'My Gord! Won three hands straight runnin,' ejaculated Hatt. 'An' one a fat jack-pot.'

'Wal, shore reckoned you'd change my luck. Play 'em for all you're worth, Elam, an' if you break this outfit I'll divvy with you.'

'Ha! he's got no chance on earth, Jim,' said Cash. 'Better set back in before we break you.'

Old Elam held his own, however, evidently to his immense gratification. Jim watched for a while, much amused, until his ever-roving glance fastened upon a newcomer to the scene.

A man had come out of the aspen thicket. He carried a rifle, which he held by the barrel over his shoulder. His gait, his build, betrayed him to Jim Lacy. This was Cedar Hatt.

Jim had been kneeling on one knee behind Elam, and now, leisurely rising to his feet, he stood at ease. Upon nearer view Cedar Hatt turned out to possess only the walk and the shape of the Hatt family. He was darker than any of them, with beardless face of clear brown tan, small glittering eyes set close, black as coal, and of a strange intensity, sharp nose and sharp chin, with a slit between for a mouth. He wore his hair long and it curled dark from under an old slouch hat full of bullet holes. His garb was greasy buckskin, from head to toe. There was a knife in his belt, but no shells for the rifle.

Cedar Hatt stood across from the circle of gamblers, and dropping the muzzle of his rifle upon his moccasined foot he leaned on it, and gave his restless sloe-black eyes scope of all present. If the players saw him they gave no outward show of it. At length Cedar put the toe of his moccasin against his father.

Elam looked up with a start.

'Hullo! You back, Cedar?'

The son made an almost imperceptible movement with his right hand toward Lacy.

'Cedar, say howdy to Jim Lacy,' went on Hatt, a little hurriedly. Nevertheless, he was not greatly concerned. 'Lacy, this hyar's my son Cedar.'

Jim nodded civilly, without speaking, and he received even less in response. A look, like a streak of black lightning, flashed over him from head to toe—then Cedar Hatt deigned him no more attention.

It was a singular thing for Jim Lacy to meet men; and in a case like this, when he knew before he had seen Cedar Hatt that he was going to kill him, the incident seemed extraordinarily potent and strange. If there was an instinct to act almost involuntarily in such a meeting, there was also an intuitive searching that followed. Lacy needed only the slightest glimpse at Hatt's eyes to know that he had not yet learned of the killing of Burt Stillwell. After that instant the meeting became only ordinary for Jim, inasmuch as Hatt could never again be formidable face to face. Jim knew him now. It was the unfamiliar that men of Lacy's caliber always reckoned with.

The game progressed, with luck shifting from one player to another, and manifestly what seemed a long, tedious, irritating waste of time to Jim was only a fleeting of precious moments to the gamblers.

Finally Cedar Hatt, without ever having uttered a word, shouldered his rifle, and stalked away with the spring of a deer-hunter to his stride. He went up the canyon to disappear around the green bend.

Whereupon Lacy strolled away himself, into the golden shade of the aspen thicket, and on through darker shade to the lichened base of the cliff. He flung himself down here and leaned against the wall. Above him the quivering aspen leaves fluttered with the marvelous noiseless movement peculiar to them. All around in the brush the lizards rustled. Nature was alive and full of treasure for the watcher, the seeker. But Jim Lacy's eyes were focused inward; his ears were attuned to a beating within. He had come there into the obscurity and loneliness of the thicket to think, to plan, to plot, to work out a course he could inevitably follow. But how useless that was! The slightest accident or incident might change the best of his plans. If he decided on a definite thing his mind would be set. His task demanded more than that; and it involved infinite patience and sacrifice, incredible command of geniality and good-fellowship with these rustlers, sight and sense that must grasp every little clue which might lead to the succes of his venture. All this when his spirit revolted and his nature demanded quick, hard, fierce action!

After supper, which was served about sundown, on the porch between the two cabins, Elam Hatt scraped his rude seat back and arose.

'You-all who want to gamble air welcome, but I reckon some of you will want to set in to a confab with me.'

He went into his cabin, followed by Burridge and Lacy. The large room was dark, except where breaks in the chinks between the logs let in light. Hatt stirred the slumbering embers in the huge yellow stone fireplace and put on chips of wood.

'Reckon they'll want the lamps, an' we don't need none,' said Elam.

The door opened to admit Cedar Hatt, who advanced with his sliding silent step, to seat himself on a bench in the shadow besides the stone chimney.

'Burridge, if thar's a lead weight on yore chest, shove it off,' invited Elam, bending down to lift a fiery ember with which to light his pipe.

'Are you open to a big deal?' queried the rustler, bluntly.

'Always open to anythin'. But I'm careful not to change the minds of ranchers about Elam Hatt,' replied the backwoodsman, shrewdly.

'Which means they think you do some two-bit brandin' of mavericks, like any cowboy, but you never tackle a real rustlin' job?'

'Reckon thet's the size of it, Cash.'

'An' that's exactly why I'm goin' to spring this deal on you. No one will ever lay it to you an' everyone will lay it to the Pine Tree outfit. Savvy? The time's just ripe. The trap's set. We can't do it half so well without you an' your sons. We don't know the country. Otherwise you bet we wouldn't let you or anyone else in on it.'

'Sounds good. I'm listenin'.'

'Tom Day an' Franklidge have throwed a big herd of stock together. Some of it's workin' with Ben Ide's big herd, the last of his stock, in what the sheepherders call Silver Meadows. They're high an' won't be comin' down before the fall round-up. That'll come anywhere along first of October. Now while them cattle are high up we plan to drive them—*on up over the Rim*—an' down into the Basin, where we could sell a hundred times as many head, with never a question asked. I've already got the buyer. To do the job right an' quick we need more riders, an' particular some who know how to find fast travelin' through them bad canyons up to the Rim. That's all. I leave it to you to call the turn on that deal.'

'How do you know Ide's stock air runnin' on Silver Meadows? Thet's Day's range.'

'I know because I saw them an' they used to be my cattle.'

'You're calculatin' thet if Ide does rare, he'll lay it onto the Pine Tree outfit?'

'Exactly. The deal is ready-made for us.'

'How much stock thar now?'

'We can bunch three or four thousand head in half a day, an' land them over the Rim in less'n two days.'

'An' you've got a buyer?'

'Waitin' an' willin'. He's drivin' ten thousand head to Maricopa. How easy to run in a few more thousand!'

'Looks too powerful easy to me,'

returned Hatt, as if sagging under an overpowering weight.

'Easy an' safe. An' listen, Elam. . . . Twenty dollars a head. In gold! One yellow old double-eagle for every steer!'

Elam Hatt paced the rough-hewn logs that constituted the floor of his cabin. He seemed to find strength in their solidity. His legs were the first part of him to weaken. His collapse came suddenly, with a crash to the bench before the fire.

'Cedar, what'd'ye say?' he asked, in hoarse low voice.

'Burridge, swear them steers air in Silver Meadows,' said Cedar Hatt, his moccasined feet coming down with padded thuds as he leaped up and leaned out of the shadow.

'Sure I swear. Three days ago. An' the grass an' water are fine. They'll work higher for several more days. . . . Ask Jim Lacy here. Reckon you'll not be intimatin' he's a liar.'

'Talk up, Jim Lacy, if you're a rustler,' called the young Hatt.

'Wal, I was with Burridge. I saw the cattle,' replied Lacy.

Cedar Hatt glided into the light of the fire, to lean over his father and strike out with lean dark hand, like the claw of an eagle.

'Papa, with ten riders I can run them cattle over the Rim in one day,' he declared. How grotesque and striking the epithet he gave his father! He seemed the epitome of lawlessness, of the hardened rustler, yet acknowledged the endearing claim of blood.

'Thet settles it, then,' returned Elam Hatt, throwing his hands as one whose price had been met.

'Hold on! Thar ain't no Greaser herder in these brakes who'd lead thet drive. An' I'm the only white man who kin.'

'Wal, what's makin' you yap so? It's settled, ain't it, 'cept the workin' out?'

'I want my pard, Burt Stillwell, in on this.'

'Reckon I see no kick to thet. But it ain't my deal.'

Cedar Hatt faced round with the swift, sinister action peculiar to him.

'Anythin' ag'in' Stillwell?' he queried.

'Wal, not any more, Hatt,' drawled Jim. 'I shore had a little grudge, but it's gone.

When I saw Burt last, I shore had a friendly feelin' for him.'

'Burridge, you had no use for the Stillwells. How're you standin' on this hyar deal I want?'

'Cedar, all I say is, sure—ring your pard Burt in—if you can get him,' returned Burridge, with something unnatural in his tone. And it was noticeable that he stepped more into the shadow.

'Papa,' hissed Cedar Hatt, and that word inspired awe as well as mirth, 'I'm double-crossin' the Pine Tree outfit to make us all rich on this big job.'

'Air you drunk, son?' asked Hatt, slowly rising to his feet. 'How'n tarnation can you double-cross them—onless you mean beatin' them to the deal?'

'Me an' Burt belong to the Pine Tree outfit.'

CHAPTER 17

A WEEK later to the day, about the middle of the afternoon, Jim Lacy stood with Cash Burridge on the Mogollon Rim, facing south over the magnificent wilderness of southern Arizona. The black timber of the basin merged in the grassy parks and flats, growing hazy in the distance, and all that wild lowland led to the bleak colored desert ranges.

'My Gord! Listen to that!' ejaculated Burridge, with red sweaty face wrinkled ecstatically. 'Grandest music on earth.'

'Cash, they'll greet you in Hades some day with that music,' drawled Jim.

'Bawlin' bulls an' whoopin' cowboys! I'll be glad to hear it, providin' it don't come too soon,' returned Burridge.

Yellow dust palls hung over the steep Maricopa trail, where it jumped zigzag off the Rim and wound down into the green depths. A mighty roar of trampling hoofs, and bellowing cattle, and crashing brush, and whooping riders waved up from that hot slope. It seemed an avalanche of sound now softening and again swelling, wild and free, harmonious with the country which made it possible. From the look of the trail, trampled and dug and widened by thousands of hoofs, it appeared that a river of live beasts had poured over the Rim.

'Lacy, it's all over but the fireworks,' said Cash exultantly.

'*Quién sabe?* It might fetch some fireworks you're not figurin' on,' admonished his companion, moving over from his heaving, foam-lashed horse to get in the shade of a pine.

'Not much. We're shakin' the dust of the brakes. Say, won't Ben Ide an' Tom Day bite nails? Biggest drive I ever had a hand in. An' all so easy! All like clockwork! All in a couple of days despite that— yellow traitor, Cedar Hatt!'

'Shore we didn't need him,' responded Lacy, thoughtfully.

'Jim, I've seen some mad *hombres* in my time, but that Cedar Hatt beats them all to hell,' declared Burridge, aghast at the memory.

'Shore he was mad. Didn't I warn you

to keep your outfit from givin' it away aboot Stillwell?'

'Yes, you did, an' I talked myself hoarse. But it couldn't be kept. They *hated* Cedar, an' the minute somebody got two drinks aboard he up an' blows that Burt Stillwell was dead. It sure made a hydrophobia-coyote out of Cedar. But he didn't know *who* shot Burt. When he spit questions at you, like a snake with a hunch, why didn't you lie?'

'Wal, Cash, I reckon you don't savvy me.'

'Why didn't you kill him, then?' went on Burridge, sharper of tongue.

'I just aboot did,' returned Lacy, reflectively. 'But I saw he didn't have the nerve to draw—so I waited.'

'Ahuh! Waited? I get your hunch. Cedar knows somethin' you're keen to find out. Bet it's that Pine Tree outfit.'

'Cash, you're figurin' fair. But on the daid square now—rememberin' the favors I've done you—cain't you tell me somethin' about that outfit?'

'No more'n we all know, Jim.'

'Shore you have some suspicion aboot who leads them?'

'Honest to Gawd, Lacy, I haven't even an idee!' returned Burridge, with truth in look and voice. 'It might be Judge Franklidge himself.'

'Holy Moses! Cash, that's a wild guess!' ejaculated Lacey.

'Sure. An' it's only a guess. But you can gamble all the coin you're goin' to get *pronto* that the Pine Tree boss is not hidin' in the brakes, like the rest of us rustlers. He's an honest member of range society. Ha! Ha! Yes he is! . . . Jim, there might be a combine of homesteaders an' ranchers in cahoots with an outfit of great riders like Burt Stillwell an' Cedar Hatt.'

'Reckon I've thought of that.'

'What's it to you, anyway, Jim?' queried Burridge, curiously.

'Reckon I've got to put my brand on the boss of the Pine Trees,' said Lacy.

'Ah! Is *that* all? Hell! I thought you might have some interest in him,' retorted Cash sarcastically. 'Jim, on the square, if you hadn't done so much to straighten me out again, I'd have suspicions about you.'

'Wal, keep them in your haid.'

Burridge laughed, and gathering up his bridle swung into the saddle.

'Come on. I don't want the outfit to get far ahead. You'll be hearin' the clink of gold before sundown.'

'Not me, Cash.'

'What?'

'I'm not goin' any farther with you.'

The rustler exhibited profound concern and amaze.

'You're not goin' any farther—what—'

'Say, Cash, are you out of your haid?' queried Jim, testily.

'Sure I am, if you're not.'

'Wal, I'm not, old-timer.'

Burridge studied his companion for a long moment, his face working. Regret began to erase the incredulity.

'What the hell are you goin' to do?'

'That's my concern now. I'm through.'

'Through! . . .But, Jim—'

'Didn't I help you out of a bad hole—the worst you was ever in?'

'You sure did, Jim. An' I—'

'Didn't I rustle cattle with you?'

'Yes.'

'Didn't I come out in the open—so everybody on this range will know I helped steal Ben Ide's cattle?'

'By Heaven! you did!' declared Burridge, with redder face. 'An' I hold that against you, Jim. I just can't figure why you did that. We could sure have laid that onto the Pine Tree outfit.'

'Wal, neither Ben Ide nor any other honest rancher will know *you* had the high hand in this big cattle steal. But my name an' my hand in it will be known. I saw to that. They'll think *I* am the boss of the Pine Tree outfit.'

'I'm damned! . . . Jim Lacy, you're too deep for me. But I'm gettin' a hunch. . . . How about your share in the divvy for this deal?'

'You're welcome to it. Take it an' go out of this country. Try bein' honest again. You might succeed next time. But don't ever come back heah!'

'Why not, Jim?' queried Burridge, strong and hard.

'Because if you do I'll kill you,' flashed Lacy, in a voice that cut like a whip.

The ruddy heat left Burridge's face, and he began to nod his head, slowly, with increasing motion, while his eyes fixed in a startling comprehension.

'*Jim—Lacy!*' he said, huskily.

'I reckon,' replied Lacy, grimly, as he turned to his horse.

'You been a pard to me, whatever your reasons,' went on Burridge, with feeling. 'I don't care a damn what they were. . . . I'll leave this country. Here's my hand on it. . . . Good-by an' good luck!'

'Same to you, Cash,' replied Jim, as they gripped hands.

Burridge wheeled his horse so violently that it reared and plunged, and then slid to its haunches in the soft ground where the trail broke over the Rim. Burridge hauled it up and used his spurs. The animal snorted and took the first descent on a jump, then steadied to a quick walk. At the first bend of the trail into the timber the rustler looked back up to the Rim.

'I'll send my compliments to Cedar Hatt an' his boss in hell!'

Lacy strode into the level shady forest, leading his horse. He had prepared for this separation from Burridge, and had tied a light pack behind his saddle. There was a spring in his step and a light on his face. The deep forest land, beginning almost at once to slope north from the Rim, seemed to receive and absorb Lacy as a transformed man. How sweet and enchanting the silence, the solitude! He listened for the last ebb of that tide of hoofs, roaring down into the Basin. Gone! The air had cleared of the dust, the heat, the din, the smell of a cattle drive.

It still wanted an hour to sunset, and the time was approaching the most wonderful of all hours on the Mogollons. Birds and game had roused from the midday Indian-summer heat; the long black shadows of the trees were slanting down across the open swales and dells, where the white grass furnished contrast to the reds and purple and golds of the autumn leaves. The tracks of man and horse showed dark through the thick covering of gold and green that carpeted the ground.

Lacy descended winding ravines and aspen hollows until one opened into the head of a canyon where the murmur of water invited him to camp.

'Reckon you're plumb tired,' he said to his horse, laying swift hands on the ropes. 'Wal, it was a day. But we're through now—through that kind of work. . . . An' I'm hatin' to hobble you, old boy.'

Jim kindled a little fire, and while he heated water in his one pot he gathered ferns for bedding. The frost had seared the long leaves, making them brittle and easy to break off. He piled a great bundle in his blanket and carried it to the edge of an aspen thicket, where, as was his habit, he made a bed under cover of the foliage.

'I'll be cold as blazes along toward mawnin', but I cain't keep a fire goin' . . . not with that Indian Cedar Hatt roamin' the woods!'

The sordid atmosphere common to the rustler gang was lacking here. Lacy did not realize it until he grew conscious of his alacrity, of his zest with the old camp tasks, in the pause to see and feel and hear and smell the forest which seemed now his alone, in his habit of talking to himself.

'Wal, now, won't there be hell around the Ide ranch some of these heah mawnin's, when riders come in with the news? Last of the Ide cattle! . . . Jim Lacy takin' to rustlin'. . . . It will be funny. I'd like to be hid an' heah Ben cuss. This'll be the last straw. He'll get as many gun-toters as he can hire, an' set out to land me in jail.'

Jim seemed immensely pleased with the thought. The hard, morose intentness of the past weeks did not inhibit his natural geniality.

'Ben is shore goin' to get the shock of his life one of these heah days,' went on Jim. 'The dog-gone old wild-hoss hunter! ... What's he goin' to say to me first off—an' then after? ... Lordy! ... An' Hettie! ... She'll call me a low-down yellow faithless ... Say, meetin' her will be about as funny as dyin'. I can feel myself cavin' in right heah!'

Jim Lacy, with his plans well in mind, had on the whole journey across country from Elam Hatt's ranch to the head of the Maricopa trail, taken careful account of the lay of the land.

It served him now. His intention was to return to Hatt's ranch, if possible without encountering even a sheepherder. Hatt had left his daughter Rose alone, unless the mysterious woman consort of Henny or Tobe Hatt, of whom Jim had heard vaguely, might be considered as company. Elam, of course, with his two sons, could be expected to get back home from the cattle drive in two days from the time Jim had left them, or even less. As for Cedar Hatt, who had deserted Burridge and Elam after the revelation of Stillwell's death, no doubt he had rushed to the secret rendezvous of the Pine Tree men, wherever that was, there to betray to them news of the impending drive of the Ide stock. It was Cedar Hatt whom Lacy had greatest interest in, at the present stage of the game; and Cedar was most likely to be found at or near home.

There was reason, too, for Lacy to have an interview with Rose Hatt, from whom he expected to force more about the man who dominated her brother and whom she feared. Moreover, Rose was to be considered on her own behalf.

Jim Lacy did not think it wise to go near Silver Meadows, where the cattle had been collected for the great drive; and therefore he made a wide détour, hoping to strike the trail he and the rustler band had made coming from Hatt's ranch. But he had to go into camp the second night of his journey without having come to this trail. The forest was exceedingly rough, he had only a general direction to go by, and often windfalls and impassable brakes threw him off. On the third morning, however, he struck the trail he was looking for, and he back-tracked it all day. On the following day it failed on high ridges, on hard ground, rocky flats, and pine-needle mats, over which Elam Hatt had led the rustlers for the express purpose of hiding their tracks.

Lacy wasted no time trying to recover them, though he believed he could eventually have done so. Sure of his direction now, he pressed on rapidly, and the next afternoon struck the deep canyon east of the one in which Hatt lived. During his sojourn with the Hatts, Lacy had hunted turkey and deer up and down these brakes, with the sport of the hunt not at all his prime motive.

Jim took the precaution to ride well back from the Rim, peeping over whenever opportunity offered from behind foliage or rock covert. He did not really expect to see any one, but that did not influence his actions. Lacy was always cautious, watchful, alert; and in this instance he might have been on a scent, so instinctive was his progress along that Rim.

Presently, down in an open bend of the deep canyon Lacy caught a glimpse of a rider. He was riding slowly up the trail, leaning down from his saddle, evidently with eyes on the ground.

'Trackin' somethin',' muttered Jim. 'Now I wonder who that is an' what he's trackin'.'

Lacy rode back away from the Rim, and urged his horse to a lope, careful to avoid rocks and brush. There were places where he had to go slowly, but in the main he covered a mile or more in short order, then again approached the Rim.

This time he dismounted and cautiously stole to a vantage-point, from which he could peer unseen. As luck would have it, there was an open grassy meadow, narrow and long, just beneath his position. The canyon was five hundred feet deep at this point, green-walled, precipitous, and unsurmountable.

Lacy watched so long without seeing the rider that he believed he had been too late to catch him crossing this open flat. But as Lacy had about decided to hurry on again, the man emerged from the lower end.

Horse and rider grew strangely familiar as they came nearer. Lacy's iron nerves were not beyond a tiny burning thrill.

'Am I drunk or loco?' he muttered.

On the rider came, his horse at a trot, and still he bent over to one side, studying tracks in the trail. He would have had an ominous look to any experienced eye. This rider was not tracking a lost horse or deer or turkey. He was a manhunter.

'*Cedar Hatt!*' whispered Lacy, his head lowering with the motion of a striking eagle. 'Talk about luck! I'm shore smothered with it. . . . Jim Lacy's luck! . . . But bad for you, Cedar—you treacherous soul!'

Lacy watched the man with a strained, piercing gaze, as if it were possible to divine his motive.

'This might be the trail Marvie Blaine rides when he comes to meet Rose,' soliloquized Jim, ponderingly. 'Shore it is. She said the brake east of where she lived.'

Cedar Hatt rode on, directly under Jim's position, and once he halted his horse, to lean far down from his saddle.

How like an Indian! Then he swung up again to peer ahead, as if calculating on something. He made a dark wild figure, suiting his ragged horse and the background of tangled brush and rugged wall. Then he rode on, more slowly.

'By God!' burst out Lacy. 'That *hombre* is sure trackin' Marvie Blaine!'

Lacy crawled back from the Rim, then rose to run for his horse. He would head off this rustler. Luckily, the lower part of the canyon was miles below the locality where Rose was in the habit of meeting young Blaine. Lacy had time to get ahead and find a place where he could descend to the floor of the canyon. Working still farther back from the Rim, he put his horse to a gallop and made a hard fast ride for several miles. Then he slowed down and headed for the Rim again. No break in sight where he might descend! The wall grew more precipitous and higher. Lacy rode on, close to the Rim now, risking detection in his search for a descent. But he had no concern that Cedar Hatt might be the one to espy him.

At length Lacy came upon an intersecting canyon, a narrow crack which ran off into the woods. He rode back to where it headed in one of the thickest ravines, so common to the country. He descended as far as possible, then dismounting, he tied his horse and hurried on. This gorge deepened into a split between toppling walls, so rough that there was not even a deer trail. But Lacy, sparing no effort, traversed it, to reach the main canyon hot and bruised and out of breath.

Under cover of the oak thicket that lined the slope from the wall he rested a few moments, listening like a pursued deer. Only the distant murmur of a stream, a dreamy hum, and the moan of wind up on the timbered ruins came to his ears.

'Reckon I'll slip down to the trail an' hold Cedar up,' soliloquized Jim. 'But I'd shore like to know what he's aboot.'

The east side of the canyon was a gentle slope, covered with white grass, brown ferns, and low pines and oaks, affording perfect cover for anyone hiding. Lacy worked gradually down toward the level of the canyon. He did not snap twigs, or scrape brush, or make any sound. At each little opening he peered out before advancing. Often he stopped to listen. Once an elk bugled—wonderful piercing note of the wild.

It was through this extreme caution and the eye of a woodsman that Lacy came upon Marvie Blaine and Rose Hatt.

They were locked in each other's arms, lost in the enchantment of their dream. But they had chosen a secluded nook, halfway up the grassy pine-dotted slope, from which they could see, by peering under the low-spreading branches, both up and down the trail. At this moment, however, they would not have become aware of the approach of an army.

Lacy seemed struck to the heart by their rapture and the poignant pang that rent his own breast. He understood. He had lived that. He knew the sweetness and glory of love. Lacy sank to his knees, feeling that he had no right to interrupt their sacred hour. Marvie bent over Rose, whose head lay back upon his breast, with her face upturned to his, eyes closed, heavy-lidded, rapt and dreamy. If they were whispering Lacy would not hear, though he was close. But he doubted that they were whispering. Both bliss and tragedy seemed to hover over these youthful lovers.

Suddenly Lacy heard a sound that cruelly disrupted both the pain and the joy he felt. In a flash he found his equilibrium. What was that sound? It had been faint, and therefore hard to locate. It could have come from either near or far. He listened, while his eyes roved everywhere. Marvie was deaf to sounds. No doubt there was a beautiful bell ringing in his soul. Rose lay entranced.

Again Jim heard a sound, which he calculated to be a swish from the tail of a horse. Of course Marvie and Rose had their horses tethered somewhere near. But the first noise had not been like the second. It was not a thud of hoof, nor a step of foot. It seemed to have been a slippery gliding sound, as of a soft substance in contact with one rough and hard. All at once an idea flashed to Jim—buckskin over rock! Cedar Hatt always wore buckskin. Close at hand there were corners of cliff, ledges, huge slabs of rock. The instant that thought stood clear in Lacy's mind he grew stiff, intense in the grasp of a sensation for which he never found an adequate name. It mounted almost to a power of divination. It always brought the icy steadiness to his nerves.

Then from the dark shadow of pines behind Marvie a lithe figure glided. Silently Jim Lacy drew his gun. The situation was clarified, and a dread of something he could not see or control faded away.

Marvie never looked up from the beloved face until Cedar Hatt halted. It was clear to Jim that Cedar's sudden violent check came from the surprise of seeing Rose in Marvie's arms.

Marvie likewise started, so suddenly and rudely that Rose rolled off his shoulder into the grass. She screamed. She swayed up to her knees, and with hands out she backed until the pine tree stopped her.

'So hyar's why you run off from me to-day?' he shouted, fiercely. The muscles of his neck swelled, his lean jaw protruded.

'Don't—don't hurt me—Cedar!' cried Rose in terror.

'I'll beat you half to death. So hyar's why you played sick to-day an' then run off. You lyin' hussy! Answer me!'

'Yes—yes, Cedar. I—I did,' replied Rose, sagging back against the tree. Her open hands fell to her sides. A paralysis of surprise began to leave her.

'This hyar ain't no accident?' he demanded, with a forceful gesture toward the stricken Marvie.

'No. I come—on purpose.'

'How long's it b'en goin' on?'

'Weeks. I—I've come eight times.'

'Who's this hyar young buck?'

'I'll never tell,' flashed Rose.

Marvie stumbled to his feet and stepped forward, livid of face, but resolute.

'I'll tell you,' he said.

'Don't—don't!' cried Rose. 'Never tell him!'

'Who'n hell air you?' queried Cedar, in amaze, as if the factor of Marvie's participation in this treachery of Rose's had just dawned upon him.

'I'm Marvie Blaine,' answered the lad.

'Blaine! Huh! thet means nothin' to me.'

'I live with Bed Ide. We're related.'

'Ben Ide! . . . Oho! You belong to them rich Ide folks, huh, as wouldn't wipe their feet on sich as us Hatts? Wal, damn your white skin, what you doin' hyar with my sister?'

'I—I love her,' answered Marvie, manfully.

Cedar knocked him down.

'I'll kick your guts out,' he snarled.

Marvie rolled out of reach, leaped to his feet, and came back, with fight struggling to master his consternation and distress for Rose.

'I seen you huggin' an' kissin' Rose. An' you got nerve to say you love her. Playin' with my sister, huh! An' you belong to them Ides!'

'Cedar, it's not—what you think,' burst out Rose, with the scarlet dyeing her face.

'Git out, you lyin' little devil. If you'll lie about one thing you'll lie about another. . . . All the time you been meetin' this young buck. Layin' hyar in his arms, huh?'

'You skunk!' retorted Rose, passionately. 'He loves me honest. . . . You're too low-down to understand what that means.'

'Didn't I ketch you layin' in his arms?' demanded Cedar, harshly, yet with a hint of wonder in his query.

'Yes, you did. An' you might have ketched me there often,' cried the girl.

'Ed Richardson will kill you fer this!' hissed Cedar.

'Let him kill an' be damned!' returned Rose, with an equal passion. 'I don't belong to him. I hate him. Did he ever talk honest love to me? Bah! But Marvie Blaine did. An' he's made a woman out of me.'

'Hatt, I've asked—Rose to marry—me,' interposed Marvie, beside himself with emotion.

'Yes, an' Miss Ide is goin' to give me a decent home till I'm old enough,' added Rose.

'Oho! Double-crossin' Ed an' all of us, hey? You black-eyed cat! ... Git your hoss, an' soon as I take the hide off this kid lover of yours, we'll—'

'Cedar Hatt, you'll have to pack me dead—if you take me one single step. ... You'll never drag me alive to your Pine Tree—'

'Shut up!' interrupted Cedar, and he struck her down.

Marvie, with furious imprecation, wildly swinging his arms, rushed at Hatt, only to be sent staggering against the tree.

'I'll blow your insides out!' yelled Cedar, reaching for his gun.

But before he could draw, Marvie closed with him, and as Hatt dragged the gun out they began a swift struggle for possession of it. Here Jim bounded out of his covert and down the slope, his gun half leveled. Neither of the contestants was aware of his presence, but Rose saw him, and she shrieked.

Jim tried to get a bead on Cedar. But he had to be sure of his aim. He did not want to risk injuring Marvie. As they whirled and wrestled, Cedar pulled his arm over his head, his hand clutching the gun. Marvie clung desperately to that arm.

Jim took a snap shot at Cedar's gun hand. Missed! He snapped another and the bullet almost tore Cedar's hand off. The gun went flying, while Cedar, backing away from Marvie, cursing hideously, suddenly froze stiff at sight of Jim.

Marvie had not yet seen his savior. No doubt he thought the shots had been fired accidentally in the struggle, wounding Cedar. Quick as a flash he snatched up Cedar's gun and, leveling it with both hands, he worked the trigger. Bang! Bang!

Cedar Hatt clutched at his breast. An awful blank surprise rendered his expression once more human. With gasps his mouth opened to emit blood. Then he reeled and fell at Marvie's feet.

Marvie began to sag, changing his crouching position. The smoking gun dropped from his limp hands. Rose, on her knees, with a red stain on her lips, rocked to and fro, mute with terror.

'Wal, Marvie, that wasn't so bad for a youngster,' said Jim, stepping forward. 'I was just about to plug him myself.'

As if a giant arm was grinding him around the lad turned.

'*Who're—you?*' he whispered, wildly, almost maudlinly.

'Reckon I'm your old pard, Nevada, of Forlorn River days,' replied Jim, and then he grasped Marvie as he collapsed. He embraced him and half carried him toward the trees, where Rose now clung, trying to get to her feet. 'Brace up, boy. It's all over. There. . . . An' you, Rose, buck up. Why, you're both showin' yellow after as game a fight as two kids ever made! . . . That's right. Let him lean against you. Wal, wal!'

Marvie, with eyes starting, cried out: 'O my God—it's you—*Nevada*!'

'Shore is, boy, an' glad to meet you again.'

'Mister Lacy—do—you—know Marvie?' faltered Rose.

'Wal, I should smile. Me an' Marvie are old pards.'

Marvie suddenly seemed to revert to a consciousness that recalled Cedar Hatt. He stared in terror at the prone rustler.

'Nevada, you—you shot him,' he said huskily.

'Me? Nope. I only shot his hand off. You see, you was dancin' around so I couldn't bore him.'

'He—he's *dead*?'

'Wal, I reckon so. Has that sort of limp look,' replied Jim. 'But I'll make shore.' And Jim rose from his kneeling posture to walk over to Hatt. 'Daid as a door nail! Marvie, he was roarin' a minute ago aboot blowin' out your insides. An' lo!—there he lays with his own insides blowed out. His own gun! Funny aboot things. . . . Don't look so sick. Wasn't he tryin' to kill you? Wouldn't he have murdered Rose—or worse?'

Marvie sat up, pallid and wet with his lower lip quivering and his eyes losing their fixed horror.

'Nevada! You were here—somewhere?'

'Shore. I was watchin' you an' Rose make love when Cedar sneaked up. Reckon I ought to have shot him *pronto,* but I wanted to heah what he'd say.'

'Marvie, it's turrible,' interposed Rose. 'My own brother! But I don't care. I'm glad. He was a devil. . . . Did he hurt you? Oh, there's blood on your hands!'

'I'm not hurt. It come off the gun. I felt it—all wet an' sliddery.'

Jim studied these two brave young people and thrilled to his heart. What had guided his steps on this eventful day?

'Rose, I reckon you can never be scared by Cedar again,' he said.

'No, Mister Lacy. I'm free—saved,' replied the girl, in agitation.

'*Lacy?*' cried Marvie, starting up incredulously. 'But you're Nevada!'

'Son, the Nevada you knew was Jim Lacy.'

'My Heaven! What will Ben say? . . . An' Hettie,' exclaimed Marvie, overcome.

'Reckon they'll say a lot—when they

know. But promise me you won't give me away.'

'Aw, Nevada, if you only knew how Ben—'

'Marvie, I'm not askin' you to keep it secret forever,' interrupted Jim hastily. 'But for a little while. Promise, old pard.'

'I—will,' replied Marvie, choking.

'An' you, too, Rose?'

'I can keep secrets. An' I mustn't let slip that you're Marvie's old pard Nevada?'

'Shore. An' now, Rose, let's get this confab over. I reckon my hunch is correct. But I need to know more.'

'I'll tell anything,' she replied, under her breath.

'You told me Dillon is haid of this Pine Tree outfit?' queried Nevada, bending down to the agitated face.

'Yes, sir,' replied Rose. 'Some of his men called him Campbell. But he told Cedar his real name was Ed Richardson. He's from New Mexico. He figured in the Lincoln County war an' was close to Billy the Kid. He fetched rustlers here with him. An' he got hold of Cedar, an' Burt Stillwell, an' Stewart, an' other Arizona riders whose names I never heard.'

'Rose, how'd you happen on this?' asked Nevada, seriously.

'Cedar fetched Clan Dillon to our ranch, an' he tried to make up to me,' went on Rose. 'I liked him first off. But I soon saw what he was up to an' I had no use for him. Wal, one day Cedar threw me on a horse an' rode me off to a cabin over in Piñon Brake. Dillon was there. He tried makin' more love to me. But I bit an' kicked an' clawed him. Then he man-handled me bad, with Cedar grinnin' by. He'd have ruined me, too, but the men they were expectin' rode up an' I got thrown in the loft. Some of them were drunk. They all had money. An' they gambled an' stayed up all night. In the mornin' they had a powwow. Then Cedar fetched me back home an' swore he'd kill me if I squealed.'

'Clan Dillon, then, is Ed Richardson—haid of this Pine Tree outfit,' said Nevada, an' Ben Ide's foreman.'

'Yes, sir,' replied Rose, bravely, with lips that trembled.

'Good Lord!' ejaculated Marvie. 'Ben swears by Dillon. He's gone against Raidy, his oldest hand. . . . Gee! I wouldn't want to be in Dillon's boots when Ben finds out!'

'Wal, Marvie, it's likely that Dillon's boots will be stickin' out straight when Ben heahs the truth. . . . Rose, is there any particular reason why you'd like to go back home again? Clothes or anythin' you care for?'

'All the duds I own are on my back,' replied Rose, ruefully. 'Cedar burned my pretty dance dress—that I bought to look nice for Marvie. My pony's all I have. An' he's here.'

'Marvie, get your horse an' put Rose on hers an' leave heah *pronto* for the Ide ranch. Look sharp an' don't run into any riders. When you reach home turn Rose over to Hettie, an' both of you keep your mouth shut.'

His compelling force wrung mute promises from both Marvie and the girl.

'My horse is on top, an' I cain't get him down heah. Rustle now.'

Marvie started to lead Rose away, when he espied Cedar Hatt's gun lying on the brown pine needles.

'Nevada—can I take it?' he queried, haltingly.

'What? Oh, Cedar's gun? Shore you take it.'

The girl turned with lips parted. 'Mister Jim—Nevada—we'll see you again?'

'I reckon. Remember, I trust you to to keep mum. Look sharp now, an' hurry along.'

Nevada did not linger to watch them find and mount their horses; however, as he started up the slope he heard them, and felt that now all would be well with them. He climbed as one with wings. How strange that the rough gully presented no obstacles! Reaching his horse, he tightened the cinches, leaped astride, and rode up to the level, where he faced north with a grim smile.

The afternoon had not far advanced. At a steady lope he covered the miles of forested ridge, downhill and easy going until he descended into the brakes. Here his horse toiled for an hour, at last to crash out into the trail. One glance at the bare ground showed him that Marvie and Rose had not yet come so far. He preferred to reach the Ide ranch before they did. His mind clamped round one thing and set there, cold and sure.

Five miles of travel, now slow, now swift, and then a hard climb took Nevada out of the brakes into the beautiful stately forest, where the pines thinned and straggled to the desert sage. How sweet the fragrance! He had once viewed from afar the Ide ranch, with its slope of sage and cedar leading up to the black benches.

The trail grew broad and sandy, so that his speeding horse thudded almost noiselessly on. Clumps of spruce and low branches of pines obscured the bends.

Nevada rode around an abrupt green curve almost to run down a horse coming toward him. He pulled his mount to a sliding halt. He heard a cry. The rider was a woman. Hettie Ide!

CHAPTER 18

'HETTIE,' said Ben Ide as he stood on the porch and spread his arms to the glorious beauty and color of the Arizona landscape, 'I once thought Forlorn River in the fall was pretty close to heaven. But Cedar Springs Ranch has it beaten a mile.'

'Ben Ide! You going back on Forlorn River!' exclaimed Hettie, in surprise.

'Well, hasn't it? Look around. What do you think, yourself?'

'Long ago, before this wonderful autumn came, I was faithless to California,' murmured Hettie, regretfully.

'Hettie, not faithless. I don't love the old home country any the less because I've learned to love this more. Lord knows I've reason to hate Arizona. But I can't. It grows on me. Here it's way in September. Frost an' icy every mornin'. Indian summer days. Look at the sage. It's purple. Look at the foothills. Anyone would think they were painted. Look at the patches of gold an' scarlet back up in the woods.'

'It's very beautiful,' replied Hettie, more dreamily.

'Sister, we mustn't forget that mother is to be taken to San Diego for the winter months.'

'I've not forgotten, Ben. But there's no hurry. This weather is perfect. Mr. Day claims it'll last till Christmas.'

'Well, if it does, I could ask no more,' said Ben. 'Then I'll send mother with you an' Ina an' the kid to San Diego till spring. But I'll stay on here. I'd be afraid to leave.'

'It wouldn't be wise, Ben. Things have grown from bad to worse. I fear you are in for more shocks.'

'Tom Day says they must grow worse before they get better. Heigho! ... Well, I'm not lettin' disappointment sour me, anyhow.'

'Disappointment? You mean—about ranching in Arizona?'

'Between you an' me, Hettie, I wasn't thinkin' of cattle at all,' replied Ben, sadly.

Hettie suffered a contraction of her heart. If Ben knew what she knew! She prayed that he never would. And she gave no sign that she divined the undercurrent of his words.

Marvie Blaine sat on the porch step, morosely cleaning his rifle, which evidently he had used that day. The lad had grown taller, thinner, more of a man these last few weeks.

'Marvie, you don't ride far away when you hunt, do you?' queried Ben.

'Lots of turkey an' deer right in our back yard,' answered Marvie, evasively.

'Humph! Much good that does you. I've yet to eat the venison you killed.'

'Ben, I've killed some turkeys,' insisted Marvie, stoutly. 'An' to-day I had a shot at a buck.'

'Seems to me you take a lot of time off,' went on Ben, 'an' I'm supposed to pay you a cowboy's salary.'

'I do the work given me. Dillon sure slights me on every job he can.'

'Weren't you pretty smart-alec?' asked Ben.

'I wasn't until he got mean.'

'An' when was that? Are you sure you don't imagine things? Dillon is the kindest of foremen.'

Marvie looked up deliberately and

fastened unfathomable eyes upon this friend of his boyhood.

'Dillon used to like me. But he changed after the cowboys told him how I'd made up to little Rose Hatt at the dance in Winthrop.'

'Rose Hatt! That child of Elam Hatt's? I saw her once. What on earth could it be to Dillon if you did flirt with Rose? As a matter of fact, he was merely worried about you. Rose was no girl for you to get friendly with.'

'Say, did Dillon tell you that?' queried Marvie, flushing.

'Yes. An' he advised me to put a stop to it. Said you might get in trouble.'

Marvie jumped up as if he had been stung by a hornet.

'Ha! Ha!' he burst out, striding away with his head back. 'Ha! Ha! . . . Ha! Ha! Ha!'

He kept it up until he went out of sight around the house.

'Well, I'll be dog-goned,' ejaculated Ben, gazing at Hettie for confirmation of his fears. 'Was that boy givin' me the horse-laugh?'

'He was surely giving you some kind of

a laugh,' replied Hettie, striving to hide her own amusement.

'Hettie, am I growin' old, thick-headed, absent-minded?' inquired Ben, wistfully.

'No, Ben,' returned his sister, dropping her head. 'You've only the worry of the ranch on your mind.'

'By George it is a worry,' he sighed. 'But, old girl, you've not been so bright and happy as you were here at first. Neither is Ina. I'm afraid I've done bad by both of you.'

'Ben, it will all come right,' spoke up Hettie, forcing a smile. 'We must take our medicine. It's Arizona medicine, which your friend, Tom Day, says is powerful strong.'

'Hettie, do you still think of—of—*him*?' asked Ben in lower tone.

'Always.' she replied, quaking inwardly. If only she had the courage and the wit to keep her secret hidden!

'I'm afraid I've given up hope, went on Ben, somberly. 'An' it's taken the sap out of me. Don't tell Ina. But I'm fallin' into the same rut as I was in last spring, over home on Tule Lake.'

'Given up hope of what?' murmured Hettie.

'Of ever findin' Nevada,' he replied, simply, as if the name was not one he never mentioned. 'That's why I came to Arizona. Once at Forlorn River, when I asked Nevada what he'd do if anythin' separated us, he said he'd go to Arizona an' take to hard ridin'. I never forgot. . . . Well, I reckon every cowboy on these ranges has hit me for a job. But sure not one of them was Nevada, nor had they ever heard of him. I reckon he's dead. Don't you ever think that, Hettie?'

'Yes. . . . Dead to us, surely,' she returned, with dry lips.

'How could Nevada be dead to us if he were alive?' queried Ben, sharply. Then he lifted his head to some interruption of his thought. 'I hear a horse . . . comin' lickety cut! Hello! it's Dillon! . . . Damn the luck! There's somethin' up!'

Hettie sustained a sharp quickening of her pulse. A horse and rider bobbed up over the bench. At the moment Ina came out of the house, to begin some speech to Ben, which did not materialize. Ben strode off the porch to meet Dillon, who rode up like a whirlwind, scattering gravel all over the porch; and he leaped out of the saddle with the lithe grace of one to whom such action was a habit.

'Mornin', boss,' he said, and tipped his sombrero to Hettie and Ina. 'You're late. So I rode up.'

'Bad news?' asked Ben.

'No, it ain't bad, but it's disturbin'. Cowboy just in from Tom Day's range. Name's Laskin. He rode a hoss to death gettin' here. I gave him another hoss, an' soon as he'd swallowed some drink an' grub he rode off for Franklidge's ranch.'

'Yes. Well, what was he ridin' so hard for?' queried Ben, as if prepared.

'Yesterday he was in camp near Silver Meadows,' went on Dillon. 'Another rider with him—whose name I didn't get. Some men rode down on them. Laskin said they wasn't drunk. Just keyed up over a big deal. They made no bones about the deal— at least their leader didn't. An' he was no other than Jim Lacy.'

'Jim Lacy bobbed up again!' ejaculated Ben, with irritation. 'Go on, Dillon.'

'Lacy said he was goin' to rustle the stock at Silver Meadows an' sent you his compliments.'

'Well, I'm a — —!' broke out Ben, choking down the last of his utterance.

'Pretty nervy, wasn't it?' asked Dillon. He appeared excited, which was a striking exception to his usual genial and imperturbable mood. Hettie gazed spellbound at him.

'Nervy? Yes, if it's true,' retorted Ben. 'But I don't believe it.'

'It's as straight as shootin', boss,' rejoined Dillon. 'I happen to know the rider who tipped us off.'

'But Jim Lacy or anybody else would be a fool to tell such a plan, before pullin' it off,' said Ben, incredulously.

'Reckon that seems so,' replied the foreman, smoothly. 'But sometimes these desperadoes like Lacy do queer things. It's not braggin'. Such men don't brag. It's just sort of a cool defiance of law—an' honest ranchin'. ... Well, Lacy has twenty-four hours' start. There was a big bunch of cattle at Silver, so Laskin said. The last of your stock, an' some of Day's an' Franklidge's. We were figgerin' on a big roundup *pronto*. But we're too late, boss.'

'Too late! Why, man, if it *is* true, we can stop that drive before it gets down to the road,' declared Ben.

'Stop nothin'. Lacy's outfit won't drive this way. They'll drive up over the Rim, an' I'll gamble there's a bunch of five thousand head on the way now.'

Ben sat down as if suddenly weighted.

'Boss, I'm sure kickin' myself for not figgerin' that very deal,' went on Dillon, and his smile was something to conjure with. Hettie caught it, but Ben saw nothing. 'You see, the cattle were workin' high up. An' grass an' water's so good at Silver that they bunched thick. Laskin swears it's only a half day's drive up the canyon which opens into Silver. . . . 'n' there you are.'

A hoarse intolerant resentment rang in Dillon's voice. To Ben Ide he must have seemed a masterful and experienced foreman, angry at this coup of the latest recruit to Arizona rustlers.

'If it's true I'll—I'll run down this Jim Lacy an' jail him. I don't care what it costs,' declared Ben. 'But I reckon we're

315

gettin' all riled up over cowboy guessin.'

'Give me a couple of days off, boss?' asked Dillon, in strange eagerness. 'I'll find out.'

'You want to ride off alone?' queried Ben.

'Sure. That's the best way.'

'No. Some of the rustlers will plug you, an' then I *would* be out of luck,' replied Ben, decisively.

'But I want to go,' declared Dillon, with the blood rising under the tan of his handsome face.

'I appreciate the risk you'd take for me, Dillon. But, no, I'm givin' you orders to take Raidy with six cowboys an' go to Silver Meadows. Hurry back to report. Then we'll see.'

Dillon had difficulty in repressing some kind of agitation that did not owe its source to respect and regard for Ben Ide. What an intent, almost derisive glance he gave Ben! Then without another word he mounted and rode furiously down toward the corrals.

'Girls, did you hear all he had to say?' asked Ben, appealing for sympathy.

'We couldn't very well help it,' replied

Ina, putting a hand on Ben's shoulder. 'Dear, I—I haven't confidence in this man Dillon.'

'Huh! Nor in me, either,' retorted Ben, shaking her hand off.

That action hurt Ina's sensitive feelings and she drew away haughtily.

'Very well, Ben Ide,' she declared. 'But when the crash comes, don't you look to *me* for sympathy.'

With that she went back into the house. Ben gazed helplessly up at his sister.

'There! Can you beat that? My own wife gone against me!'

Hettie subdued her own impatience, not without effort, and then set herself the task of meeting her brother's morbid irritation, and by agreeing with him and bidding him hope on and fight on forever, if need be, she made some little impression upon his mood.

Then Marvie appeared again, this time black in the face. Alas for Hettie! Her heart sank.

'Ben Ide, I've a bone to pick with you,' he burst out.

'Pick away, you young rooster,' returned Ben, wearily; but he was in-

terested. Marvie had never before bearded
the lion in his den.

'Did Dillon tell you a cowboy named
Laskin rode in with news about a cattle
drive?'

'Sure he did.'

'Ha! That's what he told Raidy. He's a
damn liar?'

'Marvie, take care! You're no longer a
kid. Would you say that to Dillon's face?'

'Would I? Huh! I did an' I cussed him
good,' rejoined Marvie, hotly.

'Why did you? Marv, I'm losin'
patience.'

'An' I'm losin' patience with you, Ben
Ide. Listen. I saw that cowboy. He wasn't
no rider named Laskin. He was Cedar
Hatt!'

'What?'

'Cedar Hatt, I tell you. I *know* him.'

'Marvie, you're not only loco, but
you're ravin' sore at Dillon. You'll go too
far. Take care.'

'Care, hell!' shouted Marvie, beside
himself with rage. 'It's you who's loco.'

'Marvie Blaine, you're fired,' replied
Ben, curtly. 'You can't ride for me any
more.'

Marvie underwent a sudden disastrous change of mood.

'Fired?' he said, poignantly.

'Yes, fired. Now get out of my house an' go over to Hettie's till I can decide what to do with you.'

'Aw—Ben!' gasped Marvie.

'Don't aw—Ben me,' said Ben, furiously. 'Get out of here now—you round-eyed, freckled-faced four-flush of a cowboy!'

Marvie started as if he had been lashed.

'Ben Ide, you'll be sorry for that,' he declared, solemnly, and stamped away.

Ben stared at the erect retreating figure of the lad.

'Marvie, too!' he said, huskily.

Hettie felt something of a sneak herself as she stole away, back to her own cabin and the seclusion of her room. Was she not betraying Ben by withholding facts she alone knew? Yet how impossible to crush him utterly! Jim Lacy was Nevada! She would never have the courage to tell him.

As for herself, the last hope had fled, the last doubt, the last shred of stubborn faith. Nevada was a rustler. He had fallen so low that he could steal from the friend who had once succored him. The thing was so base that Hettie writhed under the shame of her seemingly indestructible love for this imposter Nevada—this fugitive horseman who had won her under another guise—this Jim Lacy, killer and thief. But though everything else seemed dead, hope, faith, interest in life, will to go on fighting, she knew her love survived. It was the very pulse of her heart.

A long hour she lay there on her bed, until collapse and tears came to her relief. And when she again rose to face herself in the mirror she sank aghast. But there was her mother to live for, and poor blind Ben, who had loved this traitor Nevada, even as she.

Two days went by, with the Ide households under considerable strain of uncertainty.

Raidy and Dillon, with their riders, returned about noon of the third day. The news reached Hettie while she was in the kitchen, with her sleeves rolled up and flour to her elbows, but she did not lose time on account of that.

Ben was somber, nervous, silent, and he

paced the living-room, oblivious to the importunities of little Blaine, who toddled here and there, as if he was playing a game.

Presently Raidy entered the open door, sombrero in hand, dusty and unshaven.

'Howdy, boss!' he said in greeting, and bowed quaintly to Hettie and Ina.

'Took you long enough. Where's Dillon?' replied Ben, gruffly.

'Wal, you know Dillon always leaves the bad reports for me to make.'

'Did he return with you?'

'Not exactly. He left us at daybreak this mornin' an' beat us in.'

'Is he here now?'

'Sure. I told him he'd better come along with me. But he said he'd see you later. . . . Boss, Dillon is in purty bad humor. I never seen him like this. He's another fellar.'

'Drinkin'?' queried Ben, sharply.

'No. He's just black as thunder an' sore as a kicked pup.'

'That'd be natural for anyone who had my interests at heart, as Dillon has. But it's odd he didn't come to report. . . . Well, out with your bad news.'

Ben squared himself as if for a blow and frowned upon his old foreman.

'I'm sorry, Ben. It couldn't be no wuss.'

'Oh, Ben!' cried Ina, who had evidently worried more about her husband than the impending loss.

'Reckin you an' Hettie better leave us alone,' returned Ben.

Neither of the women moved a step, though Ina subsided into a chair. Raidy appeared to have lost his usual taciturnity.

'Boss, you're rustled off the range. The last of your stock, except some stragglin' steers an' yearlin's, is gone—along with a thousand head of Tom Day's.'

Ben Ide made a flashing violent gesture, as if to strike. He paled. His eyes shot fire.

'They've cleaned me?' he demanded, fiercely, as if still doubting.

'Yes, boss. I made sure, because I wasn't trustin' Dillon to give a full report.'

Hettie, standing back of Ina's chair, felt both hot and cold; and she stared at her brother fearfully, expecting him to break into an ungovernable rage. For Ben had not been himself in weeks, and lately he had been hard to live with. She had reckoned without her host, however, for although Ben turned white to the lips he suddenly became calm and cool. With uncertainty gone he changed radically.

'Ahuh. So your hunch has come true,' he said, almost with sarcasm. 'Wal, I reckon you'll get a lot of satisfaction crowin' over me an' Dillon.'

'No, boss, I won't even say I told you so,' returned Raidy.

'Give me the facts, short an' sweet,' said Ben.

'Wal, Tom Day an' his riders were at Silver Meadows when we arrived. A sheepherder had tipped them off to the drive. We split up an' rode all around the Meadows. Only a few cattle left. Them rustlers made a slick job of it. Day an' Franklidge lost over a thousand head, an' you lost all you had left. A matter of three thousand head. We took the trail up the canyon. An' say, it was a bowlavarde clear to the Rim. ... I was for trailin' the rustlers to finish a fight. But Day wouldn't let any of us go down in that hole. We'd have been ambushed an' some of us killed. Besides, he said we could never have recovered the cattle. Once turned loose in that jungle of scrub oak, mazanita, an' cactus, them cattle would have vamoosed like ticks shook off a leaf. So we turned back.'

'You told Tom Day, of course, that Jim Lacy made this drive?' queried Ben.

'Tom knowed all about it from the sheepherder. Seems thet Lacy sent Tom word he was goin' to make this big steal. Sent his respects to Tom an' Judge Franklidge an' said he'd drop in to Winthrop some day.'

'By Heaven! this Lacy is a cool one! exclaimed Ben, as if admiration was wrenched from him.

'Cool? Wal, boss, you might call Lacy thet, but I reckon he's a mixture of hell's fire an' chain lightnin!'

'I'll hang him,' said Ben, with deadly calm.

'No, Ben, if you'll excuse me, I'll say you'll never put a rope around Jim Lacy's neck. He couldn't never be jailed, either. He'll die in his boots, with a gun spoutin', an' Gawd help the men frontin' him!'

'Bah! You talk like Marvie Blaine,' retorted Ben, curtly. 'An' you Raidy—a grown man!'

'Boss, it grieves me thet I've lived to

disagree with you,' returned Raidy, with dignity.

'This Jim Lacy is the leader of the Pine Tree outfit,' asserted Ben, positively.

'Wal, me an' Tom Day reckoned so. An' for once Dillon agreed with us,' replied Raidy. 'Tom said Lacy jest got tired of layin' low an' being' mysterious. So he comes out in the open. I'll bet you he'll ride right into Winthrop.'

'Raidy, I'm glad Lacy cleaned me out. I'm through waitin' around to see what's goin' to happen next. I've sent for Sheriff Macklin an' a posse. This mornin' I got word from Struthers, the Phoenix sheriff who's made it so hot for rustlers in southern Arizona. Struthers is in Winthrop at my request. They'll arrive here not later than to-morrow. I'll have Dillon get twenty-five of the hardest men he can gather. I'll offer ten thousand dollars reward for Jim Lacy, dead or alive. I'll spend every dollar I have to run down Lacy an' his Pine Tree gang.'

'Wal, boss, you're talkin' high, wide an' handsome,' replied Raidy. 'But it's not for me to offer opinions. This ranch—an' for that matter, this whole range—ain't big enough for me an' your man Dillon. I jest have to quit.'

'Very well, Raidy. I'm sorry you see it that way,' returned Ben, coldly, and with a wave of his hand terminated the interview.

Hettie fled. As she ran out she heard Ina deliver a stinging rebuke to her husband. Then a door slammed. Hettie hurried home in a state of mind bordering on a breakdown. She finished her work in a mechanical way, while slow torment consumed her.

'What's all the row over at Ben's?' her mother inquired, placidly, from her comfortable chair.

'Rustlers, cattle, foremen, sheriffs, and Heaven only knows what,' replied Hettie, distractedly.

'Well, daughter, don't be upset. You know Ben.'

'I thought I did, mother. But I'm doubtful about it. He fired Raidy.'

'No! Why, that's dreadful! Raidy taught Ben how to ride a horse. Oh, this dreadful Arizona! . . . But I don't mean that, Hettie, I love this quiet, sweet wild country. The men, though—they're—they're loco, as Marvie says. And Ben has got it, too?'

'Mother, have you seen Marvie to-day?' asked Hettie, suddenly remembering that she had not.

'Marvie went away yesterday and hasn't come back. At least he didn't sleep in his bed.'

'Oh dear! That wild boy! Here's more to—to worry over. ... Mother, I didn't tell you that the reason Marvie came to us is because Ben discharged him—drove him out of the house.'

'Reckon we'll have Ina next,' said her mother.

'I—I wouldn't be surprised at anything,' returned Hettie tearfully.

Hettie went to her room, with the motive of indulging her grief. But sight of her riding-boots acted powerfully upon her and she decided to take a ride. Not for days had she been on her horse. Perhaps a long hard gallop would be good for her; and moreover, she might meet Marvie on the trail. Could something have happened to him? It might very well have, Hettie concluded, with a tremor. He and Rose had such great fear. The very air around the Ide ranch seemed congested, heavy, sultry, ominous with menace.

Hettie passed the quarters of the riders at some distance, not caring to be accosted by Dillon or Raidy. She saw some saddled horses, dusty and tired, that had evidently just come in. There were a number of men bunched in a circle, conversing so earnestly that none espied her. Gaining the stables, she found Pedro and had him saddle her horse. Soon she was riding fast with the wind in her face.

But neither a gallop nor a run sufficed to change Hettie's mood. She rode into the woods, and let her horse walk at will down the shady trail in the direction from which Marvie always returned.

And here, alone, under the impelling influence of the forest, Hettie realized that she was a most miserable and heartbroken girl, with a terrible sword hanging over her head. How hopeless her situation! What use to think? There was not a thought nor an action that could help her in her extremity. Courage and intelligence had gone with the loss of hope.

A purple haze like smoke hung in the aisles of the forest; the only sound was the faintest of breezes murmuring in the pines; the thickets were on fire with golden and scarlet flame of autumn leaves; the westering sun caught the glint of falling leaf and pine needle.

Nature seemed so pitiless this day. It went on, calm, sweet, beautiful, inscrutable, unmindful of the poor little lives of human beings. Hettie could not derive any solace, any strength, from either forest or range or desert.

Arizona had killed her dream, as it had ruined her brother. And the horror of Hettie's state seemed that the climax of this infernal paradox, the dénouement, the worst, had yet to come.

Suddenly she caught the rhythmic beat of swift hoofs ahead round a green curve of the trail. That must be Marvie's horse. A rush of relief swept over her. The pine boughs spread. A big black horse was upon her before she could pull a rein. She cried out. But the rider hauled back to his haunches, and that rider was Nevada.

CHAPTER 19

HETTIE clutched the pommel of her saddle. An awful stunning shock suspended, for an instant, all her faculties, and every sensibility except the physical animal instinct of holding her equilibrium. Then emotion burst the dam.

When Nevada's horse plunged up, his head came abreast Hettie's horse.

'*You!*' Hettie felt the word leave her stiff lips, but she heard it only as a whisper.

Nevada swept off his sombrero and bowed low to the mane of his horse. And as he rose erect he remained bareheaded.

'Wal, shore it's Hettie Ide,' he drawled, in the cool, leisurely, Southern accent that cut into her heart like blades.

Then they gazed at one another, as if sight was trying to reconcile the face of dreams with the reality. The face Hettie looked into had the same lean outline, the dark blue-black shade of beard against the clear brown tan, the intent light hazel-flecked eyes, like level piercing points. But

330

it did not have the soul with which her imagination and memory had invested it.

'I—I saw you—in Winthrop,' began Hettie, as if to find relief from oppression. Silence was impossible.

'Shore. I reckoned you might,' he replied. As he spoke he rolled a cigarette with steady fingers. No surprise, no emotion that Hettie could read, manifested itself in look or manner. 'Too bad you had to run into me heah!'

'Too bad! . . . It's terrible. But I'm glad,' exclaimed Hettie, quivering, shaking all over.

'Thank you, an' I'm shore sorry I cain't return the compliment,' he said, and bent his head to light the cigarette.

His cool nonchalance, that she remembered so poignantly, seemed now to inflame her.

'*Jim Lacy!*' she cried, in scornful, sad haste to acquaint him with her knowledge of his infamy.

He thrust his sombrero on, tilted back, and as he blew a thin column of smoke upwards his penetrating, inscrutable eyes studied her face.

'Why didn't you trust me? Oh, why?'

she went on, slipping farther toward an emotional outbreak.

'Hettie, there was a time, long ago, when I'd rather have been daid than let you know I was Jim Lacy.'

'You were ashamed?'

'I shore was.'

'Long ago, you said. ... Then you're *not* ashamed now?'

'Wal, it cain't matter now,' he rejoined, with a gleam of a smile.

'Why can't it matter now?' she queried.

He made an expressive gesture, and then gazed down through the open forest to the colorful desert. His horse rubbed noses with Hettie's, and gradually backed it across the trail.

'Ben doesn't dream his—his old friend Nevada is you—the notorious Jim Lacy.'

'I reckon not. ... Too bad he's got to find out pretty soon!'

'Must Ben—find out?' asked Hettie, huskily. Thought of Ben augmented her weakness.

Nevada dropped his head. His horse, nosing Hettie's, brought Nevada closer to her, so that she might have touched him. This proximity bore upon her with incalculable influence. She pulled her horse aside, to no avail, for the big black followed with eager whinny. His rider did not seem to be aware of this proceeding, or of the proximity that again ensued.

'How can you be so cool—so hatefully cool?' burst out Hettie, 'Ben loved you. I—I . . . What did he care who you were? Why didn't you always stay Nevada? . . . Ben left no stone unturned to locate you. Failing that, he came to Arizona because he hoped you might turn up. . . . You have turned up. But as Jim Lacy—as a rustler who stole from him. Stole from a friend you once saved and succored and loved! Did you know those cattle were Ben's?'

'Shore—I did,' replied Nevada, showing a faint pallor.

'Oh, it was terrible thing to do!' cried Hettie, covering her face with her hands. 'Your pard? It will cut him to the quick—embitter him forever. . . . And it'll kill *me*!'

His silence, his impertubability in its unnaturalness roused her to a sudden furious passion that burned away her tears and waved her face scarlet.

'Wal, you're a mighty healthy lady after so many years of dyin',' he drawled, tossing away his half-smoked cigarette. 'Hettie, you always was pretty, but you've grown into a plumb handsome woman . . . Reckon the cowboys are sweeter'n ever on you.'

'That must have meant a lot to you,' she flashed, breathing hard.

'Dillon, now. *He* was.'

'Yes. He has made love to me. Begged me to marry him,' returned Hettie, in fiery flippancy, hoping with a woman's strange coquetry to make him jealous.

'Wal, you don't say. He's shore a handsome *hombre*. Devil with the women. I heah. . . . Why don't you marry him?'

'I—may yet,' replied Hettie, somberly. He baffled her. In his cool, inscrutable presence she felt like a child. And a deep unplumbed emotion seemed to swell at the gates of her self-control.

'Hettie, if you do you'll be changin your mind considerable from what it was that night at the dance in Winthrop.'

'What do you know about that?' she queried, wonderingly.

'Wal, I happened to heah you tell Dillon a few things, an' I seen him try to get you in his arms.'

'*You!* You were there?'

'Shore. An' after you flounced off I introduced myself to Dillon an' most polite invited him to draw. But he didn't have the nerve, so I took a punch at his handsome face.'

'You struck Dillon on my behalf!' murmured Hettie softening.

'Wal, yes, partly. But I had it in for him before. ... By the way, is he at the ranch?'

'Yes. I saw him at the corrals as I came out.'

'Good! I'm shore a lucky *hombre*—since I took up with Jim Lacy again.'

'You were going to our ranch?' queried Hettie, quickly.

'I *am* goin', Miss Hettie Ide.'

'What—for?'

'Wal, reckon my prime reason is to shoot out one of Dillon's handsome eyes. But I've another—'

'Oh! ... You've something against Dillon?'

'Huh! I should rather smile I have, Hettie.'

'You'll—you'll *kill* him?'

Nevada's flashing eye and sweeping

gesture were the first indications of passion he had evinced.

'Reckon if you hadn't held me up heah he'd be daid now. An' that stands for me, too.'

'Ah! Then Dillon is—a—a dangerous man—as you—'

'Hettie, *he's* a bad *hombre*. Come from New Mexico. Name is Ed Richardson, once with the Billy the Kid outfit. . . . I'll kill him, shore, but he might return the compliment.'

'You—you bloody gunman!' returned Hettie, as if those few words expressed her infinite amaze and contempt for men who lived by such a creed.

'Hettie, if he does kill me you can tell Ben the truth, then come an' smooth back my hair an' wipe my bloody face. Ha! Ha!' he said, in bitter mockery.

'Hush!' Hettie reined her horse closer, so that her stirrup locked with Nevada's. 'Do not do this terrible deed. For Ben's sake, if not mine. Be big enough to abandon your feud. Give up this outlaw, rustler, gunman life. . . . Take me away with you to some far country. I have money. You can start

336

anew. I will cleave to you—live for you.'

'For Gawd's sake, Hettie Ide, are you crazy?' he returned, stridently.

'Not yet. But I will be soon—if this—goes on,' she panted, and slipped her gloved hand to his shoulder. 'Nevada, I—I still love you. I've always loved you. . . . I forgive all. I surrender all. I don't care who you are—what you've been. All I ask is that you save Ben the horror so near—that you take me away and give up this life. . . . We can plan quickly. I will meet you at some point on the railroad. . . . Say you will.'

'No,' he said, hoarsely.

'Nevada! . . . Don't you love me—still?' And she leaned to him, overcome, betraying all her woman's soul of love, and hope for him, for Ben, for herself.

'Love you? Ha! Ha!'

'Don't stare. Don't laugh. This means life or death to me. Say you love me. Say you'll take me.'

'Yes, I love you, mad woman. But I cain't accept your sacrifice. I cain't ruin you. . . . Good Gawd! Hettie, you forget I'm Jim Lacy!'

'It's because you *are* Jim Lacy.'

'Heavens!' This heah is awful! ...
Hettie, I cain't—I won't.'

'You lie, then. You do not love me. *I* am
proving mine. But you—you are false. You
have taken some—other woman. You
don't love me!'

Hettie, dim of eye, saw him loom over
her. She felt herself seized in iron arms
and dragged from her horse. Then she was
lifted over the pommel and crushed to his
breast, and bent backward, blind, and
breathless, a victim of terrible devouring
lips. He kissed her mouth, her cheeks, her
eyes, her brow, her hair, and then again
her mouth.

Hettie's senses reeled and almost failed
her. When his violence ceased she felt
herself held closely for a long moment,
then let down from the horse until her feet
touched the ground. She was falling when
he leaped the saddle. He set her on the
grass with her back against a tree, and
there, presently, her eyes opened.

Nevada knelt before her, his face
convulsed. Slowly it smoothed out and a
wild darkness faded from his eyes.

'There. You've come to. I reckon I must

ask you to excuse me for bein' rough. But I shore couldn't stand that talk aboot not lovin' you.'

'I will not believe—unless you prove it,' returned Hettie, unsteadily, as she reached for her sombrero.

Nevada rose to his feet. 'I cain't prove it your way,' he replied, and his features set stone-cold and gray.

'Oh, what have you done to me?' cried Hettie, wildly, as again passion rose strong and regained the ascendancy over her.

'Reckon nothin' compared to what you've done to me,' he responded, with somber gaze upon her. 'Dillon will just aboot beat me to a gun.'

Hettie stood up, holding to the tree trunk. 'Nothing. . . . I've loved you since I first met you. I've been true. I trusted you. I cared not for your past. I believed in your future. I prayed for you. My faith in you was as great as my faith in God. I believed you loved me. That when you rode away from Forlorn River—to escape the consequences—when you killed Less Setter to save Ben—I believed you would be true to me, to the higher self you found through Ben's love and mine. . . . But you

339

were too little. You went back to the old life—to the old comrades. Rustlers, gamblers, gunmen! You killed just because you wanted to keep that name hated and feared. You are a bloody monster. . . . No doubt you sank to the embrace of vile women—the consorts of thieves! Oh my God! it would be my death if I could not kill my love. But I will. It will lie dead as my faith. . . . You are a liar, a failure, a weakling. Basest of all is your ingratitude. You stole from my brother— who loved you.'

Nevada's eyes held a blaze like black lightning.

'Reckon that'll be aboot all I want to heah,' he said, in tones she had never heard before.

'That is—all.'

He gathered up the reins and vaulted into the saddle, then turned to gaze down the trail.

'Horses comin,' he said, briefly. 'It's Marvie with his girl, Rose Hatt.'

'Yes, I see,' returned Hettie, with a start. 'Oh, I'm—glad.'

'Wal, Miss Hettie Ide,' he said, 'you might heah somethin' from Marvie an'

Rose. Anyway, don't rustle back home too quick.'

Her lips framed a query she could not speak.

'It's aboot sunset,' he went on, with strange gaze upon the west. 'Sunset for Dillon! An' shore sunset for me!'

Then he spurred the big black, and clattering into the trail soon vanished from sight toward the ranch.

Rose. Anyway I don't rattle back. It nettled quick.

Her lips quivered so she could not speak.

ndt toward the ranch.

CHAPTER 20

NEVADA approached the Ide ranch from that side closest to the forest, where the pines and cedars trooped down the gentle slopes of the benches, clear to the most outwardly of the cattle sheds.

With his brain on fire and his heart like lead, his whole being crushed under the burning weight of Hettie's outspoken love and terrible scorn, he halted under cover of the last clump of cedars, and dismounted, answering to an instinct, true even in that hour of utter catastrophe, to the instinct which had preserved him so long as Jim Lacy. Not now, however, was it an instinct of self-preservation, but one to meet and kill Ed Richardson, alias Campbell, alias Clan Dillon, late member of the few surviving Lincoln County war desperadoes.

Wedging this purpose into his stunned brain, Nevada kept driving it deeper, while he removed saddle and bridle from his horse and turned it free. He would have no more need of a horse. Then he crouched in the cedars, under tremendous strain, driving himself to the exclusion of all thought, of all emotion, of all faculties except those few cardinally important for the issue at hand.

When he emerged from under cover of the cedars he might have been an automaton, with guidance of some grim-strung spirit.

He glided behind brush to the sage and through this to the pole fence. It led to the back of log cabins, which he marked as the bunkhouses. The sunset hour was near. Silver-edged purple clouds hung over the soft rounded foothills. Soon the sun would sink from behind the broken mass of cloud and slide down into that golden space behind the ranges. Cowboys, riders, range hands, foreman, all would be waiting the call to supper. The day had been hot. Just now, with the first cool breeze breathing down from the hill, all the men would be outdoors.

There was a fate in many meetings of life, and singularly in all those that involved Jim Lacy.

He swept his magnified gaze to the left,

over pasture and field, which were open to his sight. A few horses and colts, cows and calves, a burro, and some black pigs dotted the gray-green pastures and the brown fields. No rider in sight!

Nevada stole swiftly along the fence to the first high corral. It contained a number of horses, with saddles and packs stacked in a corner. He would have to cross this corral, and go through the others, to reach the rear of the bunkhouses. Climbing to the top log of the high fence, he peeped over. No man in sight! He climbed and ran and climbed and ran, quickly gaining the open gate of the last corral. The two small log cabins and the long one stood across the open space, with barns to the left and courtyard on the right, leading up to the Ide homes in the edge of the forest.

A Mexican boy appeared leading horses up a watering-trough; a rider came trotting down the long lane between the fields; some one was driving cows in from the pasture. From behind the cabins came the loud rollicking laughter of cowboys.

Nevada did not hesitate a moment. Leisurely he strode from the corral toward the long cabin, making for the nearest end, where cords of firewood were stacked high. That end, where blue smoke curled from a stone chimney, would be the kitchen. There would be a porch on the other side.

Nevada gained the woodpiles. They had been stacked, seemingly, to furnish him perfect passageway and perfect cover, for the fruition of this long-planned moment. It never crossed his mind that Dillon might not be there. Dillon would be there. For the men who had wronged Jim Lacy or incurred his enmity there existed a fatality which operated infallibly. Or else Lacy never made a mistake. It was something that he felt.

He glided between the high stacks of wood. Before he peeped out he saw horsemen riding down the dusty road which wound away to the north and Winthrop. Then Nevada put his eye to an aperture between two billets of cedar that protruded from the stack.

A dozen or more men lounged and sat and stood in plain sight. Cowboys in shirt sleeves, faces shiny and red, hair glossed and wet, sat on the ground, backs to the cabin. Nevada recognized Macklin, the

Winthrop sheriff, leaning against the hitching rail, in conversation with two other men, not garbed as riders. Facing Nevada was a tall man in black and he had a bright badge on his vest. He was another sheriff, a stranger to Nevada.

'We sure want to get off by sunup,' he was saying to a man near him.

This man stood with his back toward Nevada. His powerful supple shoulders showed wonderfully through his white clean shirt. Nevada recognized that lithe stalwart build, the leonine neck, the handsome head, with its clustering fair hair.

Dillon! A slight cold thrill ran over Nevada. Following it came an instinct like that of a tiger to leap.

Nevada swiftly ran his glance over the other men, standing near and in the background. Ben Ide was not present!

Then Nevada drew back behind the woodpile, loosened his gun in its sheath, and stood there an instant while the waiting forces of brain and muscle vibrated into a tremendous unity.

'Come an' get it,' sang out the cheery voice of the cook inside.

'Whoopee! Whoaboy,' shouted the cowboys, scrambling up.

At this instant Nevada bounded out swiftly and ran to a halt.

'HOLD ON!' he yelled, with all the power of his lungs. His piercing voice made statues of all, even the cowboys stiffening in half-erect postures.

In the instant of silence that ensued Dillon was the only man to move and he wheeled swift as a flash, so swiftly that the receding trace of mirth had not yet left his handsome face.

'Howdy, Dillon!' drawled Nevada, slow and cool.

Macklin shuffled erect in great alarm.

'That's Jim Lacy,' he shouted, hoarsely.

'Shore is. Careful now, you outsiders!' warned Nevada, yet with eye only for Dillon.

Every man in line with Dillon plunged off the porch or darted into the cabin. The cowboys sank back to the ground, sagging against the log wall.

Dillon stood on the porch, facing Nevada, scarcely thirty feet distant. His reaction from careless mirth to recognition of peril was as swift as his sight. But there followed the instant when his faculties had to grasp what that peril was and how he should meet it.

Nevada had gambled on this instant. It was his advantage. He did not underrate Dillon. He read his mind in those dilating eyes.

'Wal, you know me,' cut out Nevada, icily. 'An' I know you—Dillon—*Campbell!*—ED RICHARDSON!'

That was the paralysing challenge. The rustler turned a ghastly white. The frontier's bloody creed, by which he had lived, called him to his death. His green eyes set balefully. He knew. He showed his training. He had no more fear of death than of the swallows flitting under the eaves above. But he had a magnificent and desperate courage to take his enemy with him.

Richardson never uttered a word. Almost imperceptibly his body lowered as if under instinct to crouch. His stiff bent right arm began to quiver.

Nevada saw the thought in Richardson's eyes—the birth of the first message to nerve and muscle. When his hand flashed down Nevada was drawing.

Crash! Nevada's shot did not beat Richardson's draw, but it broke his aim. Boom! The rustler's gun went off half leveled. He lurched with terrible violence and his gun boomed again. The bullet scattered the gravel at Nevada's feet and spanged away into the air.

A wide red spot appeared as if by magic on the middle of Richardson's white shirt. How terrible to see him strain to raise his gun-arm!

At Nevada's second shot one of Richardson's awful eyes went blank. His gun clattered to the floor. He swayed. His arm hooked round the porch post. Then it sank limp, letting him fall with sodden thud.

Nevada was the first to withdraw his gaze from that twitching body. He flipped his gun into the air and caught it by the barrel.

'Heah, sir,' he said to the sheriff with the star on his vest, and extended the gun butt foremost. 'I reckon that'll be aboot all for Jim Lacy.'

The strain on the watchers relaxed. A murmur of wonder ran through them, growing louder. The sheriff came to a power of movement and speech.

'What? Lacy, are you handin'—over your gun?' he queried, hoarsely.

'Wal, I'm not pointin' the right end of it at you,' replied Nevada, and tossed the gun at the sheriff's feet.

'What—the hell?' gasped a weather-beaten old rider, Raidy, staring hard at Nevada.

Here Macklin came rushing up, to get between Nevada and the other sheriff.

'Jim Lacy, you're my prisoner,' yelled Macklin, beside himself with the strange opportunity presented and a terror of the enormity of his risk. He drew his gun. 'Hands up.'

'Shoot an' be damned, you four-flush officer of the law,' retorted Nevada, wearily, and turning his back to Macklin he strode to a seat on the porch steps.

'Run for the boss,' shouted Raidy to the cowboys. 'Tell him there's hell come off. Fetch him an' Judge Franklidge.'

'Hyar comes Tom Day with his outfit,' yelled a cowboy, excitedly, pointing to the horsemen entering the square. 'The whole range's hyar. Haw! Haw!'

Nevada experienced a weariness of soul and body. It was over. He did not care what happened.

'Say, give me a smoke—one of you punchers,' he said, removing his sombrero to wipe his clammy brow.

CHAPTER 21

MARVIE BLAINE came swinging down the trail at a gallop, with Rose Hatt riding close behind.

Eager excitement lent Hettie the strength to mount her horse. Nevada's strange eyes and words! What might not Marvie and Rose have to tell her?

'Hey there, Hettie!' shouted Marvie, when still some rods distant. 'Look who's comin' behind.'

Hettie complied, with emotions changing, rising again in a flood, new, bewildering, looming darkly to threaten her with panic. Marvie rode right upon her before halting.

'Say, you look like the devil!' he ejaculated, with anxious concern.

'Marv, that's the way I feel,' replied Hettie.

Rose joined them, to crowd her pony close, eager yet shy, with eyes alight and lips parted. 'Oh, Miss Hettie!' she cried rapturously. 'Marvie's brought me to you. I—I'll never go back—to the brakes.'

'My dear, you're welcome to my home,' returned Hettie, warmly, leaning to kiss the flushed face.

'Hettie, you've seen a ghost—the same ghost I seen,' declared Marvie shrewdly.

'Oh, Marvie lad—a ghost indeed!' moaned Hettie. 'Nevada! . . . He just left me—to—to kill Dillon!'

'No news to me,' shouted Marvie, fiercely. 'I've got to see that. . . . Fetch Rose. But go round. Keep away from the corrals.'

The last he delivered over his shoulder as he urged his horse into the trail and beat him into a run. In a moment he passed out of sight among the pines. The swift patter of hoofs died away.

'Come, Rose—ride,' suddenly cried Hettie, with a start, striking her horse.

The spirited animal, unused to that, broke into a gallop, and then a run. Hettie looked back. The girl was close behind, her hair flying in the wind, her face flashing. Her pony was fast and she could ride. Hettie turned her attention to the trail and the low branches of pines and the obstructing brush. Soon she was flying at a tremendous gait through the forest. The speed, the violence added to her agitation.

Where the trail emerged from the pines to drop down on the sage and cedar slope adjacent to the ranch land, Hettie turned her horse and kept to the top of the slope. Soon she passed Nevada's big black horse grazing on the sage. Her heart took a great bursting leap. *'An' shore sunset for me!'* Nevada's words of resignation and sadness rang in her ears like bells of doom.

Suddenly she imagined she heard a shot. She turned her ear to the left. Another! A gun-shot—then two sharp cracks, clear on the breeze. She reeled in her saddle. Almost she put her horse at the ranch fence. But she kept on in wild flight, forgetting Rose, clutching with left hand at her breast, where uncertainty augmented to supreme agony.

Her fast horse, keen at the freedom afforded him, swept on as in a race, on by the corrals and gardens, up over the low bench, and through the woods to her cabin, where her mother stood waving frantically from the porch. Hettie rode on, over the swaying bridge, into the shady green glade before Ben's house.

Here she pulled her iron-jawed horse to

a snorting halt. She saw men running. She heard Rose's pony come clattering over the bridge. Then Marvie's horse appeared over the rise of ground toward the corral. What breakneck speed! How he thundered up the drive!

One sight of Marvie's flashing face answered Hettie. She could have screamed in her frenzy. Marvie reached her at the moment Rose came up. His horse reared and pounded. Marvie jerked him down with powerful arm, and closed with Hettie.

'Nevada's down there—handcuffed!' he whispered, pantingly. 'Dillon's dead! . . . Oh, there'll be—hell now! . . . But not a word from—you an' Rose!'

The boy's heated face, the horses, Rose so white and rapt, the running riders, the houses and the pines—all blurred in Hettie's sight. She had to fight fiercely to recover. She felt the girl's strong hand on her, steadying her in the saddle. The deadly faintness passed. Her eyes cleared and her breast lifted to give rein to a tumult there.

Ben and Judge Franklidge were striding out to meet the running cowboys.

'Judge, I told you I heard shots,' Ben was saying. 'Somethin's happened!'

'Seems like. But don't let it upset you,' replied the judge.

'There's Marvie. . . . Has he gone loco?' exclaimed Ben, in amaze, as the boy, riding wildly, scattered the men coming up the slope.

'By thunder! Ben,' replied Franklidge, suddenly espying Hettie and Rose, as they rode in upon the lawn.

At that juncture the first cowboys reached Ben to blurt out:

'Boss, Jim Lacy's here! He just killed Dillon.'

'Wha—at?' shouted Ben, incredulously.

As the cowboy repeated his news Raidy arrived at the head of three more of Ben's hands, and all began to jabber pantingly.

'One at a time,' ordered Ben, harshly. 'What the hell's wrong? Raidy!'

The old foreman drew himself up steadily, though with heaving breast.

'Boss, I have to report—Dillon's been killed—Jim Lacy!'

Ben Ide leaped straight up in sudden ungovernable fury. His face turned dusk red. He clenched his fists high above his head.

'On my own place?' he thundered.

'Yes, sir. Right on the cook-house porch.'

'Dillon dead?'

'He is indeed, sir,' replied Raidy. 'Lacy shot him through the middle—then put out his right eye.'

'Murder!' gasped Ben.

'Not much! . . . It was an even break. Lacy dropped out of the clouds, seems like. Dillon was game, sir, an' quick—but not quick enough.'

'Killed! My best man,' rasped out Ben, stridently. 'Where's this Jim Lacy?'

'He's sittin' on the cook-house porch,' replied Raidy. 'Handcuffed, sir. . . . The sheriffs put him in irons.'

Ben cracked a hard fist into his palm. 'They got him, then. . . . Judge Franklidge, I knew we'd land that gunman rustler.'

'Ide, it's a little embarrassing to know what to do with this—this Jim Lacy—now we've got him,' replied the judge, dryly.

'Damn him! I'll show you.'

'An', boss,' interrupted Raidy. 'Tom

Day has rid in with his outfit. They wanted to lynch Lacy. But Tom roared at them like a mad bull. Reckon you'd better hurry down.'

Ina came running from the house. 'Ben, what—in the—world's happened?' she asked, in alarm.

'Ina, it's all over, so don't get scared,' returned Ben. 'Dillon has been shot by that bloody devil, Jim Lacy. Why, the man must be insane! Comin' here to carry out his queer feud! Right at my back door!'

'Dillon? Is—is he dead? asked Ina, fearfully.

'Yes, ma'am,' interposed Raidy, touching his sombrero.

'Oh, how dreadful!' Then Ina caught sight of Hettie and Rose. She ran to them. 'Hettie, isn't it awful? That Dillon! I wonder. . . . You look sort of wild, Hettie. Who's this girl with you?'

'Rose Hatt. Marvie's friend,' replied Hettie, bending down. 'Oh, Ina, I've—'

Ben, striding away with his men, turned to call out, 'Ina, stay back, an' keep those girls with you!'

'But why can't I come, too?' burst out Ina.

'No place for women,' he returned curtly. 'There's one dead man now an' soon there'll be another.'

Ina halted with a revulsion of feeling too strong for curiosity.

'Hettie, we mustn't go,' she said.

'Listen, old girl. Chucks for Ben Ide. There's not enough men in Arizona to keep me away,' declared Hettie, wildly. Then she bent down over Ina to whisper. 'Jim Lacy is Nevada!'

Ina put a hand over her mouth to stifle a scream. Then she gasped, 'No!'

'Yes! I've known it for long. And I *met* him to-day. . . . O God! . . . But I—I can't talk now. Come.'

Hettie, with Rose on her left, rode at the heels of the striding men. Ina ran beside Hettie, clinging to the stirrup, looking up now and then with dark bright eyes.

They traversed the short lane to enter the wide square, on the other side of which stood the quarters of the ranch hands. There were ten or more saddle horses standing bridles down. Hettie's startled sight included a dark group of men massed in front of the cook-house. There! Nevada must be there—soon to be confronted by Ben. How terrible for Ben—for both of them! Hettie's state became one palpitating suspense, of nerve racking torture. Yet an overwhelming, incomprehensible curiosity consumed her.

They reached the crowd of cowboys and men strange to Hettie, some of whom faced around.

'Open up here,' shouted Ben, in loud hard voice. 'Spread out. . . . Let me see this man.'

The crowd split in a hurry, leaving a wide V-shaped space, at the apex of which sat the prisoner on the edge of the porch. The dead man lay on the ground, covered with a blanket.

Hettie recognized Nevada, though his head was bowed and his sombrero hid his face. His hands, in irons, hung over his knees. What a strange, pathetic figure! Hettie's sore heart failed her. What mystery was here? The moment seemed charged with indefinable and profound portent.

Macklin, the Winthrop sheriff, beaming and bristling with his importance, advanced a stride, with pompous gesture.

'Wal, Mr. Ide, here's your man. I've got him in irons,' he boomed.

Ben advanced, his gaze passing from the dead man on the ground to the slumping prisoner.

'Jim Lacy,' he called, sternly.

There was no movement from Nevada, except that he seemed to contract. Nobody else stirred. The air was fraught with tragic suggestion, with inscrutable meaning that yet transfixed the on-lookers.

'Lacy, I'm goin' to hang you!' rang out Ben Ide.

Still no response from this notorious gunman, whose daring, whose cold nerve, had long been a subject for campfire gossip.

'Stand up. Let me look at you,' ordered Ben, suddenly.

With a violent wrench the prisoner jerked out of his dejected posture, to slip off the porch and stand erect. He ducked his head, removing the sombrero, which fell to the ground. Composed and pale he faced his judge.

Ben Ide seemed struck by lightning.

'My God! . . . Who—is this—man?' he faltered, almost inaudibly.

There was no answer. The crowd of onlookers gazed spellbound.

'*Who are you?*'

'Wal, Ben, I'm shore sorry we met this heah way,' came the reply, in the old slow cool accents. 'But I reckon it had to be.'

'NEVADA!'

With the hoarse wondering cry, Ben leaped forward to clasp his old friend in a close embrace and hold him so a long moment.

Hettie saw Ben's face in convulsion, his eyes shut tight, his expression one to bewilder the staring bystanders. To her it was beautiful and somehow soul-satisfying. Her eyes were dim, her heart pounding.

'My old pard! Found at last! ... Thank God!—I feared you were dead. ... All these long years! But I hoped an' prayed ... An' here you are. It's too good to be true. I reckon it's a dream. Say something to me— you old wild-horse-huntin' pard, Nevada!'

Ben held him back, hands on his shoulders, oblivious to all but that lean stone-grey face.

'Yes, Ben ... Nevada to you—but to all

362

the world—only Jim Lacy,' replied
Nevada, sadly.

'*What?*' cried Ben, with a violent start.
Then his nervous quick hands ran down to
Nevada's iron. 'God Almighty! ... You
Jim Lacy?'

'Yes, to my shame—pard.'

Ben's transition to reality was swift and
passionate. Suddenly white, with blazing
eyes, he tore at Nevada's handcuffs. 'I
don't care a damn who you were. You're
Nevada to me—my friend—my pard. An'
so you'll be forever.'

'Wal, Ben—it's shore good to heah you,'
replied Nevada, his voice trailing off.

'Macklin, unlock these irons,' ordered
Ben.

'What? ... But, Mr. Ide—he's my
prisoner!' protested the sheriff, aghast.
'He's wanted for rustlin'. He killed your
foreman. The law—'

'To hell with your law!' interrupted
Ben, fiercely. 'Unlock his irons!'

'You hired us to ketch this man!'

'Quick. Before I throw my gun on
you!'

His hand went to his hip. The crowd
stirred with restless feet and whispered

exclamation. Tom Day stepped out to get between Macklin and Ben.

'Easy now, Ben. Let old Tom have a word,' he said, in his big voice, now full and resonant. 'We've had enough gunplay for one day. . . . Macklin, give me the keys to these irons.'

The sheriff, red of face, flustered and intimidated, complied with poor grace. Day unlocked the irons, removed them, and somewhat with contempt cast them at Macklin's feet.

Nevada rubbed his wrists and then looked up to smile at Day.

'Put her thar, Texas Jack,' boomed the old rancher, with a wonderful smile wreathing his rugged face. 'We're shore from the old Lone Star State. Let me be the first to shake the good right hand thet did for Dillon.'

'Wal, Tom, shore you needn't rub it in,' drawled Nevada, as he yielded to the vigorous onslaught of the older man.

'Come heah, Franklidge,' called Day, beckoning to the judge. 'I reckon it's aboot time.'

Ben Ide stood motionless, his jaw

dropping, his eyes expressive of an incredulous wonder that he could not voice. His feeling was surely shared by others there. As for Hettie, she seemed to feel her blood and brain whirl madly. Texas Jack! That warm, splendid smile of the old rancher! Judge Franklidge moving forward with dignified step and grave, kindly face!

But the other black-garbed sheriff intercepted him.

'Mr. Ide, these are sure most extra-ordinary proceedings,' he said, authoritatively.

'Hell, yes!' burst out Ben. 'But it's an extraordinary case.'

'The law must take its course. Even if this Jim Lacy was an old pard of yours, he's now a criminal. Reckon his gun-play was always on the level. But he's a cattle an' hoss thief. We set out to hang the leader of this Pine Tree rustler outfit. Sure Lacy is him. His killin' of Dillon proves that. If this is no hangin' case, it sure is one for jail.'

'Struthers, I hired you to come up here,' returned Ben, deliberately. 'I admit I wanted Jim Lacy shot or hanged. But I've changed my mind. He's my friend. I owe my life, my fortune, my family, all to him. There's some mystery—some mistake here. That's for me to learn, an' not for you.'

'All right. But I'll take Lacy to Phoenix for trial,' replied Struthers.

'If you do, it'll be over my dead body. Take care, Struthers. This isn't Phoenix. You're up in the brakes.'

Thus Ben Ide answered to his few months in Arizona. The situation looked grave again. But Judge Franklidge interposed to push Struthers back.

'You have no jurisdiction here unless I give it,' he said. Then he turned to Ben with courtly kindness. 'My son, don't distress yourself further. Just have a little patience.'

'Patience!' ejaculated Ben, as if he had not heard aright.

Judge Franklidge advanced to place his left hand on Nevada's shoulder and extended his right, which Nevada quickly met.

'Jack, you may be from Texas, as old Tom here brags, but you sure belong to Arizona,' he said, heartily.

'Wal, I should smile,' corroborated Day, heartily.

Judge Franklidge turned to indicate in slight gesture the dead man on the ground.

'Dillon, of course, was the leader of this Pine Tree rustler gang,' he asserted. 'Otherwise you would not have risked revealing yourself here?'

'Wal, I reckon I wouldn't,' replied Nevada, with a smile that held no mirth.

'Dillon!' boomed Tom Day, his eyes rolling at the dead man. 'Who was he, Jack?'

'Ed Richardson, late of New Mexico.'

'Richardson? I know aboot him. Lincoln County war *hombre*? Billy the Kid outfit?'

'That's the man, Tom.'

'Wal, I'm a son-of-a-gun!' ejaculated the old rancher. 'I begin to see light. Dillon was thick with Stewart. An' Stewart never worked the same for me after Dillon became foreman heah at Ben's. This mawnin' he was gone. An' he knowed where we was bound for. . . . Jack, what you make of thet?'

'Stewart was one of the three Arizonians

that Richardson took into his New Mexican outfit.'

'Ahuh! Who's the other two?'

'Burt Stillwell an' Cedar Hatt.'

'Stillwell . . . Jack, didn't you—meet thet *hombre* just lately?' queried Day, his eyes glinting.

'Yes. It was Stillwell who stole Ben's horse, California Red. I made him send Red back. Reckon that riled Stillwell. . . . An' Marvie Blaine shot Cedar Hatt to-day. So the Pine Tree outfit is shore broke.'

Ben Ide, in bewildered state, crowded closer to the speakers.

'Marvie Blaine shot Cedar Hatt?' ejaculated Judge Franklidge.

'Good Lord!' added Day in his booming voice. 'What next? Ben, you listenin' to all this?'

'Tom—I'm stumped,' replied Ben, hoarsely.

'Spill it, Jack. Tell us about Marvie. Heaven help us now!' went on Day.

'I happened on Cedar Hatt to-day,' replied Nevada. 'He was ridin' down in one of the brakes an' I was on top. Wal, I soon saw he was trailin' some one. So I

368

worked ahaid an' got down off the Rim. There I happened to run on Marvie an' his girl, Rose Hatt. They were spoonin' under the trees an' never saw me. I was lookin' for Cedar an' I knew Cedar was lookin' for them. So I kept quiet. Pretty soon Cedar slips up, right on to them. An' he begins to rave. Rose talked back an' shore Marvie showed spunk. Cedar knocked him down, an, then Rose, too. That riled Marvie an' he tore into Cedar. It looked bad, with Cedar pullin' at his gun. He got it out, but Marvie fought him for it. . . . An', wal, in the fight Cedar dropped the gun an' Marvie quick as a cat snatched it up. Usin' both hands, he throwed it on Cedar an' shore bored him twice.'

'Whoop-ee!' yelled one of the cowboys at the back of the crowd.

'By thunder! I'd whoop myself if I had any voice left,' returned Tom Day. 'Where's Marvie? Come heah, you gun-slingin' kid!'

'Rose Hatt is heah, too,' said Nevada. 'An', Tom, it'd be wal for you an' Judge Franklidge to talk to her. Rose is a good honest girl. Dillon was after her. An' Cedar Hatt had dragged Rose away from home to meet Dillon. That was how Rose found out aboot the Pine Tree outfit. An' she confessed to me.'

'Wal, I'll be darned!' replied Day, feelingly. 'The lass looks a little scared an' white, Judge. I reckon we needn't heah her say now, in this crowd. But that kid Marvie—he shore don't look scared.'

'Come here, my lad,' called Judge Franklidge, beckoning.

Marvie slipped off his horse and stalked forward to confront the three men. Hettie thrilled at sight of him, yet she could have wept and screamed with mirth. Marvie, if he were any character at all, was surely Nevada. In look, in walk, in manner! He had a big black gun in his chaps pocket, and another smaller one in his belt. What a moment for Marvie Blaine!

'Son, what's this we heah?' asked Day, bluntly. 'Did you shoot Cedar Hatt?'

'Reckon I did,' replied Marvie. 'Here's his gun. It happened just about as Nevada told you.'

'Who's Nevada?'

Marvie laid a hand on his friend.

'Oho! You mean Jim Lacy heah?'

'No, I mean Nevada,' replied the lad,

stoutly. 'That Jim Lacy handle doesn't go with me.'

'Marvie, you speak for me,' interposed Judge Franklidge. 'He may indeed be Nevada and Jim Lacy. But for me he will always be Texas Jack. He has worked for me for two years. And before that for Tom Day. We found him to be the best cowboy who ever threw a rope for us. And more— a splendid honest man whom it is my privilege to call friend—and whom I would be happy to take into my cattle business.'

'Hey, you sheriff rustlers,' boomed Tom Day, with loud satisfaction, 'did you heah that? Wal, listen to some more. Texas Jack volunteered to clean up this Pine Tree outfit. He had my backin'. He had Judge Franklidge's office behind him. He had a free hand to become a rustler an' thief, to drink an' gamble an' shoot his way into the secret of the Pine Tree outfit. Do you savvy? Or are you wearin' your hair too long? There won't be any arrest. There won't be anyone danglin' on a rope.'

CHAPTER 22

HETTIE lay upon her bed, face to the open window, with the cool sweet sage-laden wind blowing in upon her. Dusk had fallen. The last rose and gold of the afterglow of sunset lingered in the west. She never knew how she had gotten from Ben's courtyard to her room. Dimly she remembered faces and murmuring voices that had no meaning for her.

The door opened—closed. Ben knelt beside her bed—took her hands—kissed her face.

'Hettie, I came as quick as I could get away,' he said, with deep agitation. 'I was knocked off my pins. But happy—oh, girl, never so happy before, except on the day Ina married me! . . . When I could think I remembered you. So here I am.'

'Oh—Ben!' she whispered, and clung to him, her slow overburdened heart lifting painfully.

'Hettie dear—joy never kills,' he replied, tenderly.

'If it were—only joy,' mourned Hettie.

'Child, there's nothing *but* joy,' he rushed on. 'It was a terrible shock. To find out old Nevada—was Jim Lacy. But we always knew he was somebody bad. No, not bad. But somebody wild an' great. You knew—Hettie. . . . An' now he's turned up. The wonder of it is that he had hidden the old identity. He had given up the old wild life. He had found honest work an' had lived clean an' fine. As we knew him in those happy days at Forlorn River. So you see all your love an' faith an' hope were justified. He *was* worth it. Thank God I never lost—'

'Hush! You're killing—me!' gasped Hettie, writhing from his embrace.

'Hettie! Why, sister, this isn't like you,' he expostulated, in anxiety. 'You're overcome. It has been too much for you.'

'Not the joy—not the excitement,' she returned. 'I've been a poor miserable creature! . . . A coward! A selfish, headstrong woman! Jealous, little! . . . Oh, so poor in love—in faith!'

It came out then, gradually, sometimes incoherently, the story of her meeting with Nevada; and Hettie, in her self abasement, magnified all the shame and ignominy—all the bitter invective and scorn which she had flung into his face.

Ben drew her head back to his shoulder and smoothed her disheveled hair.

'Well! . . . I understand now. Too bad! But there are excuses for you. Didn't you believe in him—love him—keep yourself for him all these years? Some things are too much for anybody.'

'He—will—never—forgive,' she sobbed, with the relief that came through his sympathy, his championship.

'Nevada? Why, that fellow would forgive anythin'.'

'I—can never—forgive myself.'

'Hettie, it will all come right. Don't you remember how you harped on that? Beat it into my poor thick head! . . . An' lo! it has come right. . . . Nevada could not hurt you.'

'I have—hurt myself. I've lost something. My ideal has failed me.'

'No—no. You're just overwrought by this sudden crash. Please, Hettie. I don't mean cheer up. But brace up an' see it through. Where's your Ide spunk?'

'Gone—gone.'

'Well, then, get it back. I swear to you Nevada will be just like I am now. On my knees to you!'

'Where is he?'

'I left him in the livin'-room, playin' with Blaine. The kid took a shine to him *pronto*. An' Nevada. Lord! no one would ever dream of him bein' what we've learned to understand by the name Jim Lacy. ... Hettie, there's somethin' so simple an' great about Nevada. He's just himself now as we remembered him. He's Nevada, that's all.'

Hettie lay awake many hours, with anguish slowly wearing away to regurgitation of something quite as full of pangs. The night wind moved through the pines, sweeping, swelling, lulling. Coyotes added their lonesome chorus. White stars shone from the dark blue sky. When she fell asleep she dreamed vague, unreal, distorted dreams, in which she seemed the central shadow among shadows of Nevada, Marvie, Rose, Ben, and that mocking handsome Dillon. But she awoke to a new day—new as the bright morning, and with a dawning hope, like the gold and blue of the Arizona sky.

She had no time for her own thoughts. Marvie rushed in upon her, in the kitchen, to be followed by Rose, shy, sweet, modest as the wildflower for which she was named. Already they had been out in the woods and now they were as hungry as bears. Mrs. Ide looked upon them with wonder and favor. They wanted to go to Winthrop. Would Hettie go? Rose must have clothes and books and things. How Marvie's face glowed under his freckles! And Rose was in a transport. Had she forgotten that sordid home down in the brakes?

'Not to-day,' replied Hettie, to their importunities. 'To-morrow, maybe, if Ben consents.'

'What has that Ben Ide to do with my affairs?' demanded Marvie, loftily. 'I'd like to have you know *I* can ride for Franklidge or Tom Day or any other big rancher in Arizona.'

Hettie sensed trouble for Ben when he came to attempt reconciliation with Marvie. Ben would surely need her aid.

'Marv, boy, of course I know,' she said.

376

'But you must use some sense. Rose is to have a home with me. And I shall take her to San Diego for the winter. I should think you would want to be near her this fall, and also go to San Diego, at least for a while.'

Marvie wilted under that. What a master-stroke, thought Hettie.

'Well, if Ben crawls to me I'll consider comin' back,' replied Marvie, condescendingly.

After breakfast Tom Day came over to pay his respects to Hettie and her mother. How bluff and genial and substantial he was!

'Wal, lass,' he said at partin, 'I reckon the Ides an' the Days can go back to ranchin' again, thanks to thet Texas Jack of ours. Shore, we'll have rustlin' bees again an' mebbe for years to come. But there'll be a spell now, like these Indian-summer days. Folks can sleep an' be happy. An' you youngsters can make love. Haw! Haw! . . . Hettie lass, I've been a-wonderin' aboot you. I'm shore a keen old fox. Wal, *adios*, an' God bless you.'

Later in the morning Ben came to her so utterly abject that he was funny.

'Now what?' queried Hettie. 'You needn't come to me for sympathy.'

'Aw, Hettie, that's what Ina said, an' she stuck to it,' said Ben. 'But I've got to tell somebody. An' Nevada is moon-struck or somethin'. He never heard me.'

'All right, Bennie,' smiled Hettie, relenting.

'You know I fired Raidy—well, of course I had to go to him an' ask him to come back. Reckon the old fellow was hurt deep. He didn't rub it in, but he was sure cold. For a long while I apologized, made excuses, swore, an' did about everythin' before he would take back the old job. But at that he was nothin' compared to Marvie Blaine.'

'Indeed! Yes, I remember you fired Marvie, too,' said Hettie.

'You would have died laughin' to see that kid,' went on Ben, ruefully. 'I sent for him. Did he come? Not much. He sent word back by my messenger that if I wanted to talk to him I could hunt him up. So I had to. An' I'm darned if I don't believe he watched me an' kept dodgin' me. Well, anyway, I found him at last an' asked him to forget our difference. Whew! ... Say, he's expanded in this Arizona air. He had an argument that floored me. It *was* logic, though I wouldn't admit it. He made me crawl. By George! You know I love Marvie an' I could never let him leave Ina an' me till he's grown up. He had more dignity than Judge Franklidge an' more conceit than any cowboy I ever saw. He swelled up like that Sheriff Macklin. Well, after he got his job back at a higher salary he put on the screws some more. He actually hit me for the reward I offered for any clue leadin' to the apprehension of the Pine Tree outfit. That reward was a thousand dollars. Marvie claimed Rose was his clue. The cheeky little rooster! But Nevada backed him up. An' as a matter of fact, 'most everythin' came through Rose. So I promised it to him. ... Now what do you say?'

Hettie leaped up gladly. 'Good for Marv! Now, Ben, run over and crawl to Ina. Then we—*you* all can be happy again!'

'Ahuh! I get the hunch that "you" aren't included. I'll bet before this day ends you'll be as crazy as Marv an' as mum as his little wood mouse, Rose.'

Still Hettie was not to have any of the solitude she craved. No sooner had Ben gone than Judge Franklidge appeared.

'I've come over to bid you and Mrs. Ide good-by,' he said, in his kindly way. 'It has been a rather staggering time. But we're on our feet again, and "ridin' pretty," as the cowboys say.'

Then leaning closer to Hettie he continued in lower tone: 'You recall one day at my home—when you said somethin' mysterious to me then, but pertinent now. It was about—*Nevada*.'

'I remember—Judge Franklidge,' murmured Hettie, trembling.

'Well, would I be correct if I—sort of put two and two together—or perhaps I should say one and one? . . . Nevada and Hettie, for instance?'

His persuasive voice, and his linking together the two names, quite subdued her poor and rebellious resistance. She dropped her head, murmuring a faint affirmative.

'I'm glad I hit upon the truth,' he said,

with eagerness. 'I watched you yesterday and I believe I saw then something of your ordeal. And I see now in your face the havoc that tells of your pain. It is my earnest hope to soothe that pain, Hettie Ide, and I know I can do so. Listen. It has been a terrible shock for you to find in your Texas Jack—or Nevada, as you call him—no other than the infamous or famous Jim Lacy. This is natural, but it is all wrong. There need be no shame, no fear, no shrinking in your acceptance of this fact. I've met and trusted no finer man than this same Jim Lacy. But I did not come to eulogize him. . . . I want to make clear in your mind just what such men as Jim Lacy mean to me. I have lived most of my life on the frontier and I know what its wilderness has been, and still is. There are bad men and bad men. It is a distinction with a vast difference. I have met or seen many of the noted killers. Wild Bill, Wes Hardin, Kingfisher, Billy the Kid, Pat Garrett, an' a host of others. These men are not bloody murderers. They are a product of the times. The West could never have been populated without them. They strike a balance between the hordes of ruffians, outlaws, strong evil characters like Dillon, and the wild life of a wild era. It is the West as any Westerner knows it now. And as such we could not be pioneers, we could not progress without this violence. Without the snuffing out of dissolute and desperate men such as Dillon, Cedar Hatt, Stillwell, and so on. The rub is that only hard iron-nerved youths like Billy the Kid, or Jim Lacy, can meet such men on their own ground. That is all I wanted you to know. And also, that if my daughter cared for Jim Lacy I would be proud to give her to him.'

'Thank you, Judge Franklidge,' replied Hettie, lifting her head to look straight into his eyes. 'But you misunderstand my—my case. I do not mind—that Nevada has been Jim Lacy.'

'For Heaven's sake! Then, why all this—this—I don't know what?' burst out the judge, in smiling amaze.

Hettie glanced away, out into the green black-striped forest.

'I scorned him. I believed him lost to—to . . . I failed in faith. And I fear he will never forgive.'

'Hettie Ide,' returned Franklidge, with

solemn finality, 'this Texas Jack won't even know he has anything to forgive.'

Before Hettie could recover from this ultimatum Marvie waylaid her. Full of importance and authority, added to something of mystery, he hauled Hettie off the porch and out under the trees.

'Hettie,' he whispered in her ear, 'I fixed it for you.'

'Marvie! . . . Are you—Oh, if you—'

'Keep in the saddle,' he interrupted, shaking her. 'Nevada just told me he was dyin' of love for you. . . . There now, Hettie, don't look like that. I'm dead serious. Honest to God! Cross my heart! . . . Didn't you make my Rose happy? Why, I'd go to hell for you. An' Nevada knows it. He's sufferin'. He thinks you ought to send for him, if you can forgive him for being Jim Lacy.'

Hettie could only cling mutely to this glad-eyed boy who was torturing her.

'So I fixed it. You run out there across the bench,' he went on, pointing with eager, trembling finger. 'You know. There among the pines where I always find you. Go now. Nevada is watchin'. He'll come. I swore I'd get you there if I had to pack you. An' I will.'

Hettie kissed his brown lean cheek, then ran wildly into the shelter of the pines. First she meant only to escape Marvie and all of them. But an irresistible magnet drew her to the secluded nook where she went so often alone to gaze out under the low cover of green to the purple sage and changing radiance of the desert.

Nevada was there—somehow the Nevada of old. Hettie ran into his arms.

'I—love—you!' she cried, imploringly. 'Forgive me. It was my one failure. I was the weak one—not you.'

Hours passed and sunset again widened its golden effulgence down over the sage hills to the rolling slopes. Purple clouds like ships sailed in a sea of gold and rose.

Hettie and Nevada sat with their backs to the great pine tree, their cheeks together, their hands clinging.

'Ben sprung somethin' on me,' Nevada was saying. 'Why not all of us rustle down to San Diego! Shore, it floored me. . . . But I'd like you to get away from heah just now, for a little. . . . So, darlin' Hettie, would I be askin' too much if—if—'

'No. Ask me anything,' murmured Hettie.

'If I'd asked you to marry me?'

'If! . . . Do you?'

'Shore. I reckon I'm darin' to.'

'No,' said Hettie.

He accepted that in startled silence.

'I mean no—you are *not* asking too much. . . . Oh, Nevada! Yes! Yes!'

The last golden flare of sunset burned from over the darkening range.

'Arizona is smilin' at us,' said Nevada, gazing at the sunset glow upon her rapt face.

'Nevada is smiling down upon me,' she replied, dreamily.

THE END

WESTERN TITLES IN THE ULVERSCROFT LARGE PRINT SERIES

FICTION TITLES IN THE ULVERSCROFT LARGE PRINT SERIES

Wyatt's Hurricane	*Desmond Bagley*
Landslide	*Desmond Bagley*
The Spoilers	*Desmond Bagley*
Green Hand	*Lillian Beckwith*
A Man of His Time	*Phyllis Bentley*
The Episode at Toledo	*Ann Bridge*
Letter from Peking	*Pearl S. Buck*
The New Year	*Pearl S. Buck*
Mandala	*Pearl S. Buck*
The Three Daughters of Madame Liang	
	Pearl S. Buck
The Melting Man	*Victor Canning*
The Green Fields of Eden	*Francis Clifford*
The Long Corridor	*Catherine Cookson*
The Unbaited Trap	*Catherine Cookson*
Hannah Massey	*Catherine Cookson*
Love and Mary Ann	*Catherine Cookson*
Fanny McBride	*Catherine Cookson*
Kate Hannigan	*Catherine Cookson*
The Menagerie	*Catherine Cookson*
The Nice Bloke	*Catherine Cookson*
A Song of Sixpence	*A. J. Cronin*
A Pocketful of Rye	*A. J. Cronin*
Shannon's Way	*A. J. Cronin*

Devil's Cub	*Georgette Heyer*
The Corinthian	*Georgette Heyer*
The Toll-Gate	*Georgette Heyer*
Black Sheep	*Georgette Heyer*
The Talisman Ring	*Georgette Heyer*
Bride of Pendorric	*Victoria Holt*
Mistress of Mellyn	*Victoria Holt*
Menfreya	*Victoria Holt*
Kirkland Revels	*Victoria Holt*
The Shivering Sands	*Victoria Holt*
The Legend of the Seventh Virgin	*Victoria Holt*
The Shadow of the Lynx	*Victoria Holt*
Wreckers Must Breathe	*Hammond Innes*
The Strange Land	*Hammond Innes*
Maddon's Rock	*Hammond Innes*
The White South	*Hammond Innes*
Atlantic Fury	*Hammond Innes*
The Land God Gave to Cain	*Hammond Innes*
Levkas Man	*Hammond Innes*
The Strode Venturer	*Hammond Innes*
The Wreck of the Mary Deare	*Hammond Innes*
The Lonely Skier	*Hammond Innes*
Blue Ice	*Hammond Innes*
Golden Soak	*Hammond Innes*
The River of Diamonds	*Geoffrey Jenkins*

NON-FICTION TITLES IN THE ULVERSCROFT LARGE PRINT SERIES

THE WHITEOAK CHRONICLE SERIES TITLES IN THE ULVERSCROFT LARGE PRINT SERIES

by Mazo De La Roche

The Building of Jalna
Morning at Jalna
Mary Wakefield
Young Renny
Whiteoak Heritage
The Whiteoak Brothers
Jalna
Whiteoaks
Finch's Fortune
The Master of Jalna
Whiteoak Harvest
Wakefield's Course
Return to Jalna
Renny's Daughter
Variable Winds at Jalna
Centenary at Jalna